EX LIBRIS

VINTAGE CLASSICS

NICHOLAS BLAKE

Nicholas Blake was the pseudonym of Poet Laureate Cecil Day-Lewis, who was born in County Laois, Ireland, in 1904. After his mother died in 1906, he was brought up in London by his father, spending summer holidays with relatives in Wexford. He was educated at Sherborne School and Wadham College, Oxford, from which he graduated in 1927. Blake initially worked as a teacher to supplement his income from his poetry writing and he published his first Nigel Strangeways novel, *A Question of Proof*, in 1935. Blake went on to write a further nineteen crime novels, all but four of which featured Nigel Strangeways, as well as numerous poetry collections and translations.

During the Second World War he worked as a publications editor in the Ministry of Information, which he used as the basis for the Ministry of Morale in *Minute for Murder*, and after the war he joined the publishers Chatto & Windus as an editor and director. He was appointed Poet Laureate in 1968 and died in 1972 at the home of his friend, the writer Kingsley Amis.

ALSO BY NICHOLAS BLAKE

A Question of Proof

Thou Shell of Death

There's Trouble Brewing

The Beast Must Die

The Widow's Cruise

Malice in Wonderland

The Smiler with the Knife

Minute for Murder

Head of a Traveller

The Dreadful Hollow

The Whisper in the Gloom

End of Chapter

The Worm of Death

The Sad Variety

The Morning After Death

NICHOLAS BLAKE
THE CASE OF THE ABOMINABLE SNOWMAN

VINTAGE CLASSICS

1 3 5 7 9 10 8 6 4 2

Vintage Classics is part of the Penguin Random House group of companies

Vintage, Penguin Random House UK, One Embassy Gardens,
8 Viaduct Gardens, London SW11 7BW

penguin.co.uk/vintage-classics
global.penguinrandomhouse.com

Copyright © Nicholas Blake 1941

The moral right of the author has been asserted

First published in Great Britain by Collins (The Crime Club) in 1941
First published in Vintage Classics in 2012
This paperback edition reissued in 2025

Penguin Random House values and supports copyright. Copyright fuels creativity, encourages diverse voices, promotes freedom of expression and supports a vibrant culture. Thank you for purchasing an authorised edition of this book and for respecting intellectual property laws by not reproducing, scanning or distributing any part of it by any means without permission. You are supporting authors and enabling Penguin Random House to continue to publish books for everyone. No part of this book may be used or reproduced in any manner for the purpose of training artificial intelligence technologies or systems. In accordance with Article 4(3) of the DSM Directive 2019/790, Penguin Random House expressly reserves this work from the text and data mining exception.

A CIP catalogue record for this book is available from the British Library

ISBN 9781529971118

Printed and bound in Great Britain by Clays Ltd, Elcograf S.p.A.

The authorised representative in the EEA is Penguin Random House Ireland,
Morrison Chambers, 32 Nassau Street, Dublin D02 YH68

Penguin Random House is committed to a sustainable future
for our business, our readers and our planet. This book is made
from Forest Stewardship Council® certified paper.

CHAPTER ONE

'Oh that I were a mockery king of snow.'
SHAKESPEARE

THE great frost of 1940 was over. The great thaw had set in. For nearly two months the flat lands around Easterham Manor had been lying under a monotony of snow which, like an enchanter, turned even the most familiar landmarks into strange and silenced shapes. Gazing out from behind the blurred panes of the nursery window, John and Priscilla Restorick could see Easterham village, a mile away, gradually emerging from its snow-white trance. In this country of level fields and winding, hedgeless roads there had been little else but the villages to arrest the steady flow of the blizzards. Easterham had been half obliterated by drifts. As often as men had dug passages through its one street and their own backyards, the snow had come to fill them up again. To-day, Easterham resembled a series of half-finished excavations in a white desert: the snow, sliding off its red-tiled roofs and melting to a yellowish slush where the inhabitants walked, pattering down from the vicarage elms, wearing threadbare on the allotments, was beginning to reveal the outline of the village the children knew.

But John and Priscilla had little attention to spare for the village. They were staring, with all the intense absorption of their age, at the snowman on the lawn just beneath their window.

'Queen Victoria is being liquidated,' murmured John, who had a knack for picking up well-worn words from his elders and minting them afresh. He used this word *sotto voce*, knowing that his father did not at all approve of it. It was, no doubt – like 'strumpet' and 'bloody' – one of those words which were all right for Shakespeare and grown-ups to use, but did not do for children. At any rate, Will Dykes, their mother's friend, who was staying in the house, had used it at lunch one day; and their father had closed his eyes slowly in the gesture of rebuke so painfully familiar to John and put on a shocked, not-before-the-children expression.

'Queen Victoria is being liquidated,' John murmured again, savouring the word pleasantly on his tongue and watching another patch of snow slide off the disintegrating widow.

'Queen Victoria is being decontaminated,' exclaimed Priscilla, not to be outdone. She rubbed the misty mark on the window where her snub nose had pressed.

'You're a fool,' said John amiably. 'Decontaminated is what they do when you're covered with mustard gas. Or else you come out with bloody great blisters and they go pop.'

'You shouldn't use that word.'

'I don't care. Anyway, Aunt Betty was always using it.'

'She was grown up. Besides, she's dead.'

'I don't see that makes any difference. I say, Mouse, don't you think it was awfully queer about Aunt Betty?'

'Queer? What do you mean, Rat?'

'Well, having policemen here and the whole household whizzing about like mad.'

'They didn't whizz. They all sat around looking as if – as if they were waiting for a train. Yes,' Priscilla elaborated, 'it was like when we're going off for the summer holidays. Everyone keeps sitting down and then standing up and rushing off somewhere, and they're too busy to play with us, and you never know if they're going to be extra decent to you or snap your head off.'

'But you don't have policemen whizzing around when you're going off for the holidays.'

'I like Mr Strangeways. He's my best policeman.'

'He isn't a policeman, you spotted pard. He's a private impersonator.'

'What's that?'

'It's – well, it's a private impersonator, like Sherlock

Holmes. He puts on a false beard and tracks the criminal to his lair, when the police are baffled.'

'Why can't he track the criminal to his lair without putting on a beard? I don't like beards. Dr Bogan tickles when he kisses me.'

'Don't be an ass. He puts on a false beard – oh well, it's one of the things you'll understand when you're older.'

'I've never seen Mr Strangeways in a false beard. And anyway, I'm as old as you, twin-rat.'

'You were born ten minutes after me.'

'Women are always older for their years than men. Every one knows that.'

'Oh, tripe and onions! You're not a woman. You're an infant cheeild.'

'Don't copy Miss Ainsley. She's a stuck-up vampire.'

'She's not. She helped Uncle Andrew and us to build the snowman.'

'She is. She's got bloody fingernails and sharp white teeth.'

'The better to eat you with. Aunt Betty used to do her fingernails red. *And* her toenails. I saw them that night she came in.'

'What night?' asked Priscilla.

'The night she died and went to Heaven. She came in and looked at me, and then she went out again. She thought I was asleep. Her face was white as death. I could see her in the moonlight. She looked all frozen, like a snowman.'

'I expect it was her ghost.'

'Don't be an ass,' said John, a shade less robustly. 'How could she be a ghost when she wasn't dead?'

'Well, it wouldn't be the first time a ghost had walked in this mouldering mansion.'

'I say, what are you drivelling about?'

'It's a secret. I heard Daddy and Mr Strangeways – ssh, someone's coming!'

Hereward Restorick entered the nursery. The twins' father

had retired Army and Country Gentleman written all over him. His flaxen, drooping moustache, worn rather longer than the cavalry fashion, reminded one of his Saxon ancestry. The Restoricks of Easterham are older than Domesday Book.

Hereward glanced round the nursery with a preoccupied eye: he had the look of an officer inspecting his men with something else on his mind.

'Whatever's all this?' he asked, indicating a conglomeration of toys and games on the floor.

John stuck out his underlip, as if bracing himself for trouble. But Priscilla was not at all dismayed. She tossed back her dark curls, in a winning, independent gesture caught from her American mother, and said:

'We're tidying out the toy cupboard, Daddy.'

'Tidying? Hm. Oh well, John can finish that. It's time for your music lesson, moppet.'

The deep-lying snow and quarantine for measles had kept the children away from school this term, and their parents had been giving them occasional lessons. Hereward Restorick, rather surprisingly to those who saw in him the very type of the outdoor sportsman, possessed a talent for the piano.

Priscilla, running to him, took his hand and dragged him excitedly towards the door. As they were going out, he glanced back at his son who was now staring out of the window again.

'Get on with it, old man,' he said – not unkindly, but with an undertone of suppressed impatience in his voice that made the boy stiffen a little. 'Tidy it up. You can't stay mooning there all the morning.'

'We were watching the snowman melt.'

'Well, that's all right. He'll be there still when you've tidied up. That air-gun of yours isn't loaded, is it? Are you sure?'

'Uncle Andrew said I could shoot at birds out of the window when he gave it to me.'

'I asked you was it loaded, son.'

'I have to keep it ready in case I suddenly see a bird, and –'

'I've told you before, John, never to keep a gun loaded, haven't I? You're ten years old, and it's time you learned sense about firearms. Very well, let me see you take the shot out now, before you forget.'

John did as he was told. He was a fearless child: but he knew better than to provoke the raging, terrifying temper which any insubordination aroused in his father. Instinctively he realized that, though his father was normally a patient and kindly man, this temper was a hair-trigger affair which the lightest touch might explode. And lately, there was no doubt of it, his father had been somehow different. It was all part of the changed atmosphere in the house since Aunt Betty died, part of a bewildering picture which for John included also his absence from school, the coming and going of policemen, the burst pipes, the snowman, the hushed conversations of grown-ups which were apt to break off abruptly when he or Priscilla entered the room. The general unsettlement of a household that normally ran as smoothly as an eight-cylinder engine.

Putting the air-gun away in a corner, John returned to the window. He opened it and leaned out. Everywhere the thaw was perceptible: in the snow flaking off the evergreens behind the tennis-court, in the dank, mild air that brushed his face so softly, and most of all in the tinkling water-music made by the running gutters, the stream tumbling over its miniature waterfall at the bottom of the rock-garden, the whole melting landscape beyond.

Only the snowman seemed to resist this universal dissolution. Its surface was beginning to look pocked and granulated, but its lumpish figure still retained something of the contour given to it by its creators; and the snow all round it, trodden hard by many feet, reminded John of its fashioning and his dream. He remembered that afternoon, several weeks ago, when Uncle Andrew, Mr Strangeways, Priscilla, and himself had built it. Miss Ainsley was there, too, wearing scarlet woollen gloves and furry snow-boots, making a lot of silly, queer remarks he didn't understand. She was the sort of woman who sat about making remarks. She had even brought out a kitchen chair to sit on, but Uncle Andrew soon tipped her off that and rolled her in the snow, and Miss Ainsley had laughed a lot and been quite sporting about it, though John fancied she didn't really enjoy it as much as she pretended. Then Uncle Andrew took the chair for the snowman to sit on. He said it was a throne, and the snowman would be Queen Victoria; and Miss Ainsley said something vulgar about the Good Queen getting piles if she sat out in the cold. The children rolled up great balls of the clinging snow, which Uncle Andrew lifted into position and scraped and prodded till he had produced a figure really just like the Queen in John's history book. Then they stuck halfpennies in the face for eyes, and Miss Ainsley found an old widow's bonnet and veil in the acting cupboard to place on its head. But, for some reason, Daddy didn't approve of that part of it when he came out to look, and they had to put the bonnet back again.

As he gazed down at the snowman now, John felt a queer sort of exultation. It was as though he were God, looking down from Heaven and commanding the snowman to melt. One of the halfpennies dropped silently out of an eye socket. 'It is the Lord's doing, and wonderful in our eyes,' John muttered dreamily. He willed a crack to appear on its head: and presently, sure enough, the crack did appear. 'Look, Mouse, Queen Victoria is cracked!' he exclaimed, forgetting that his sister was not in the room.

Once again, he remembered his dream. It was over a week ago, but still extraordinarily vivid to him. He had dreamt that he woke up in the middle of the night and went to the window. It was a moonless night, but bright with stars. A few miles away, the serried searchlights of the Outer Defences stood straight up into the sky, a palisade of light. On the lawn below he could just see the glimmering, stocky outline of the snowman. But, in his dream, it kept appearing and disappearing, as though (he thought next morning) someone was passing to and fro in front of it. It was almost as if someone were building another snowman, but the next morning Queen Victoria was still there, without a consort; a little bulkier and more ragged, perhaps, for more snow had fallen in the night, but still recognizably the same figure of majesty.

He had not mentioned this dream to anyone but Priscilla, and, in the excitement of getting an air-gun from Uncle Andrew, it had been temporarily forgotten. But this morning, when there were no plump, feather-ruffled birds on the lawn to pot at, for the thaw had sent them back to their normal winter ways, John seemed for a moment to be living in the dream again.

It was odd, he reflected vaguely, that he had not been at all frightened by it, only interested, and – in a remote way – excited, as though part of himself had been down on the lawn while part watched from the window.

The sound of Priscilla playing the piano in the drawing-room below now stopped. Everything was silent except for the musical shush and tinkle of thawing snow. John's pony in the paddock away to the right suddenly kicked up its heels and galloped to the hedge, sending up snow like spindrift. Priscilla was running up the stairs. Mummy appeared, in Wellingtons, talking to the gardener. John remembered there was something he wanted to ask Priscilla.

'I say,' he called when she entered the nursery, 'What was all that bilge about a ghost?'

'Bilge yourself. I heard them talking about it. Well, Scribbles saw the ghost anyway, Mummy said.'

'Cats don't see ghosts.'

'Scribbles is a very wise cat.'

'Scribbles is a naughty old stinkerado. Saw it where, anyway?'

'In the Bishop's room. That's all I heard. They dried up when they saw I was there listening. Oh yes, and someone said it was funny the way Scribbles kept bouncing off the walls.'

'Bouncing off? Oh, you're crackers! I say, Mouse, come and look at Queen Victoria. She's cracked, too.'

The children, side by side, leaned out of the window. As they watched, the crack at the top of the snowman's head deepened. A segment of snow slid, smoothly as a camera shutter, off its face. Its face ought to have gone. But it was still there. The squat, shapeless snowman still had a face – a face almost as white as the snow which had covered it, the dead, human face of someone who shouldn't have been there at all.

John and Priscilla gave each other one frozen, terrified glance. Then they raced for the door and went pelting downstairs.

'Daddy! Daddy!' John yelled. 'Come quick! There's someone inside the snowman! It's . . .'

CHAPTER TWO

*'Ingenious Fancy, never better pleas'd
Than when employ'd to accommodate the fair.'*
COWPER

Nigel Strangeways' introduction to the macabre and tragic events which he later named 'The Case of the Abominable Snowman' came, several weeks before the snowman revealed its secret, in the shape of a letter to his wife Georgia. She handed it to him across the breakfast table in their Devonshire cottage, grinning with amusement. The letter was written on thick, cream paper, headed 'The Dower House, Easterham, Essex', and written in a script of peculiar character and delicacy. Nigel began to read it aloud:

'Dear Cousin Georgia, – It would give an old woman much pleasure if you and your husband were to do her the honour of visiting her. I live, as you know, not much in the world, and it would be vastly agreeable to me to have your company for a week, could you engage yourselves to make the journey in such desperate times. I am not insensible of the inconvenience to which my request may put you: but, leaving aside the gratification your visit would cause me, I have a little problem which, I take leave to suggest, your husband, whose fame has reached even to my rural seclusion, would find intriguing. The problem, to be brief, concerns a cat – '

'Oh, but really now,' Nigel protested. 'I can't traipse over to Essex to find a missing cat.'

'Go on. There's more to the cat than that.'

' – a cat,' resumed Nigel, ' belonging to Hereward Restorick, of Easterham Manor. I am not, I hope, fantastic in declaring that there was more – to use a cant phrase – than meets the eye in this cat's behaviour. Unpredictable as are the ways of its tribe, we may yet have cause to wonder when such a creature generates universal alarm by transforming itself into a delirious Dervish. Though in the autumn of my years, I conceive I am not yet so much deprived of wit that I should attribute to the Supernatural what may surely be resolved by Reason. Should the ingenious Mr Strangeways lend his counsel to my own poor observations, he would, I make no doubt, bring *lux e tenebris* and in so doing ease the curiosity – nay, the worse apprehensions of

>Yr. obliged cousin,
>CLARISSA CAVENDISH.'

When Nigel had got his breath back after the perusal of this extraordinary missive, he remarked to Georgia:

'Well, really, you do have the most eccentric relatives. Who is this eighteenth century fantastic?'

'I've not seen her for years. Not since she went to live at Easterham. Some great-uncle of mine left her a fair packet of money and she bought the Dower House, so they tried to clap her into a bin.'

'Darling Georgia, please don't talk shorthand at this hour of the morning. Why should they clap her into a bin for buying a Dower House? And who are "they"?'

'The cousins who thought they should have got the legacy, of course. And it wasn't because she bought the house, but because she acted so strange after buying it.'

'As for instance –?'

'Oh, you'll see all that when we've got there.'

'Now, Georgia, please. The ingenious Mr Strangeways is not going all the way to Essex, in wartime, to stay with an aged lunatic and investigate a cat which transforms itself into a delirious Dervish.'

'He is. And she isn't. What I remember of her, she was remarkably sane. And altogether charming. If she prefers to live in the reign of George III, rather than Queen Victoria's like most old ladies, that doesn't mean she's soft in the head.'

So it was settled. A few days later they arrived at Chelmsford where, as Miss Cavendish had announced in a stately telegram, a conveyance could be chartered to carry them the last stage of their journey. They had not, however, bargained for the severity of the weather in this part of the country; though in Devonshire it had been harsh enough. An icy east wind flailed at them as they emerged from the station; snow was piled everywhere; under the pewter-coloured sky all life seemed at a standstill.

'Brrh,' muttered Nigel. 'So we're to be frozen alive at the start of this wild-cat chase. Let's go home again.'

Even Georgia, whose experience as an explorer might have inured her to such rigours, felt a qualm of regret for their warm, thatched cottage in the south-west. However, they found a taxi-driver willing to brave the perils of the Easterham road, and set forth. The ten-mile journey took over an hour, by the time they had dug themselves out of a couple of drifts and narrowly escaped sliding into a river at a right-angled turn. When, finally, they reached Easterham it was almost dusk.

The Dower House overlooked what must have been the village green, though the ubiquitous snow had obliterated all such features. It could not, however, entirely efface the charm of Miss Cavendish's home, a red-brick building whose symmetry of window and chimney, sharply-pitched roof and snug dormers, portico, fanlight, and wrought-iron gate, muffled up as they were with snow, still retained, like an elegant woman heavily furred, the essential assurance of beauty.

'What did I tell you?' whispered Georgia. 'Nobody could live in a perfect house like this and keep their insanity.'

Nigel was doubtful of the logic of this remark. But his brain, numbed by the cold, had room for only one thought – how huge a house this was to accommodate so tiny a woman. For Clarissa Cavendish, who received them in the hall, was a mannikin, a mere wisp and miniature of a woman, as delicate in filigree as a snowflake, with white hair piled high on her head, and a complexion that was a triumph – whether of art or nature, Nigel could not be sure.

'It is vastly horrid, this snow, is it not?' she remarked in a crisp, tinkling voice all of a piece with her appearance. 'You must be fatigued after your journey. I will show you your room. Then we will take a dish of tay, Georgia. Mr Strangeways will no doubt prefer clarry.'

Nigel protested that he did not drink claret at four-thirty in the afternoon.

'The bottle will serve for dinner, then,' said Miss Cavendish – a reply whose significance Nigel was soon to realize.

After tea, their hostess offered to show them over her house. Nigel, already fascinated by the many beautiful pieces he noticed around them in the drawing-room – the Hepplewhite chairs, a Bartolozzi engraving, a set of miniatures by Cosway, a side-table bearing several superb examples of Battersea enamel, a cabinet filled with fans, toys, snuff-boxes and knick-knacks of elaborate craftsmanship, the silk hangings and the Adam fireplace – accepted eagerly.

It was certainly a big house, bigger even than he had imagined. Miss Cavendish, a tiny figure erect as a ramrod, went in front, leading them from room to room. Each room had the lovely proportions of its age. Even the electric lights which Miss Cavendish switched on, with a cavalier disregard for the black-out, making the crystal chandeliers sparkle like frozen cascades, did not destroy the illusion of another age: the doors were mahogany, the walls washed in delicate tints of green, yellow, blue, and dove-grey.

'Lovely,' Nigel kept repeating mechanically: 'a perfect room.' He kept pinching himself, too, to make sure that he was not dreaming. Georgia he did not dare to glance at. For every single room they entered, with the exception of the drawing-room, a small morning-room, Miss Cavendish's and their own bedrooms, was stark staring empty. Not a single piece of furniture, not a curtain or a carpet adorned their exquisite symmetry. When they had returned to the drawing-room, Nigel cast about vainly for some comment which would do justice to the situation and no violence to Miss Cavendish's sensibilities. Georgia, however, with her customary directness, went straight to the point.

'Why do you keep all those rooms empty, Cousin Clarissa?' she asked.

'Because I cannot afford to furnish them in the style they demand, my dear,' was the reasonable reply. 'I had rather live in the part of a beautiful house than in the whole of an ugly one. You will allow that an old woman has a right to her fancies.'

'I call it very sensible,' said Nigel. 'You have an elastic house. You can expand or contract within it according to the fluctuations of your income.'

'Mr Strangeways,' announced Clarissa Cavendish, 'I perceive we are going to understand each other.'

'You could put a grand piano in each of those rooms, and have ten pianists down to stay, and play them all together. The resonance would be remarkable with those high ceilings,' said Georgia dreamily.

'I nauseate the piano. It is an instrument fit only for tradesmen's daughters to practise upon. The spinet is very well. The harpsichord will do. But the piano I believe to be a very vulgar pretentious noise. I am surprised at Restorick for playing it.'

'Restorick?'

'Hereward Restorick owns Easterham Manor. It has been in his family for a tolerable time now. It was they who built the Dower House.'

'Oh yes,' said Nigel. 'He's the chap whose cat has brought us together, isn't he? Will you tell us about the cat, Miss Cavendish?'

'After dinner, Mr Strangeways. It is a story which must wait upon good digestion. I am an old woman, and not to be rushed.'

In their bedroom two hours later, dressing for dinner, Georgia said to Nigel: 'I hope I've not done wrong, dragging you down here.'

'Darling, I wouldn't have missed it for anything. But what made her like this?'

'It's all coming back to me. Clarissa was one of the first blue-stockings – a don at Girton, I think. She made her name as an historian: the eighteenth century was her period, and she just soaked in it. Then she had a complete nervous breakdown – overwork, and I believe there was an unhappy love-affair: when she recovered, a part of her had got permanently stuck in the Georgian age. Of course, she had to give up her position; and she had a hardish time, teaching as a governness, till the legacy came along.'

A faint, fragile chime, like the notes of a musical-box, came up the stairs. Georgia and Nigel went down for dinner. The white panelled morning-room set off their hostess's grace and brilliant complexion; her eyes sparkled with sedate pleasure. Nigel was touched, seeing in this old woman the intelligence, the gay independence of the girl she had once been. To think of her as a governess, at the mercy of brusque or patronizing employers, gave one a really sickening qualm.

A village woman, looking oddly fancy-dressed in her mob cap and short, muslin apron, waited upon them. The food was excellent, though the helpings were fined down to Miss Cavendish's physique – a slip of sole, a tiny round of a tournedos, and wafer-thin fritters.

'We must celebrate your first night here,' said their hostess. 'Annie, the bottle of clarry.'

It was, quite evidently, the one and only bottle of claret in her cellar. But it proved to be an excellent Chateau Beychevelle, and Nigel complimented her upon it.

'It is a wine Harry was most partial to, I remember,' said Clarissa Cavendish; a faint twinge of some emotion, to which Nigel could not put a name, showed on her enamelled face. 'You will forgive me,' she went on, 'if I drink champagne. I cannot drink any wine but champagne.'

Annie half filled her glass from a bottle that had been opened before this evening. The champagne was flat as stale water. Clarissa Cavendish squirted soda-water into it, raised the glass gravely to Nigel, and said:

'A glass of wine with you, Mr Strangeways.'

The blizzard howled outside the shutters. The old house stood firm as a rock. It seemed a night, desolate without, warm and reassuring within, made for ghost stories, and, as if she had taken the thought from his mind, Clarissa Cavendish, leading the way into the drawing-room, said in the crisp tones of a don probing her pupil's knowledge –

'Mr Strangeways, I desire to know whether you accept the supernatural.'

CHAPTER THREE

'A harmless, necessary cat.'
SHAKESPEARE

'I BELIEVE there are more things in heaven and earth –'

'Come, sir,' interrupted Miss Cavendish, rapping her jewelled fingers smartly on her side-table. 'I am not to be evaded by quotations.'

Nigel tried again. 'Well, then, I believe we do not yet fully comprehend the laws of nature, that nature may even make exceptions to its own laws, but that it is our duty to look for rational explanations of all phenomena.'

'That is better. I conclude, then, that if you were to see a cat attempting to batter its brains out against a wall, you would not in the first place assume it to be possessed by a devil or attacking some ghostly apparition visible only to its own eyes: you would rather suppose it be rendered phrenetic by some internal disorder.'

'Cat's rabies,' suggested Georgia flippantly.

'Yes,' said Nigel. 'The creature must have fits. Or else it was in agonizing pain.'

'Scribbles never has fits,' said Miss Cavendish severely. 'And a few minutes after its droll display, it was fast asleep.'

'I think you had better start at the beginning,' Nigel said.

The old lady, drawing herself even more upright, composed her fingers in her lap. Every now and then they made little gestures, as though toying with a fan. For the rest, nothing of her moved during her strange narrative except the mouth and the dark brown, scintillating eyes.

'My story opens on the fourth day before Christmas. I was taking tay with Charlotte Restorick, Hereward's wife. She is a – an American,' (Nigel was convinced that Miss Cavendish had been on the point of saying 'a colonist'), 'but I find her civil enough, and she is generally accounted a handsome sort of female. Lord knows why she married Restorick: he's a poor thing – all moustache and decorum: the Restoricks are sadly inbred, of course. Presently, the house party assembling, the conversation turned on the subject of ghosts. There is a room at the Manor, called the Bishop's room, which is reputed to be haunted, and Elizabeth Restorick proposed that we should assemble there one night and – as she expressed it – beat up the bish.'

'Elizabeth Restorick?' asked Nigel. 'Who is she?'

'She is a trollop,' rejoined Miss Cavendish briskly. 'Hereward's sister, but a great deal younger than he, and a shocking forward chit. If Hereward inherited the Restorick fortune, Elizabeth inherited its vice. She was educated in America, to be sure, so we must not judge her too harshly. You are to know that Harold Restorick, Hereward's father, was attached to the embassy in Washington, and, being as he was to live there for some years, he was under the necessity of taking his family out to America, so that the children only received what rudimentary education the country can furnish. A sad pity. For Elizabeth and Andrew both had talent.'

'Andrew? That's another brother, is it?'

'Yes. He was Harry's favourite son, though Hereward of course was the heir. Andrew, alas, disappointed his father. He turned out a rolling stone, a lover of low company. He's a vastly handsome lad, though, and there is no real vice in him, unless it is a vice not to abide his brother's sermons. He and Elizabeth have always been great cronies.'

'Was he in the house party at Christmas too?'

'He was. The company was made up by Elizabeth's latest conquest, a Mr Dykes – a tedious, ill-bred person, a writer of romances – and Miss Ainsley, a nondescript sort of fribble. Oh yes, and I am forgetting Dr Bogan. Dr Bogan is, I apprehend, a quack.'

'It seems to have been a queerly assorted house party to find under so conventional a roof,' Georgia commented. 'A trollop, an Anglo-Saxon squire, an American wife, a rolling stone, a fribble, and a quack.'

Clarissa Cavendish inclined her head. Her fingers fluttered, and composed themselves again in her lap. 'Harry would not have countenanced it. But Hereward has no backbone. If Charlotte wishes to invite a person, then it is to be so. She is a snob, poor girl, and believes every freak duckling a swan. Well then, we fixed to assemble in the Bishop's room on the night of Christmas Eve.'

'What were you expected to see?' Nigel interrupted.

'It is a foolish, idle tale. The Bishop of Eastchester was staying at the Manor, in 1609. One morning he was found dead in that room. Some ill-conditioned persons alleged he had been poisoned by his host, and there was a scandal put about. But the Restorick of that time affirmed that the bishop, who was notoriously a gross liver, had taken a surfeit of venison the night before and died of it. I make no doubt this was the truth of the matter. However that may be, the superstition is that groans are heard by night from the Bishop's room, and the bishop has appeared to the credulous in a cambric nightgown clutching his belly and groaning mightily.'

'It sounds rather a frivolous ghost story to me,' said Georgia.

'At half an hour before midnight on Christmas Eve we all repaired to the Bishop's room. It is a horrid cold room, used now as a little library, and Charlotte Restorick had brewed a bowl of punch to warm our vitals. A great deal of wine had been drank at dinner; so, what with this and the punch, Elizabeth and Miss Ainsley were getting quite tipsy. I recall that Restorick rebuked Betty for sitting in Mr Dykes' lap, and she retorted that the bishop had done worse than that in his day. Her pertness started a very strange, vulgar scene. She is strangely violent at times. A positive virago. But what a beauty! Well, at the worst of the quarrel – though indeed the quarrel was all Elizabeth, and Restorick only trying to quieten her – the clock struck twelve. Andrew Restorick said, "Pipe down, Betty, or the bishop will cancel his visitation." After that she was quiet. His words seemed to sober the rest of the company too. We were sitting in a row of chairs along the wall opposite the fireplace. Someone suddenly said, "Look at Scribbles." '

Clarissa Cavendish paused effectively. In the silence, Georgia and Nigel could hear the howl of the east wind tearing past the house. Miss Cavendish shivered a little, so that her necklace made a sound like a faint tinkling of icicles, and resumed her story.

'The cat had been lapping a saucer of milk which had been brought in for her. She was now purring aloud – a mightily harsh, disagreeable sound, as if the creature was a rusty clockwork and someone winding it up. Then she walked into the middle of the room, her legs strangely rigid, arching her back and still making that infernal purring. We were all struck dumb with amazement. Scribbles held the floor. She was crouching now, like a tiger, kneading the carpet with her paws, glaring into the far corner of the room. On a sudden she sprang at this corner. I wish I might not have seen it. She sprang, and struck the wall with her head, and rebounded like an indiarubber ball. This queer behaviour she repeated three or four times, with every circumstance of ferocity, flinging herself against the bare walls or the bookcases till we had thought she must dash out her brains against them. The party was vastly discomposed at the spectacle. One of the females – Miss Ainsley, I fancy – began to sob and caterwaul, shrieking that the cat was seeing some horror invisible to us.'

'And what did *you* think?' asked Nigel sharply.

'I thought the cat was not frightened, but enjoying her hunt.'

For some reason this comment, delivered in Miss Cavendish's light, crisp voice, froze Georgia's blood.

'After some while,' the old lady resumed, 'Scribbles seemed to tire of these odd assaults. She prowled back to the centre of the room, suddenly commenced to chase her tail and went whirling round like a mad Dervish or a teetotum; then curled herself up in front of the whole company and fell asleep.'

There was a long silence. Nigel was staring down his nose, unwilling to meet the old lady's eyes. Georgia fidgeted with her cigarette-holder, for once at a loss for words.

'Why have you told us about this?' said Nigel at last, looking up.

Clarissa Cavendish's scintillating eyes held his. There was an excitement in them he could not fathom; they seemed to expect something from him, too, as though she were a teacher who could hardly restrain herself from prompting a pupil towards the correct answer. She said:

'First, Mr Strangeways, what is your own opinion of the incident?'

'Either the cat was seeing a ghost, or she wasn't. If it had been a ghost, she'd have been frightened, arched her back, spat, but surely not have delivered a series of assaults. Besides, we are agreed to shelve the supernatural until we are sure no rational explanation can be found. The violence of the animal's behaviour – how old is she, by the way?'

'Three years old,' said Clarissa.

' – precludes us from attributing it to mere kittenishness. Suppose she was drugged. You say she'd just been given a saucer of milk. I don't know what poison would produce such symptoms without leaving more severe after-effects. But suppose someone doped the milk, or gave her an injection before your séance began. Why should he do it? To frighten the party, seems the only possible answer. A practical joke. Or to frighten *one* of the party, seriously.'

'It sounds to me rather elaborate and cruel for an ordinary practical joke,' said Georgia. 'If the joker had dressed up in a cambric nightdress, and clutched his belly and groaned – but the phantom bishop seems to have got left on the side-lines.'

Miss Cavendish nodded vigorously, and gave the arm of her chair a little applauding pat.

'If the joke was a more serious one,' resumed Nigel, 'aimed at some particular member of the party, it must mean that there was something about the cat's behaviour which would be understood by the victim and frighten him more than the others. Was anyone especially upset, apart from Miss Ainsley?'

'You are familiar with the play, *Hamlet*, Mr Strangeways?'

Nigel admitted it.

'You recollect the play within the play – how the King watched the players, and Hamlet watched the King. On Christmas Eve we were not all engaged with the antics of the cat. I chanced to look aside and noticed Andrew Restorick gazing fixedly at another member of the party.'

'Which one?'

'That I cannot tell you. The chairs were arranged in an arc. Andrew was sitting on the extreme left, and gazing at some one of those at the other end, it might have been his sister, Elizabeth, or Dr Bogan, or Mr Dykes.'

'You were not altogether engrossed in the play yourself, then, Miss Cavendish?'

'La, sir, you are very pertinacious!' she exclaimed, with a coquetry that did not quite conceal a certain discomfiture. 'I have my understandings still, I hope. I may be allowed to use my eyes.'

'And did any of those three appear particularly upset?'

'I cannot pretend so. Betty looked dumpish, I thought she was too tipsy for alarm. Mr Dykes seemed to be swearing to himself. Dr Bogan maintained an air of reserve. I saw him and Betty with their heads together afterwards, though.'

'Have there been any repercussions since?'

Miss Cavendish gazed at him blankly, as though the word did not come into her vocabulary.

'You spoke in your letter of being apprehensive,' Nigel persisted. 'Are you afraid there's more to it than a cat's hallucinations? Was that only a beginning?'

The old lady seemed strangely unwilling to speak. Her eyes,

unfocused now, stared vaguely and painfully in front of her. She looked lost. At last, rising from her chair, leaning heavily upon her tasselled, ivory stick, she moved across to the far end of the room, ran her finger over a print upon the wall and, with her back turned to Nigel and Georgia, said:

'Yes. I *am* afraid. There is something rotten in that house. I cannot put my finger upon it, but I know it is so. I have' – her voice faltered slightly – 'I have special reasons for being interested in the family – in Elizabeth and Andrew particularly. My reasons are of no consequence, I beg leave to say no more of them. This I *can* tell you – that I had rather face the devil and all his angels than the influence, whatever it may be, which is at work in Easterham Manor.'

'I understand,' said Nigel gently. 'You wish me to – '

Clarissa Cavendish swung round from the wall, and pointed her ivory stick at Nigel like a rapier. Her voice now had an incisiveness that brought him upright in his chair.

'I wish you to find out what is wrong. I wish you to find out what Dr Bogan is doing in that house: I reckon him to be an objectionable creature. And what Hereward Restorick is afraid of. And what was in Andrew Restorick's heart that night when he paid no attention to the cat but was staring so fixedly at one other person in the room. And I wish,' she added in a whisper that Nigel only just caught, 'you may save Elizabeth from damnation.'

She returned to her chair, and gazed expectantly at Nigel.

'They're all there still – the house party?'

'They come and go. But at present they are all at the Manor, and like to stay. The roads in winter are very dirty.'

'But, you know,' Nigel pointed out gently, 'I have no authority to –'

'I have arranged for that. There is, I understand, a society for Psychical Research. You are to be a member of it. I have asked you to stay with me so that you may investigate the incident of the cat in the Bishop's room. It is all arranged.'

'But I don't know the first thing about psychical research.'

'I have purchased some volumes on the subject from my bookshop. You will study them to-morrow, and in the evening we are invited to take dinner at the Manor.'

Nigel gasped a little at Miss Cavendish's high-handedness. He would have liked to feel more sceptical about the extraordinary statements she had made, but against his will he had been impressed. Moreover, she had inspired him with a strong curiosity, an impatient desire to fill in the shadowy outlines of the characters she had described.

'What is this Dr Bogan a doctor of?' he asked.

'Medicine, I dare say. I hope I may not have to take any of his medicines.'

'Who invited him, do you know?'

'Elizabeth brings many unsuitable persons to stay at the Manor.'

'She comes down quite often herself, then?'

'Yes. She is a sadly erratic girl, I fear. But Hereward can scarcely forbid her the house.'

Miss Cavendish's replies were not very revealing, thought Nigel. He tried another track.

'Were any explanations of the cat's behaviour offered at the time? Did anyone think of examining the saucer?'

'I am not to know what the party said of it later. At the time, Hereward took upon himself to break up the assembly. He is the sort of man that chooses to ignore what he cannot understand: he would pile on a hundred mattresses rather than search for the pea. I do not know whether the saucer was examined.'

'You say that Dr Bogan and Elizabeth Restorick put their heads together after the incident. Did you hear anything they said?'

'Nothing material, I am sure. I am a little deaf, but adept in lip-reading. I fancied Dr Bogan said to Elizabeth, "Stick it, E." – but I was not paying them much attention. And now, my dears, we have had an exhausting day. You will forgive me if I retire. If you desire a dish of chocolate before retiring, pray ring for Annie. I am happy to have you both in my house.'

With remarkable dignity, the old lady rose, kissed Georgia, offered Nigel her frail, jewelled fingers, and took herself and her ivory stick up to bed.

CHAPTER FOUR

'O'er all there hung a shadow and a fear.'
THOMAS HOOD

EASTERHAM MANOR, as they emerged next evening from the car which Hereward Restorick had sent to fetch them, was no more than a blacker bulk against the blackness of the night. Nigel had to take Clarissa Cavendish's word for it that the house had been built in Queen Elizabeth's reign and little altered since. The Virgin Queen and her subjects, he reflected, never suffered from such a black-out. The car drove off, the chains round its tyres clinking, a faint fume of snow marking the course of the invisible wheels. The front door opened. Easterham Manor was evidently the kind of house where the front door opened without your having to ring the bell. There ought to be a slap-up dinner. Nigel squeezed Georgia's arm as they scurried inside, and the butler closed the door quickly behind them.

A maid-servant led Georgia and Miss Cavendish upstairs to take off their wraps. For Miss Cavendish this would be a formidable undertaking, since, in spite of their host's solicitude in sending a car, and the shortness of the journey from door to door, she had snugged herself up as if for an Arctic expedition, putting on a bonnet, a fur coat, and a leather golf-jacket over her party dress, and six or seven petticoats – to judge by her Mrs-Noah-like figure – beneath it.

While the disrobing was going forward, Nigel had leisure to observe the hall in which he had been left. It was big enough to have been set down in the World Fair and create a sizable obstruction there, it was warm as toast ('American wife; central heating; plenty of cash,' said Nigel to himself), but otherwise almost overpoweringly Elizabethan with its great oaken and cedar chests, rush mats, iron flambeaux, and coats of arms upon the walls – the kind of hall that Charlotte

Restorick would probably have described as 'just too cute'.

Yes, she certainly would, thought Nigel, a few moments later, when Mrs Restorick, superbly gowned in gold lamé, swam forward to meet them. He had the utmost difficulty in not addressing her as 'Mrs Rittenhouse', for she resembled to the life the stately, arch, sorely put-upon hostess of *Animal Crackers*.

'So nice to have you here, Clarissa,' she boomed in a voice like a stag belling. 'And this is the famous Georgia Strangeways. Hereward, haven't I always said I was dying to meet Mrs Strangeways?'

Hereward Restorick assented, in a well-bred mumble, pulling at the ends of his moustache.

'Pleasure,' he was understood to say. 'Distinguished woman. Read your novels.'

'Oh, how provoking men are!' exclaimed his wife archly. 'Mrs Strangeways is not a novelist, Hereward. She's the explorer, *you* know. Welcome to Easterham Manor, Mr Strangeways. I think psychical research is just too cute. Hereward, the sherry – these poor things are dying of cold. Now, Mrs Strangeways, I want to have you know Mr Dykes. Will Dykes, *you* know, the proletarian novelist. I'm sure you'll have so much in common, you two clever people. Eunice, this is Mr Strangeways, who is going to find out all about our ghost for us. Mr Strangeways, Miss Ainsley.'

Presently the note of a gong, hardly less portentous than Big Ben, was heard, vieing not altogether successfully with Mrs Restorick's bell-like tones. Two men came into the room, one slim, bronzed, with a light, athletic tread; the other sallow, stooping, and bearded. They were introduced as Andrew Restorick and Dr Dennis Bogan. It was at this moment that, amid the confused bubble of conversation, Clarissa's voice sounded like a tinkling icicle.

'Where is Elizabeth?' she said. 'Is she not to be with us?'

The effect of this innocuous question was quite extraordinary. It created a momentary silence which set all Nigel's nerves tingling, as though Clarissa had made some unforgivable accusation. He noticed several of the party glancing covertly at each other, as if to estimate the effect of Miss Cavendish's question upon their neighbours. Everything, for an instant, seemed frozen into the helpless unreality of a nightmare. Then their hostess said:

'So sorry. Elizabeth is not well. She's had one of her attacks and won't be able to come down to-night. So disappointing for her. How is she, Dr Bogan?'

'The pulse is still a little high. But I hope we shall be able to get her up to-morrow.' The doctor's voice was smooth as oil upon troubled waters. By rights, it should have put an end to the odd little situation, but Clarissa Cavendish said:

'Too many cocktails. You should forbid them to her. They undermine the system.'

It was an outrageous remark, and doubly so coming from Miss Cavendish – thought Nigel – who was normally so very much the mistress of ceremony. Its reception, however, showed that she was more intimate with the household than he had realized. It seemed to relax the tension rather than increase it, though Nigel felt it had been quite out of character. Several of those in the room laughed indulgently, and Andrew Restorick said:

'Miss Cavendish, you're incorrigible. I believe you would rather see us all under the table with sherry or claret than sipping one tiny glass of watered-down gin and angostura.'

'In my day,' replied the old lady briskly, 'gin was drank only by the low. A penny a quartern. Drunk for a penny, dead drunk for tuppence, was the saying.'

Once again Nigel's scalp crawled. It was uncanny – that 'in my day' – referring to a time two hundred years back, a century from which Clarissa Cavendish, sitting bolt upright in her flowered dress and aura of elaborate courtliness, might have been a revenant.

'A penny a quartern!' exclaimed Miss Ainsley. 'Those were the days! But I thought it was loaves you sold by the quartern.'

Miss Cavendish surveyed the flushed, jerky young woman through her lorgnette with considerable disdain, but offered no reply. Will Dykes muttered audibly.

'Anyone'd think Betty was a dipsomaniac, the way some people talk.'

'Really, Dykes,' protested Hereward Restorick, massaging his moustache even more vigorously. 'I'm not aware that anyone suggested –'

'Oh, no. We're not suggesting anything. We're just sitting round being polite ladies and gentlemen, pretending not to notice the bad smell in the room.'

'A rough diamond,' Charlotte Restorick murmured in Georgia's ear. 'But such talent, such native honesty, poor fellow. He was born in the gutter, but literally in the gutter, my dear. So wonderful, don't you think?'

Georgia was saved from having to express an opinion on the miraculous birth of Mr Dykes, by the butler's announcing dinner. Nigel found himself seated beside his hostess, with Dykes opposite him. The novelist, whom he could now study at more leisure, was evidently a fish out of water in this company, and did nothing to conceal his incompatibility. His hair lying in an oiled quiff over a broad forehead, his coarse skin and jutting underlip gave him an unattractiveness which was redeemed by the lively, searching eyes and a voice of unusual resonance. Nigel judged that he was neither trading on his proletarian origin here, nor at all awed by his surroundings. There had been something appealing in the way he had taken up the cudgels for Elizabeth Restorick. Was he in love with her, perhaps? What else could account for his coming into a society so obviously uncongenial to him? And, a still more teasing question, why had the mention of the absent Elizabeth produced such sharp and varied reactions from these people? Yes, there was a spectre at this festal board all right;

and Nigel fancied it had nothing to do with the hallucinations of the cat, Scribbles.

Nigel had the gift, more common amongst women than men, of being able to take active part in a conversation while his attention was directed elsewhere. Now, though he was on the alert towards the other diners, he was also keeping his end up quite adequately with Mrs Restorick. Indeed, once he began to disentangle her from his initial associations with Mrs Rittenhouse, he found her a real enough person. She had that positive snobbery of the American, so much more agreeable than its negative English counterpart because it proceeds from a zest and appetite for experience.

'We shall all go up to the Bishop's room after dinner,' she was saying. 'You will want to reconstruct the scene of the crime, I'm sure, Mr Strangeways.'

The remark was accompanied by a light, conventional laugh, but also by a look from her sapphire-blue eyes that brought Nigel up all standing. Now just what does she mean by that, he wondered. What an odd way to talk about the haunted cat. He said:

'I'm afraid I'm only an amateur, you know, Mrs Restorick. You mustn't expect too much from me. Don't be disappointed if I fail to bring your ghost out into the open.'

'Ah, yes. The ghost. I suppose every old family in this country has its' – she paused a moment – 'its skeleton.'

'The Bishop must be a very substantial skeleton, by all accounts. Have you seen or heard anything in that room yourself, Mrs Restorick?'

'No. I'm afraid I can't be psychic.' She turned her head to include Will Dykes in the conversation. 'Do you believe in ghosts, Mr Dykes?'

Nigel attended with one ear to the novelist's pugnaciously dogmatic reply. But he was also listening to the conversation at the other end of the table where Hereward Restorick, Andrew, Georgia, and Clarissa were sitting. Mrs Restorick's remark about 'the scene of the crime' must have started a subject over there. Hereward and Georgia were discussing a detective novel they had both read. Suddenly Andrew broke in with:

'The trouble about detective novelists is that they shirk the real problem.'

'The real problem?' asked Georgia.

'The problem of evil. That's the only really interesting thing about crime. Your ordinary four-a-penny criminals, who steal because they find it the easiest way to make a living, who murder for gain or out of sheer exasperation – they're of no interest. And the criminal in the average detective story is duller still, a mere king-pin to hold together an intricate, artificial plot, the major premiss of an argument that leads nowhere. But what –' here Andrew Restorick's quiet voice took on a louder, compelling note which made the whole table listen – 'what about the man who revels in evil? The man or woman whose very existence seems to depend upon the power to hurt or degrade others?'

There was a shocked silence. That phrase, 'the man who revels in evil', arrested the whole company in a stony silence, as if Andrew had produced the Gorgon's head out of his table-napkin. Yet again, Nigel was conscious of a general shrinking – an apprehension far greater than the remark should have produced; not so much an apprehension, perhaps, as a shrinking horror at the appearance of something which they had all been expecting. Nonsense, said Nigel irritably to himself, you're getting as bad as Scribbles. Hereward was heard to say:

'Oh come, Andrew, old chap. There aren't people like that. Not in real life. There's so much good in the worst of us – how does it go?'

'What about Hitler?' Miss Ainsley inquired vapidly.

Will Dykes said, 'Restorick is right. It's too bookish. You don't get 'em in real life – not characters like the valet and the governess in *The Turn of The Screw*.'

Andrew Restorick turned the screw a little tighter, saying:

'Oh, but you're wrong. I've knocked about the world a bit, and I tell you I've met such creatures. Three of 'em, to be precise. One was an American, in Constantinople; a blackmailer. The second was a sadist storm-trooper in Breslau – he got tight one night and confided to me that he simply lived for the tortures he was allowed to inflict on prisoners.' Andrew Restorick paused.

'And the third?' prompted Miss Cavendish coolly. 'You are saving up something excessively horrid for your climax, I am assured.'

'The third,' said Andrew Restorick deliberately, in a voice that seemed to Nigel to be dragged up out of an abyss of pain and deep bewilderment, 'the third, since you ask me – unless I'm very much mistaken – can be found here in this house to-night.'

'Oh la, Andrew!' exclaimed Clarissa Cavendish. 'You are too odious. I protest you have turned me goose-flesh all over.'

'Andrew, you're very naughty!' said Mrs Restorick, plunging in like a roguish titan to save the situation. 'Andrew is such a dreadful leg-puller. Now he's trying to work us up into a panic for our little séance to-night. I won't have it, Andrew. Mr Strangeways wants us to approach it in a calm, scientific spirit.'

'Sorry, Charlotte. My imagination running away with me,' said Andrew Restorick, lightly seconding her effort. 'But I still maintain there are such people. What do you say, Dr Bogan? You must have a wide experience to draw on.'

The doctor, who had been following these exchanges with an alert, whimsical eye, tugged gently at his beard. His eyes became abstracted, as though he were turning over case-histories in his own mind.

'I'm inclined to agree with you, Restorick. Of course, in my profession, we do not have the same values. There is no good or evil for us. There is just sickness or health. We never judge. But yes, I believe there may be minds which are incurably sick, which live – as you put it – for evil. I reckon so.'

But at this point their hostess firmly put an end to the morbid discussion by collecting the ladies' eyes. The gentlemen being left alone, Nigel had more leisure to look about him. The dining-room was large enough to be called a banqueting hall; a musicians' gallery stood at the far end. The table was lit by electric candles in heavy iron sconces, and in the huge fireplace several trees seemed to be burning.

'A wonderful old house this must be,' he said politely to Hereward Restorick.

'Like to show you over it. Bit of a rabbit warren really, y'know. Come up to-morrow morning. And your good wife. You must meet the kiddies, too.'

Nigel somehow hadn't connected the statuesque Charlotte Restorick with the idea of children. He said he would be delighted.

'And I say, Strangeways,' continued his host, looking rather like a melancholy spaniel caught out in some delinquency, 'this show of yours to-night. My wife's deuced keen on it, otherwise I'd – what I mean is, with everyone a bit het up – this war, y'know – and we don't want the women folk frightened, so I thought – well, what d'you think?'

Nigel gathered from these incoherent mumbles that his host wanted to have the psychical research called off, without being held responsible for calling it off himself. Nigel would have been only too ready to fall in with his host's wishes, particularly in view of a certain penetrating, sceptical look he had noticed in Dr Bogan's eye – a look which boded ill for impostors; but the situation at Easterham Manor was so mysterious that curiosity got the better of caution, and he compromised by telling Hereward Restorick that he thought he ought to go forward with it, since his hostess expected him to, but it would be all very mild and unsensational – just a preliminary reconnaissance of the facts.

So, an hour later, they all trooped up to the Bishop's room. It was an unprepossessing apartment, gloomy and cold in spite of the fire burning in the grate. Bookcases lined the walls at intervals, filled with fusty volumes in calf and bound copies of dim nineteenth-century periodicals. The ceiling was so low that Nigel had to stoop to avoid being brained by some of its more massive beams. Chill draughts ran like mice along the floor and hurried up one's ankles.

None of this, however, cramped Charlotte Restorick's style. Rising from her seat, hands clasped on her massive bosom and an expression of anticipative ecstasy on her face, she announced to the semi-circle of chairs – as if they had been the whole embattled Four Hundred – that she was happy to be able to present Mr Strangeways, the well-known expert in psychical research, who with their help was going to solve the mystery of the Bishop's room.

The combined effect of this announcement and the room itself was to make Nigel's blood seem to be alternately boiling and freezing in his veins. However, he took the floor, ignoring a flagrant wink from Georgia and firmly avoiding Dr Bogan's eye, and opened up. Mrs Restorick had exaggerated his credentials. He was a mere amateur of psychical research. But the episode of Christmas Eve had interested him strangely – and where, by the way, was Scribbles?

Charlotte Restorick, flushing, said wasn't it tiresome of her, but in the excitement she had quite forgotten to have the cat brought up. She spoke into the house telephone. Nigel half expected the butler to arrive bearing the cat on a salver, but Scribbles entered in the arms of a housemaid who was evidently distraught with panic at the idea of being in the haunted room, and, dropping her burden on the floor – where it instantly curled up and fell asleep at Nigel's feet – fled downstairs again.

In the meanwhile Nigel, judging that this was the simplest way to conceal his own ignorance, had begun to ask each of those present to give his or her own account of the Scribbles episode. Their testimonies varied but little. Eunice Ainsley, it is true, shuddering strongly from blonde head to dainty toe, protested that she had seen a too foully weird shadow pass along the wall where the cat had been battering itself. 'Auto-suggestion,' murmured Dr Bogan, taking the words out of Nigel's mouth. Andrew Restorick gave an embellished account of Scribbles' behaviour, an account which must have been second-hand if – as Miss Cavendish had asserted – he had been observing the effect rather than the agent of that Christmas Eve alarm. Hereward Restorick contributed a prosy synopsis of the history of the Bishop's room. Everyone seemed a little deflated, a little ashamed of the strong reactions they had felt on the previous occasion. Nigel received the impression that something vital was missing – the presence, perhaps, of the elusive Elizabeth Restorick.

'So much for the facts, then,' he said. 'Now we've got to consider the possibility that the whole thing was a hoax. Who suggested the experiment originally?'

'Betty did,' said Charlotte Restorick. She wagged a roguish finger at her brother-in-law. 'Andrew, are you quite sure it wasn't one of your and Betty's practical jokes? You two children are so naughty.'

'Innocent this time,' replied Andrew, smiling amiably.

'But, damn it,' said Hereward, 'you couldn't make the cat behave like that. It was extraordinary. Gave you the creeps.' A sudden little chill came over the assembly. Hereward went on hurriedly, 'Not that there's anything in it, I mean. Brute must have eaten something that disagreed with it.'

'Who gave Scribbles the saucer of milk?' Nigel inquired.

After a moment's general indecision, Will Dykes said:

'Betty did.'

'Oh, but that's absurd,' said Miss Ainsley. 'Betty never would. She loathes animals.'

'Can't help that. I saw her,' maintained Will Dykes.

'Perhaps someone asked her to.' Nigel looked round at the guests inquiringly. They all shook their heads or remained silent.

'Well, I shall have to ask her myself then.'

'God damn it!' Will Dykes suddenly exploded. 'Is this a

police inquiry, or what? It's always Betty who's got to be blamed for everything.'

'Don't be a bloody fool, Dykes,' said Miss Ainsley viciously. 'Just because Betty's got you on a string, you imagine she's a holy angel. I could tell you –'

'Hold your tongue, you bitch!' shouted Will Dykes.

The scene was incredible, bursting out like a thunderclap from a clear sky. For once, Nigel felt utterly at a loss. Even the premonitory breezes over the dinner table had not prepared him for such a storm. Nerves seemed to be so raw in this house that the least touch provoked an outcry. Mrs Restorick, however, pulled herself together and rode – or rather, contrived to seem quite oblivious of – the whirlwind. The company was shepherded downstairs. Final drinks were served. Hereward's chauffeur drove the Dower House party home. Nigel and Georgia had been invited to come up again early next morning.

Half an hour later, in their bedroom, they compared notes.

'Darling, I rather wish we hadn't come,' Georgia was saying. 'I don't like it. I've never been so frightened in my life.'

This was something of an admission from Georgia, who had faced more dangers in her thirty-five years than most men meet in their whole lifetime, and Nigel took it at its face value.

'What frightened you most?'

'Andrew Restorick, when he said there was somebody in the house who "lived for evil". One of his three instances. You see, he meant it. He wasn't pulling any legs then.'

'That's what I thought, too,' replied Nigel soberly.

'Clarissa knows about it. The cat business was just an excuse for getting you down here.'

'Who did Andrew mean, I wonder. Elizabeth, do you think? What did Clarissa say? "I wish you may save Elizabeth Restorick from damnation." I think it's all a bit above my weight.'

'Did you notice, just after we arrived, when Clarissa asked if Elizabeth was going to be with us to-night – what an odd effect it made? The queer way people glanced at each other?'

'Yes. It makes me think that each of them had his own secret about her, and was covertly trying to estimate whether the others guessed it. What I mean is, when a number of people have a secret *in common*, their protective reaction is very studiously to avoid each other's eyes.'

'Which rules out the idea that Elizabeth was being kept from us by a kind of common conspiracy. She must be a remarkable creature. You could hardly mention her name to-night without someone acting strange or blowing up.'

'Well, there's no use speculating about it till we know more of the background. I wonder will she be well enough for me to see her to-morrow. I should like to know what Dr Bogan is treating her *for*, I must say.'

Nigel was to see Elizabeth Restorick to-morrow, but under circumstances very different from what he had imagined. When they presented themselves at Easterham Manor next morning, after a floundering walk through the snow, the door was opened by the butler. His fat, white face was quivering like a blanc-mange. In a voice almost out of control, he said:

'Mrs Restorick wishes me to bring you to her room. Oh sir, the most terrible thing has happened. Miss Elizabeth –' His voice failed him.

'Is she – worse?'

'Dead, madam. Milly found her this morning. She was dead.'

'I *am* sorry. We'd no idea she was so ill. I'm sure they won't want us to – please give our deepest sympathy to –'

'Mrs Restorick particularly asked for you to come in. You see, sir,' the butler gulped, 'Miss Elizabeth has – has hung herself.'

CHAPTER FIVE

A neck God made for other use
Than strangling in a string.
A. E. HOUSMAN

As they waited in Mrs Restorick's room, Nigel's mind went back to an earlier case of his, a case whose solution had depended upon a young Irish girl who had killed herself years before and in another country. At the start, he had known as little about that Judith as now he knew about this Elizabeth. Judith had been a face seen in an old snapshot. Elizabeth was still almost as shadowy a figure; he knew little about her except what Miss Cavendish had told them two evenings before – that she had inherited the vice of the Restorick family, and that she was a beauty. And, last night, every time her name was mentioned there had been a curiously violent reaction.

Charlotte Restorick now appeared. Shock and sorrow had stripped from her those little artificialities of speech and gesture, and left her a quiet dignity which impressed Nigel very much. He fancied, looking at her haggard face, that she had been taking most of the strain of the tragedy in her household. Georgia tried to express their sympathy. Charlotte received it with a gentle nobility which made it seem all the more inadequate, then she turned to Nigel.

'Mr Strangeways, I have a request to make which you must feel quite free to refuse. A request and a confession. I'm afraid I asked you here last night under false pretences. Miss Cavendish had told me you were a private investigator, and I asked her to have you stay at the Dower House. The episode in the Bishop's room seemed the best pretext. Only Miss Cavendish and myself, to the best of my knowledge, are aware of your real profession.'

'You were expecting – something to happen?'

'I didn't know. I've been in great distress – but we'll talk about that later. What I want you to do is' – her hands gripped the back of the chair so that her knuckles whitened – 'is to go and look at Elizabeth. Just that. I know something is wrong, but I can't figure out what it is. Then come back and talk to me. Maybe I've just been imagining things these last weeks – everything's been so unsettled. I –'

She was slipping a little towards incoherence, and, as if to arrest herself, turned more briskly to Georgia, saying:

'I wonder would you go and keep the children company for a while. It would be a great kindness. Priscilla's governess is on vacation, and they don't take to Miss Ainsley. I don't want them to be wandering around the house just now.'

Georgia willingly agreed. Mrs Restorick sent a message to her husband, then took Georgia off upstairs. Presently Hereward appeared and conducted Nigel to Elizabeth's room. On the way, he apologized – vaguely and rather ludicrously – for the trouble to which they were putting Nigel. He seemed much more distraught than his wife, as though he had nothing but his conventional good breeding to oppose to the tragedy, and it was not equal to the strain.

'I suppose you've sent for the police?' Nigel asked.

Hereward winced. An expression of distaste came over his features. 'Yes, I'm afraid there's going to be a dreadful scandal. Y'know what it's like in the country. Scandal and gossip. Of course, Dixon'll do his best to hush it up. He's the Chief Constable. Friend of mine. Very good fellow. Mind your head through this door.'

Upstairs the house, as Restorick had said, was a rabbit warren. Dark little passages that seemed to twist and turn till you lost all sense of direction. Low doors. Steps up or down where you least expected them.

'Sent for a doctor, too?'

'Oh, didn't think that necessary. Got Bogan here, y'see. He was looking after her.'

He cast a dubious glance at Nigel, which said as plainly as words – deuced embarrassing situation, this; total stranger;

why Charlotte wanted to drag him into it I can't imagine. He looked so pathetically inadequate that Nigel tried to help him out.

'My uncle's Assistant Commissioner at New Scotland Yard. I've had a certain amount of experience of this sort of thing. Perhaps I can be of some help.'

'Quite. Quite. Very good of you. Well, here we are. Andrew said we should leave everything untouched. I'll – er – leave you to it. Robins – that's our constable – he'll be along soon: was out somewhere when I rang up. Difficult to get about in this snow,' said Hereward Restorick, and, opening a door, retired hastily from the scene.

It was perhaps the weirdest scene Nigel had ever witnessed, for everything here – even the central figure – seemed to contradict the idea of tragedy. It was a gay room, the ceiling higher than most of those at the Manor, decorated with a pretty flowered wallpaper and bright curtains of the same pattern. The black-out curtains had been pulled back, so that the shine off the snow pervaded the room with an unearthly radiance. Bright clothes were littered on the chairs, a crimson slipper in the middle of the floor took the eye, and the mirrors on the dressing-table reflected a crystal array of scent bottles and toilet preparations. A clean, pleasing odour of some sandalwood-smelling scent hung in the air. It might have been a young girl's room, breathing innocence and a light heart.

And Elizabeth Restorick, hanging from a beam in the centre of the room, a thin rope twined double round her neck, might have been a young girl still. She was stark naked. Her body had a vernal perfection, even in death, that took the breath away. Shining in the light from the snow, the red-lacquered toenails so close to the floor that she seemed almost to be standing on tiptoe, her body challenged the eye and humbled it. Nigel understood what havoc the living girl could have caused.

But she was a woman, not a girl. Her face showed that. Though little distorted by the manner of her death – peaceful, indeed, and remotely smiling – the features bore the mark of experience. There were fine wrinkles under the brown eyes, and the skin over the temples had a tired, brittle look. For a few moments Nigel was so fascinated by the beauty, the incurious regard of the dead woman, that the strangest thing about her failed to strike him. Her face was made up. Once he had realized this, his mind kept returning to it, even while he was going through the commonplace preliminaries of his investigation. Her face was made up, thoroughly if not quite perfectly – the lipstick did not quite follow the lines of the mouth. Well, one would not expect her hand to have been steady just then. It seemed to tell him a great deal about Elizabeth – that she should have tired her face for this assignation with death.

But perhaps she hadn't. Perhaps she had never removed her day make-up. Why should she bother to, indeed, if she had this in mind? No, it was of no significance, Nigel decided. He had just lost his sense of proportion for a moment, seeing that lovely, artificial face with the dark hair tumbling about it, the wanton head drooping over the body that might have been an innocent girl's.

Everything, Hereward said, had been left untouched. Then she had written no farewell message, unless Hereward, in his morbid horror of scandal, had found one and decided it had better be suppressed. Hereward, or some other interested party – a suicide note from Elizabeth might easily damage more persons than one – Nigel fancied. Well, it was not unprecedented for suicides to leave no message. And maybe it was in character that Elizabeth should have hung herself naked, flaunting her beauty to the end. There was nothing more for Nigel to do till he had discovered some of the facts. He went out, and found his way downstairs.

As he approached Mrs Restorick's room, he saw her husband in the hall below, talking to a policeman who was furtively trying to kick some of the caked snow off his boots. If Hereward was so sanguine about persuading the Chief

Constable to hush things up, it seemed more than likely he would have the village constable in his pocket too. And what about Dr Bogan? Were his lips to be sealed also? Nigel anticipated a difficult job. But, of course, he had no reason yet to believe that there *was* anything to hush up – anything beyond the suicide of an erratic relative. Or did Hereward want to have it made out an accident?

Charlotte Restorick was seated at her desk. 'Your wife is a dear,' she said, 'the children are quite crazy about her already. Now, come and sit over here, and tell me what you think about it all.'

'May I ask you some questions first?'

'Why, of course.'

'Who found the body?'

'Milly. She's the maid who was looking after poor Betty. She called her at nine o'clock this morning – Betty liked to sleep late. Milly found her like that, and we heard her screaming.'

'What happened then? Did you all run upstairs?'

'Hereward, Andrew, and I went up. We saw – what had happened. I wanted to have the poor thing taken down, but Andrew said nothing in the room must be touched.'

'She left no farewell note for anyone?'

'No. At least, we couldn't find one. It might be locked away somewhere. We thought we'd better not have anything opened till the police came.'

'Did you make sure she was dead? At once?'

'Oh, Mr Strangeways, we knew. But Andrew sent Hereward to fetch Dr Bogan, almost at once.'

'Was the door locked when Milly went in?'

'I don't know. She would have her own key, of course. Shall I ring for her?'

Presently the girl appeared, red-eyed and shaking. She said, yes, the door had been locked. No, she hadn't touched anything in the room, she wouldn't have dared, not if you'd offered her a hundred pounds.

'What about the black-out curtains? Were they open or closed?' asked Nigel.

Milly said she'd been far too terrified to notice.

'They were closed,' said Mrs Restorick. 'We could see Betty by the light through the door, but Andrew flung them open to give us more light.'

'It was fairly dark, then? I mean, the electric lights in the room weren't on when you entered?'

Both Mrs Restorick and Milly agreed that they were not.

'Now, Milly,' asked Nigel, 'what time did you see Miss Restorick last?'

'Ten o'clock last night, sir. I went up to help her get ready for bed, the poor soul.'

'Oh, she wasn't in bed? I understood she was unwell last night.'

Mrs Restorick shot a quick, warning glance at him. 'She didn't feel up to joining us at dinner. But she hadn't been in bed yesterday. She just kept to her room. Dr Bogan wished her not to have any change of temperature.'

'I see. You helped her to retire, Milly? You didn't put her clothes away though, I noticed.'

'She told me not to, sir.'

Nigel raised his eyebrows. 'Do you remember her exact words?'

'She said, "You needn't bother with my clothes to-night, Milly. Run along now, there's a good girl," she said. Well, of course I went downstairs then, but I did think it was funny – Miss Elizabeth always liking to have her dresses put away tidily.'

'Did she seem tired? Depressed?'

The girl pondered for a moment. 'Well, sir, that's funny too, seeing as what the poor lady meant to do. But she didn't seem sad. I thought she was excited, like.'

'And that was the last you saw of her – till this morning? Had she her nightdress on when you left her?'

'Yes, sir. She was doing her face at the mirror, in her night-dress and peignoir.'

Nigel's eyes suddenly sparked, and his tone made the girl start as he said:

' "Doing her face"? Making up, d'you mean?'

'Oh no, sir. She had taken off her make-up and was putting on cold cream. She did that every night.'

'I see. Yes,' said Nigel after a short pause. 'Now, Milly, can you keep a secret?'

'Oo, yes, sir. What was it you – '

'I want you to tell nobody – nobody at all, you understand – what we've been talking about.'

The girl promised, and was sent away. Nigel was aware of Charlotte Restorick's eyes shrewdly scrutinizing him. Getting up he walked over to the mantelpiece and began to fiddle absentmindedly with a Lalique fish that stood upon it – a delicate, grotesque piece of glass work, but no more grotesque than the idea which had come into his head.

'I'm afraid I understand only too well what direction you're moving in,' whispered Mrs Restorick. 'But it's not possible. You *must* be wrong, Mr Strangeways.'

'How well did you know Miss Restorick? Did she confide in you? Had you any reason for thinking she might kill herself?'

'I didn't know her very well. I admired her – she was a lovely creature and so full of life. But I don't think any woman,' Mrs Restorick faintly accented the word, 'could have got to know her well. I want to be frank with you. You'd find it out for yourself, in any case. Elizabeth was a man's woman, every inch of her. Some of us are like that, others aren't. No, she didn't confide in me. We never saw her for long. Of course, there was always a room for her here, but she was erratic and secretive – she used to come and go – she had an income of her own, by her father's will, and she spent most of the time in London or travelling.'

'You never suspected she might put an end to her life?'

'She had been out of sorts and very nervy lately.'

'Lately?'

'We noticed it particularly this visit. She came down just before Christmas.'

'What was her illness?'

Mrs Restorick looked a little confused. 'I think you had best ask Dr Bogan about that.'

'I will. Do I take it he was officially in attendance upon her? Has he been here all the time? Did you know him before?'

'I don't know a great deal about him. Elizabeth used to bring people down here very casually. He was a personal friend of hers, I believe, and she consulted him professionally too. He's some kind of specialist, in London. He's been down here every week-end since Elizabeth came.'

'And the other members of your house party – have they all been here since just before Christmas?'

'Andrew arrived a week before the others. Will Dykes and Miss Ainsley came the same day as Elizabeth. They were to have stayed a fortnight or so, but now –'

'Did they all know each other previously?'

Charlotte Restorick rose from her chair and walked over to Nigel. Her fine, full face kept its dignity, though she made no attempt to conceal her distress.

'Mr Strangeways,' she said, 'all these questions of yours – let's not pretend to each other any longer. You don't believe my sister-in-law committed suicide.'

Nigel gazed back at her straightly. 'You saw the body. The face is made up. Milly told us that Miss Restorick was removing her make-up when she left her. Milly said she sounded "excited". Can you believe that Elizabeth, that any woman would take off her make-up, *and then make up her face again*, just before hanging herself?'

Mrs Restorick's hands gripped the shelf of the writing-desk behind her back.

'I think you had better say it all,' she whispered.

'Elizabeth was "excited", not depressed. She wanted to get

Milly out of the room quickly, as if she expected a visitor any moment, so she told her not to bother about putting away the clothes. She had begun to remove her make-up, because she didn't want Milly to guess that she – expected a visitor. When you found her this morning, her face was made up and her body naked. There's only one explanation. She *did* expect a visitor that night, and someone *did* visit her – a lover. And that someone killed her.'

CHAPTER SIX

*'There are worse occupations in this world
than feeling a woman's pulse.'*
STERNE

A FEW minutes later, Mr Restorick took Nigel to interview the members of the household. It was, Nigel thought, a rather horrible travesty of last night's occasion; there was the same embarrassment and artificiality about the company now assembled in the drawing-room, the same touch of formality in the way Charlotte Restorick introduced him; while Nigel, himself, was only a little less uneasy about his status quo than he had been the night before. Mrs Restorick had agreed that neither of them should hint at the dreadful interpretation he had put upon Elizabeth's death; so she was now introducing him, with that air of making something between an informal and a set speech which even under the present circumstances her dignity contrived to carry off, as a friend who had some experience in these matters and had kindly consented to give them all the help he could.

'Mr Strangeways seems to be a man of parts,' murmured Andrew when Mrs Restorick had finished. 'A psychical investigator. A friend in need. An expert in – er – police matters.'

Hereward shifted in his chair and glared at his brother. Miss Ainsley was staring at Nigel, her mouth dropped unbecomingly open, nicotine-stained fingers pulling at her lower lip. Dr Bogan, gazing at the floor, combed his beard. It was Will Dykes, Nigel noticed as he glanced round the company, who seemed to have taken the blow hardest; he was staring out of the window, isolated in grief, tears running down his cheeks; the others were keeping up an elaborate pretence of not noticing this exhibition. So Dykes was in love with her, thought Nigel, there's no doubt about that now. Dragging his attention away from the novelist, he addressed the company at large.

'I hope you won't look upon me as an intruder. The police are bound to ask questions presently, and it'll be more satisfactory all round if you're prepared for that. It's not a question of cooking up a story, of course, but of having clear in one's mind the essential points.'

Nigel paused for long enough to realize how very unconvincing this preamble sounded, then continued:

'Now first, did any of you suspect that this might happen? Had any one heard Miss Restorick threatening to kill herself? Is there any reason why she should have done so?'

An uncomfortable, dismal silence followed. Hereward Restorick, as if he felt it the duty of a host to relieve the awkwardness, finally said:

'I never got the impression personally that – but, of course, Betty was a rather – well, I mean she was rather – '

'– a neurotic girl,' supplied Andrew, in a tone so harsh that even Nigel started and glanced at him in surprise. Andrew's thin, brown face looked bleak as the wintry sky outside. His words, like the key log loosened from a log jam, set everything moving.

'Betty was what the world made her. She lived in a rotten environment, and she couldn't help being tainted. But at heart she was sound. I tell you, in her heart she was innocent. And she'd far too much courage to take the easy way out. I don't understand it.'

Will Dykes seemed to be talking to himself. His voice was low and monotonous, like the voice of a man mumbling through a nightmare. When he'd finished, it was as if the act of speech had woken him out of his dream. He looked around in a dazed way and, suddenly aware of the tears on his cheeks, brushed his sleeve over them. There was a moment's outraged silence. Then Eunice Ainsley said:

'Well, considering I heard her tell Mr Dykes only a week ago that she couldn't go through with it, I should have thought – but she could always make men believe black was white.'

'Come, child, you're overwrought,' said Mrs Restorick firmly.

'Is that true, Dykes?' asked Andrew.

The novelist stiffened in his chair, an incongruous figure in this company with his oiled quiff of hair and provincial clothes.

'What Miss Ainsley hears through keyholes is hardly evidence. But Betty did say that to me.'

'What? Good God! But why didn't you – ?' Hereward stuttered to a standstill.

'It's not relevant,' said Dykes stubbornly.

'Not relevant?' asked Andrew. 'Surely the police or Mr Strangeways are the best judges of that?'

'When Betty said she couldn't go through with it, she was not talking about suicide. She was talking about marriage.'

'Marriage?' It was evident from Charlotte Restorick's tones that it was the first she had heard of it.

'Yes,' said Will Dykes, throwing up his head and challenging the whole lot of them, 'she was going to marry me, but –'

'Marry *you*?' Miss Ainsley's voice rose in a kind of tittering scream. 'Betty marry *you*?'

Dykes flinched a little, but maintained his air of defiance. Is he telling the truth, wondered Nigel. Or defending her 'good name' at the cost of making himself look ridiculous? The latter would be in character. In Nigel's imagination, that delicate, luxurious body hanging upstairs set itself beside the uncouth figure of the novelist. Hereward Restorick was saying inadequately:

'Well, of course, must be a terrible shock to you, Dykes. Had no idea the wind was in that quarter. A rotten business for us all. Poor Betty –'

'Now we've cleared up that misunderstanding,' came Andrew's incisive voice, 'we can look elsewhere. Perhaps Dr Bogan will state his views.'

The doctor's eyes slowly lifted to Andrew Restorick. They were at once melancholy and reserved. Nigel fancied Dr Bogan's practice must be largely among women – the melancholy would appeal to their maternal feelings, the deep reserve would intrigue the Pandora in each of them.

'My views?' said the doctor slowly.

'Did you consider Betty a suicidal type?' Andrew asked.

'I am not disposed to think there is such a thing as a suicidal *type*. If you ask me whether the conditions making for self-destruction were present in Miss Restorick's mind yesterday, I should have to answer in the affirmative.'

'You mean, she was ill in her mind as well as her body?' asked Nigel. 'Or was it only for mental illness you were treating her?'

'Now we're getting down to brass tacks,' said Andrew. 'Just what *was* wrong with Betty? Or, to put it another way, what is Dr Bogan a doctor of?'

Nigel's mind flashed back to a recent occasion when the same question had been asked – by Miss Cavendish. Dr Bogan did not seem put out by Andrew's aggressive tone. He replied equably:

'I specialize in nervous diseases of women.'

'Ah!' exclaimed Andrew outrageously. 'A lucrative profession. What is it Laurence Sterne said? "There are worse occupations in this world than feeling a woman's pulse."'

'Really, Andrew! Dr Bogan is a guest in my house. I must ask you to remember that,' said Charlotte Restorick.

'Yes. Bad form,' added her husband. 'We must all try and pull together just now. No recriminations.'

'I quite understand your brother's feelings,' said Dr Bogan, lightly yet formidably. 'He has an antipathy for me, which results from a fixation upon his own sister. He has resented my presence here because of the influence I exercised professionally upon Miss Restorick. It is a quite normal, commonplace reaction on his part.'

For once Andrew Restorick seemed altogether put down. He evidently did not relish the idea that any reaction of his could be commonplace.

'Can we go back a little?' suggested Nigel. 'If you will tell us more precisely the nature of your patient's illness, and explain your belief that – how did you put it? – the conditions for self-destruction were present in her mind yesterday, perhaps the business'll clear itself up.'

Dr Bogan pondered for a moment. 'Miss Restorick, besides being a friend of mine, consulted me professionally. She did not wish the nature of her nervous disorder to be disclosed, otherwise she would have told you all about it herself. I should, therefore, be breaking the seal both of friendship and professional secrecy if I divulged what she was unwilling to tell even her own folks. As for –'

'Just a moment, doctor,' Nigel interrupted, 'you are an *old* friend of Miss Restorick's? Did you meet her in America originally?'

It was now the doctor's turn to look, for the first time, discomposed. It showed itself in the slightly unfocused expression of his eyes.

'In America? Why –'

'You *are* an American, aren't you?' Nigel persisted. 'Some of your turns of phrase –'

'I've lived in the States quite a bit,' said the doctor. 'But I'm not an American citizen. Mongrel Irish and Italian, I'm afraid. No, Mr Strangeways, America's a big place, and I didn't know Miss Restorick while her family was living there. That was ten or fifteen years ago, remember.'

'I see. Well then, without infringing professional etiquette, perhaps you can tell us more exactly about your patient's suicidal tendencies.'

'Suicide only takes place, as I believe, when the will to live has temporarily lost – how shall I say? – its margin of power over the death-will.'

'The obvious. Decorations by Sigmund Freud,' murmured Andrew, but not softly enough to escape Dr Bogan's ears.

'It will sound obvious only to a superficial mind, Restorick. There is neither a suicidal type nor a suicidal tendency. There is nothing but the predestinated and unremitting war between life-will and death-will – a war which must always end in victory for death, but where sometimes the positive forces desert to the enemy before the battle is half over.'

Dr Bogan, more by his vibrant voice and presence than by his actual words, was holding the attention of all. Even Andrew Restorick regarded him with a look of wary respect.

'Elizabeth,' continued the doctor, 'was a woman of strong impulses. As you all know, she was apt to disconcert folk sometimes by taking them at their own word. She took herself at her own word, too. Last night, when I went to see her just before dinner, she said something which ought to have warned me what she had in mind.'

'That's what we – Strangeways is trying to get at,' interrupted Hereward Restorick. 'She was depressed, you mean? Hinted at –'

'She hinted at suicide, yes – I realize that now. But she wasn't depressed. She was, you might almost say, excited. Lit up. She said, "Dennis, I expect you'll be glad to have one hysterical woman off your hands." I thought then that she was referring to the success of my treatment. That was my mistake.'

'Your treatment was showing good results?' asked Nigel.

'I believed so. Physically. But I didn't realize the strength of the death-will in her. The old cliché about having nothing left to live for means more than we often think.'

'But if she was going to marry – ?'

Dr Bogan's almost imperceptible shrug dismissed Charlotte's argument. 'She lived, forgive me, at a white heat. When the fire showed the first signs of sinking, she was ready to depart. Her nervous condition, if you like, predisposed her to the act. But it was the emptiness of life stretching before her, the sense that experience could now be only a series of stale repetitions, which allowed the death-will to enter the citadel.'

'No!' came an anguished cry from Will Dykes. 'No! That isn't true! She *had* something to look forward to, something different, a better life. You won't catch me with all this high-flown talk about life-wills and death-wills. I tell you, she –'

Dr Bogan had raised a soothing, deprecating hand. But it was the butler's entrance which made Will Dykes break off short. The man approached Hereward, inclined his head solemnly, and whispered something to his master.

'The Chief Constable's here,' said Hereward, rising. 'Afraid we must – er – postpone the rest of this discussion. I expect he'll want a word with you, Bogan. And will you come along too, Strangeways?'

The Chief Constable, Major Dixon, was accompanied by a superintendent of police – a large, raw-boned man called Phillips, who looked as if he had been born and bred on a farm. Both men treated Hereward Restorick with a deference that indicated his influence in the district. Introductions being made, the party went upstairs. The policeman on guard outside Elizabeth's room saluted and opened the door for them.

'Good God!' exclaimed Major Dixon, his hard-bitten countenance flushing furiously when he saw what the room contained. 'Good God, she's –! This is a shocking business, Restorick. Shocking.'

Shocking, for him, in more senses than one, thought Nigel. Well, Elizabeth contrived to be as sensational in her death as in her life. The red lips of the girl hanging there seemed to be touched with the faintest smile of mockery.

'Andrew said we oughtn't to touch anything,' Hereward was saying apologetically, 'so we didn't – er – cut her down. Bogan, of course, made sure there was no hope.'

'She must have been dead for at least five hours when she was found,' said the doctor.

'I see. Yes. H'm.' Major Dixon looked at a loss. 'Well, Phillips, you'd better call Robins in and get on with it.'

While the two policemen set to work, the Chief Constable began to ask routine questions, his eyes obviously restrained by an effort from the challenging lifeless body. Had Miss

Restorick left no message for them? Had she given any indication of contemplating suicide? Who had found the body, and when? Who had last seen her alive?

Phillips and Robins had cut the body down, laid it on the bed and covered it with a sheet. They were about to untie the rope, knotted under the side of the jaw, when Nigel said,

'Excuse me. Just a minute. Before you go any further, I would like a word with Major Dixon.'

The Chief Constable looked startled, but there was a compelling note in Nigel's voice which overruled any objections he might have been going to make. Nigel motioned him outside. As he closed the door, he saw the two policemen straightening up from the bed, staring at him in undisguised amazement. Hereward and Dr Bogan looked equally surprised. That group in the room was to be repeated again many times during the next few weeks, with its air of suspended activity, of waiting uneasily and ineffectually for some new circumstance over which it could have no control.

Taking Major Dixon a little way down the passage, Nigel repeated briefly the statement he had made to Charlotte Restorick.

'So you see,' he concluded, 'there's strong evidence that this is not suicide. I don't want to butt in, but I suggest a post-mortem is justified – and a good look at that rope through a microscope.'

'The rope?'

'Yes. You noticed it was twined double round her neck. Of course, she might have done it that way herself. But equally a murderer might have done it, so as to overlay with the marks of the double ligature any bruises he made while throttling her into unconsciousness. If the body was hauled up by laying the rope over that hook in the beam, a microscopic examination of the rope will show the fibres lying upward, in the opposite direction of the pulling. You noticed a certain amount of slack had been wound round the hook. Then the knots at the hook or the girl's neck may tell us something. That's why I weighed in when I saw your Super was just going to untie the knot. The object of cutting down the body would have been quite defeated if he'd done that.'

Nigel had reeled this off in his most dispassionate, incisive voice, while Major Dixon's eyes regarded him with increasing consternation.

'Afraid I didn't catch your name,' said the Chief Constable when he had found his tongue. It was – Nigel realized with secret amusement – a polite variant of 'Who the devil are you, sir, to interfere like this?' – a variant adapted to the Chief Constable's deference for anyone staying at Easterham Manor.

'Strangeways. My uncle, Sir John, is Assistant-Commissioner at New Scotland Yard. I've done a fair amount of this sort of work. Mrs Restorick asked me to take a look at things.'

'Jiminy, this is going to kick up a dust,' said Major Dixon presently. 'Suicide was bad enough. But murder! What Restorick'll say, I hate to think.' He gazed at Nigel for a moment with an appealing, bothered look which seemed to say, 'Couldn't we just forget the last two minutes?' Then he took a grip on himself, paused in front of the bedroom door as if on the brink of an icy bath, and plunged into the room.

'Phillips, don't untie that rope, cut it. Then wrap it up carefully for examination. Restorick, I'd like a word with you. But first, may we use your telephone?'

'Certainly. But –'

'Robins. Ring Dr Anstruther and ask him to come over at once.'

'Anstruther?' Hereward Restorick stiffened. His voice took on an autocratic tone which showed Nigel another side of him – the influential landowner, not the rather colourless husband of Charlotte Restorick whom he had seen so far. 'I assure you, Dixon, Dr Bogan here is fully qualified to do what is necessary – death certificate and so on. My sister was his patient. I fail to see –'

'Sorry, Restorick, but one or two complications have arisen.' Major Dixon held his ground against the formidably mounting anger in Hereward's eye. 'You were treating her, Dr Bogan? What was the nature of her illness?'

'She was suffering from a nervous disorder, which I had some difficulty in diagnosing. I am not at liberty to reveal its cause,' said the doctor stiffly.

'You may be asked to do so at the inquest.'

'Then I shall have to consider the position afresh.'

Neither of them was giving an inch. Nigel, standing by the window, suddenly turned and asked:

'Would you be willing to tell us the nature of your treatment?'

'By all means. I was giving her sedative drugs to alleviate the attacks, and a course of hypnosis to try and eradicate the —'

'You were *what*?' exclaimed Hereward Restorick. 'D'you stand there and tell me you were mesmerizing my sister?'

It ought to have been ludicrous. But the temper flashing in Hereward's blue eyes, the aggressive pose of his body which quite visibly shook with rage, brought Superintendent Phillips up to his shoulder ready to intervene. Dr Bogan, however, showed no sign of being rattled.

'Hypnosis is not an uncommon form of treatment nowadays,' he said with quiet assurance. 'There's no black magic about it.'

'It's criminal!' stormed Restorick. 'If I'd known this was going on, you'd have been packed out of my house double quick.'

'Miss Restorick agreed to the treatment. She was a free agent.'

Hereward glared about him. He seized the Chief Constable's arm in a grip that made him wince.

'Hypnotizing her! That's the way you get hold of somebody body and soul. How do we know the fellow didn't put her to sleep and then tell her to – to hang herself? Eh?'

CHAPTER SEVEN

'O Rose, thou art sick!'
BLAKE

THAT scene between Hereward and Dr Bogan was one of many which made Easterham Manor resemble a battlefield. Even before Elizabeth's death, on the previous night, Nigel had heard the premonitory rumblings of conflict. Now, war was openly joined. But, like the war that was convulsing Europe, it would be an affair of long boredoms, broken by sudden brief spasms of violent action.

Nigel and Georgia were walking back to the Dower House through the snow. Andrew Restorick, who wanted to buy tobacco in the village, accompanied them. Georgia had been delighted by the Restorick children, John and Priscilla, who had entertained her most of the morning, quite ignorant of what was happening in the house around them.

'I think Mrs Restorick is very sensible, not letting them know,' she said. 'Children have an instinct for smelling out trouble, of course, and they realize something has happened. But they won't take it too hard if the knowledge comes to them gradually. Some modern mothers, who have this absurd theory about treating children as grown-ups and equals, would have put the whole business before them in black and white. Taking your children into your confidence. I don't believe in it: it puts too much of a load on them, too much responsibility.'

'I wonder,' said Andrew after a pause. 'Making everything easy for the young. Does it come off?' He kicked his feet through the snow, his mind going off on a personal tangent. 'Look at us. We had an ideal childhood. Parents who were kind and sympathetic without being over-indulgent. A beautiful home. A tradition. Good schools. A free country life in the holidays. Then travel. My father was appointed to the

Embassy at Washington and took us all with him. We had everything a child could want. And look at us now. Hereward running to seed in the country, fiddling about on war agricultural committees, and half-demented because they won't let him back in his old regiment yet. Myself, a sort of amateur beachcomber, the family ne'er-do-weel who's never even attained the romantic notoriety of being an outright black sheep. And Betty –' his voice wavered for an instant – 'Betty hanging up there like dead mutton.'

'You were very fond of her, weren't you?' asked Georgia gently.

Andrew's voice was savage with pain. 'Betty was the most arrant little bitch and the most glorious creature I ever – Oh, God damn it, she was my sister – I can't think of her in words; they don't mean anything; you couldn't describe her – she ought to have had a poet, Shakespeare, to do it, or Donne. And I did nothing for her. I let her do this.'

His slight, wiry body was trembling uncontrollably. Georgia, saying nothing, took his arm. He didn't seem even to notice the contact.

'Do you really think she killed herself?' said Nigel flatly. His words did not penetrate for a moment. Then Andrew stopped dead in his tracks, staring at Nigel.

'Say that again.'

'Do you really think she killed herself?'

'Explain that,' demanded Andrew, with an extraordinary, controlled kind of ferocity.

'I believe she was murdered,' said Nigel. 'And the murderer rigged it up to look like suicide.'

He felt Andrew's eyes, the whole ferocious attentiveness of his body, almost like a scorching wind on his own flesh. Frozen reeds around a pond beside which they had halted, stirring in the wind, brushed harshly against the absolute silence.

Nigel outlined, once again, the points he had made to Charlotte Restorick. 'Surely you felt there was something wrong with the suicide tableau?' he concluded. 'Or why did you impress upon everyone that they mustn't touch anything?'

'Oh, that was a sort of automatic reaction. Drummed into one by detective novels, I suppose. Hereward and the rest were knocked right over. Somebody had to take charge. But it didn't occur to me it could be anything but suicide. Not at first.' He gave them one of his speculative, sidelong glances. 'Well, my reaction when first I saw her was – No, it's not possible, Betty wouldn't do it, she'd never take that way out. Which amounts to the same thing, I suppose.'

'Weren't you expecting something to happen, then?'

'How d'you mean? Let's move on. It's infernally cold, standing over this Stygian marsh. I wonder why the Christian tradition makes Hell hot, it ought to be cold – cold as this foul countryside, cold as malice and all uncharitableness.'

Nigel led him firmly back to the point. 'You all seemed thoroughly on edge last night at dinner. That's why I ask weren't you expecting something to happen.'

'You didn't know Betty. She'd been ill and edgy ever since she came down this time. And when she was like that, everybody felt the vibrations. You see, she was a person who simply radiated life, not a blood-sucker draining the life out of everyone else: the delicate instrument goes out of order, and you all feel seized-up.' His voice died down to a whisper harsh as the rustle of the reeds they had passed. 'O Rose, thou art sick! I wonder who it was that found out her bed of crimson joy.'

'You weren't expecting anything particular, then?'

Andrew whirled round upon him. 'Do you suppose, if I'd had the faintest suspicion that so much as a hair of her head was in danger, I'd not have –'

'Well, who *were* you talking about? At dinner? Did you just make up that purely evil person – the person who revelled in evil, as you put it?'

'Oh, I was just pulling their legs,' replied Andrew, a little too negligently. 'Many a true word spoken in jest.'

'I'm afraid the police will go into that jest pretty thoroughly, Restorick.'

'Let them. I've lived too rackety a life to be afraid of a blue uniform any longer.'

'Have it your own way.' Nigel poked his walking-stick at a snow-furred signpost on the edge of the village, which they were now entering. 'Lovely place-names Essex has. Why do you hate Dr Bogan so much?'

Andrew Restorick laughed, with the sort of spontaneous gaiety which might possess a skilled duellist at the first flick and jar of his opponent's weapon.

'No, no, Strangeways. You can't jump me like that. I dislike Bogan very much, certainly, because I believe he's a pretentious fake, and I believed he was doing Betty no good, but I am not therefore assuming he killed her.'

He tipped his hat to Nigel, grinned saucily at Georgia, and stepped aside into the tobacconist's.

'Well, what d'you think of *him*?' Nigel asked.

His wife paused to consider. 'I think, if he finds out who killed his sister before the police do, there'll be a second murder at Easterham Manor,' she replied soberly.

'He's like that, is he?' said Nigel, who accepted implicitly Georgia's judgements on human character.

'Yes. Upbringing, temperament, and the kind of life he's lived – they'd all incline him towards taking the law into his own hands.'

'Hereward's got a touch of that temper, too.'

'Yes. But respectability and the family tradition are his mainsprings of action. By the way, he's a devoted father, a little too exacting with the boy, but both the children worship him, and he treats them very sensibly.'

'What about Charlotte?'

'She puzzles me a little. That *grande-dame*, hostessy façade. A simple, shrewd, realistic mind beneath it, I'd say. I don't know how well her two selves run in harness, though. Hereward, I fancy, married her partly for her money – it needs a good deal to keep up a place that size nowadays, and his farms must be subsidized. I'd say she and Hereward got on pretty well, he's not the type to want an intense emotional relationship – each of them has his own province and sticks to it.'

'He can't much like the sort of people she fills her house with. Proletarian novelists, hypnotists, Eunice Ainsleys.'

'Hypnotists?'

'Dr Bogan uses hypnosis in his treatments.' Nigel described the scene that had taken place between Hereward and the doctor. 'Hereward's very naïf. He connects hypnotism with shady practices in back streets, or Doctor Mabuses – a black art to get possession of one's victim, soul and body. Body particularly in Elizabeth's case.'

'Well, there may be something in it. In Elizabeth's case.'

'Oh now, Georgia, darling. A respectable Harley Street specialist?'

'Whose word have we for that?'

'He wouldn't say he was a London specialist if he wasn't. Too easily disproved. We'll verify it, of course.'

'"Respectable" is the operative word. You must be as naïf as friend Hereward if you think a man who happens to be a specialist is automatically respectable. I could tell you things –'

'Now, now, Georgia! None of your In-Darkest-Wimpole-Street reminiscences!'

They were turning in at the wrought-iron gate of the Dower House.

'It's just occurred to me. Clarissa won't have heard yet. You must break it to her, my dear. She'd a very soft spot for Elizabeth Restorick, whatever she might say about her.'

While Georgia went to find her cousin, Nigel sought the seclusion of their bedroom. Miss Cavendish's domestic arrangements were going to be a bit awkward if he had to stay on some while in Easterham. His commission from Mrs Restorick was vague, but, he realized it now, he had come under the spell of the dead woman, and would not be happy till he knew all about her death. No, not her death; it was her life that most mattered, both to him and for the solution of the case. The police could look after material clues. His job would be to recreate for his own imagination, in all its lurid, fascinating, pitiable detail, the story of the girl he had seen hanging in that sandalwood-scented room, a cryptic shadow of a smile upon her red lips.

Fumbling in his pocket, Nigel took out a pencil and paper. When Georgia came up twenty minutes later, she found him sprawled upon the window seat, staring out at the snow-piled village green. She took up the paper from beside him, and began to read.

'(i) Where does Clarissa come into all this? Did she know, or merely suspect, that E. was in danger? "I wish you may save Elizabeth from damnation." Did Charlotte R. ask her to invite me down?

'(ii) Yes, she told me so. She knew what my profession is. Just *what* was C. expecting to happen?

'(iii) What was the nature of E.'s "nervous disorders", and why is Bogan so reticent about it? (Answer fairly obvious. Post-mortem will make it clear.)

'(iv) Is the cat relevant? Get Uncle John inquire from experts whether any drug could send cat temporarily haywire. Shakespeare – "I would like to be there, were it but to see how the cat jumps" – transfer into past tense, and the Bard expresses my own heartfelt wish.

'(v) Why does Andrew so dislike Doc. Bogan, and why does the Doc. not resent his nasty cracks more? Who is this "person who revels in evil" that A. talked about? A. himself, perhaps. That was no leg-pull, or my name's Adolf Hitler.

'(vi) How far would Hereward go to hush up a first-class family scandal, even at the cost of creating a minor ditto? H. by no means a nonentity.

'(vii) Will Dykes. Was it E. or Mrs R. who invited him down? How long had he known E.? Was she really engaged to him? Was he aware of the nature of her "nervous disorder"? How is his bedroom situated in relation to E.'s? Ditto for the rest of the household.

'(viii) Why do Dykes and the Ainsley creature row? What is her position in the general set-up?

'(ix) And, to go back to Scribbles, who was it suggested to E. that she should give the cat a saucer of milk on the night of the séance in the Bishop's room?'

'I shall really have to give you a nice note-book,' said Georgia, after working her way through the microscopic writing that covered both sides of the paper. 'You need more room to spread yourself.'

'I don't want a nice note-book. It'd ruin the shape of my suit.' Nigel patted with some complacence the pocket of his new tweed suit that was already beginning – like all his clothes – to look as if he had slept the night in it.

'Clarissa is very upset. But I somehow felt the news was not altogether a shock to her. She wants to talk to you after lunch. Maybe you'll get the answer to your question 1.'

Clarissa Cavendish did not appear for lunch herself. But shortly afterwards she sent for Nigel to her own room. She was sitting bolt upright, her hands resting on her ivory cane, her snow-white hair peeping from under a mob-cap. Her face was still lavishly made-up, and indeed she presented the same picture of herself as on the previous night; but, when she began to speak, it was evident that the news of Elizabeth's death had shaken her out of that eighteenth-century character more than a little, for its mannerisms of speech were far less pronounced.

Asking Nigel to give her a full account of what had taken place, she sat expressionless, motionless, her bird-like eyes fastened upon him unwinking. When he had finished, she remained silent for a moment. Then she said,

'You believe that poor Betty was murdered?'

'Yes. Provisionally. The police will soon have final evidence, one way or the other.'

'The police may pursue their own courses. It is to be expected. But there are things beyond their comprehension. You will never know who killed poor Betty unless you know Betty.'

'That's what I thought. You will help me?'

'I shall be obleeged to you if you will place that cushion at my back. I am a little fatigued.'

Nigel did as she asked. The straight, brittle little figure relaxed, with the ghost of a sigh. It was characteristic of her that she broke straight into the gist of the matter, without hesitation or apology.

'I am an old woman. I have been silly in my day, too – a silly, fond creature like poor Betty. But Betty found many men she could love, none she could respect; while I found one man I could respect, and his love was not for me. That man was Betty's father, Harry Restorick. You will perceive why, for all her faults, I looked upon Betty as my own daughter.'

The old woman began to tell Nigel about Elizabeth's childhood. She had been a fascinating, fearless child, devoted to her brother Andrew, who was two years older than herself. The two had, indeed, been more like twins. Their charm had extricated them often from the consequences of the escapades into which their wild fearlessness led them. During the early years, Miss Cavendish had seen a good deal of them, for she used to stay at Easterham Manor and look after the children whenever their governess was on holiday. Then, after the Great War, Harry Restorick took his family out to America. In 1928, when Elizabeth was fifteen years old, the blow had fallen. Fate struck at that happy, fortunate family, which had possessed everything the human heart could ask for, through her who had seemed its most fortunate member.

'How it happened, I was never precisely to know,' said Miss Cavendish. 'But Elizabeth, who was at a high school out there, became pregnant. Her child was still-born. She refused to tell her parents who was its father. Harry resigned his post and came home. He was very nice in his sense of propriety, but it was not the scandal that broke him, it was Betty's attitude. The child, he told me, showed no remorse, no understanding of the enormity of her behaviour. She had become sullen, her heart closed to him, but – alas – open to the worst influences. I own I hardly credited this till I saw Betty myself: she returned later with her mother. She was indeed an altered creature, all fire and beauty now, but the fire was a sullen smouldering, and the beauty corrupted. She might have been won back to her better self, only that two years later Harry and his wife were killed in a motor-car accident. Hereward and Charlotte took her under their wing, but, as soon as she came of age and had control of the income her parents left her, she was off. Since then her career has been' – the old lady's voice trembled – 'as bright and headlong as Lucifer's.'

Miss Cavendish paused. Her jewelled fingers tapped once or twice on the handle of her stick.

'I hope I am not censorious,' she declared at last, with a return to her old manner. 'Betty, I believe, after her parents died, looked upon me as her one link with the past – she did not agree with Hereward, and Andrew was seldom in England. She found me willing to accept her as she was. Perhaps I was too indulgent. But you could not resist her loveliness. She came to visit me from time to time. Yes, she used to tell me about her lovers. It was difficult to reprobate something which – how am I to describe it? – seemed to be, for her, a matter of pure rejoicing. Glorying in wickedness, the world would call it, but I am a foolish old woman, I was so dazzled by the glory I could not see the wickedness. Ah well, right or wrong, it doesn't signify now.'

'But, this last time you saw her, something was different? You spoke of "saving her from damnation".'

'You are thinking she was past saving. Perhaps that is true. But, as you say, something was different. I had not seen her for some six months. When she came here, just before Christmas, I was shocked by her appearance and her manner. I saw a terrible strain in her eyes, it was more than illness – more as if she was fighting some sickness within her soul. I had never seen her like that, since the time when she had just been brought back from America. Indeed, sir, I saw something in her eyes I not had seen even then.' Miss Cavendish paused. Then she whispered one word: 'Disgust'.

CHAPTER EIGHT

'Did you ever hear about Cocaine Lil?
She lived in Cocaine Town on Cocaine Hill,
She had a cocaine dog and a cocaine cat,
They fought all night with a cocaine rat.'
ANON.

RUMINATING that afternoon on Miss Cavendish's story, Nigel found himself most intrigued by the incidents she had related of Elizabeth's childhood. It was not the highly coloured Elizabeth of later years that came most vividly before his imagination, nor the sullen, corrupted girl who had returned from America, but the child plotting with Andrew to climb up inside the huge chimneys of the Manor and appear out of the chimney-pots while a garden-party was in progress on the lawn below, the child setting her pony at an impossible fence with a look in her eyes that said – as Clarissa had put it – 'Stop me if you dare.'

Nigel was still turning over these memories when Superintendent Phillips called in. What with his countryman's gait and his slow country speech he gave the impression of having endless time at his disposal. In fact the snow, lying deeper and deeper every day, compelled the inquiry to take a leisurely tempo which suited him better than Nigel or Scotland Yard. If the superintendent was slow, however, he was thorough enough. He made Nigel go over his own part in the affair, including his original commission – the investigation of the Scribbles episode, beaming at him the while with the encouraging look of a teacher drawing out a nervous child. Nigel rather took to him. He was a pleasant contrast to the jumpy, unpredictable people up at the Manor with whom he had been dealing so far.

'Well now, that's very helpful, Mr Strangeways. Very helpful indeed,' he said when Nigel had finished. 'You and me should get this affair to rights between us. But Major Dixon, he talks of calling in the C.I.D., so many of the parties involved being London folk. Mind you, I reckon we could handle it down here, but 'tis a bit awkward – Mr Restorick being a well-known gentleman in these parts. He needs handling with tact.'

'You've established that it was murder?'

'We can't be sure till we've had the expert's report on the rope. But there's indications.' Phillips gave Nigel one of his dazzling beams. 'Indications. Yes.' With maddening deliberation he extracted a note-book from his pocket, licked his thumb, turned over page after page: when he had found the right one, he beamed at it as if it were a long-lost friend. The gist of his matter followed at leisure.

First, a careful examination of the snow-covered grounds had established that no unauthorized person visited the Manor on the night of the murder. There was no signs of a struggle in Miss Restorick's room. The bed had been occupied that night, but was not unduly disarranged. A rumpled nightdress lay on it. This meant nothing, for a murderer might not be expected to tidy up behind him. One scarlet slipper was found on the floor close beneath where the body had hung, the other under the bed. A number of fingerprints had been photographed and were now being worked upon. There was no sign of a suicide-note, but the police were going over a number of letters and bills found in the bureau. The bedrooms most adjacent to the dead woman's were occupied by the Restorick children, a maid who was looking after them in the absence of their governess, and Andrew Restorick. The rest of the house-party slept in the opposite wing. No one had heard any suspicious sounds during the night.

'You asked the children too?' Nigel put in.

'Mrs Restorick did not wish them to be upset, sir. So she put the questions in my presence. Neither of them heard steps passing their door last night, they said.'

'I suppose the household in general must have gathered what you were driving at.'

'I told them it was all in the way of routine, but some of 'em looked at me a bit odd.'

'Which ones?'

'Dr Bogan, sir. And that Miss Ainsley. Of course, Mr and Mrs Restorick knew already we wasn't satisfied.'

'And I told Andrew.'

'Oh, you did, sir, did you? I wondered. A cool customer, that. But he's a pleasant-spoken gentleman. Remember him when he was so high, I do. A proper handful, he and poor Miss Betty were.'

'How did Mr Dykes take it?'

'Dazed, sir,' said the superintendent, after a suitable pause for finding the *mot juste*. 'He was dazed. Didn't seem to understand what was going on. A writing gentleman, they tell me. I like a nice book myself, now and again.'

'Well, Super, so far so good. But I fancy you've got something up your sleeve yet.'

Phillips cocked a winsome eye at Nigel. 'Maybe I have. First, sir, we had a report in this morning, from Mr Eaves – he's a farmer and one of they Special Constables. Says he was patrolling last night, and saw a chink of light showing from a window at the Manor. This was at ten minutes past midnight. He was going to knock them up, but as he approached the house the light went out, so – seeing as Mr Restorick is an important gentleman hereabouts, this Mr Eaves decided he'd just pass a word to him quiet next morning. Well, along he comes, and I get him to show me which window it was. Mind you, it was tolerable dark, and we can't be sure, but he pointed to Miss Restorick's window.'

'Crikey! That's significant. Someone turned out her light at 12.10. Suppose it was Elizabeth herself, still alive. If she intended suicide, she wouldn't be likely to turn off the light for a spell of sleep before she did it. If she was about to hang herself straight away, she probably wouldn't do it either – it's a very rare thing for people to commit suicide by hanging in the dark – practically, it's difficult, and psychologically experience has proved it abnormal. The strong probability is that she didn't turn out the light then. Which leaves us with a murderer. You tested the light switches for prints?'

'Yes, sir,' replied Phillips with slow satisfaction. 'The switch of the bedside lamp and the switch by the door showed no fingerprints. They both show a blurred surface as if gloves had been used.'

'Do they just? Your murderer takes pains.'

'Then there is the matter of the door, Mr Strangeways. It's a double-locking door, by the way. The maid's own passkey could open it though the inside key was still in position. Milly deposed it was locked this morning, which suggested suicide. But you know as well as I do there's more than one way of turning an inside key from the outside. String and pencil he used. We found string marks on the paint of the door.'

'Don't tell me you found the pencil too. I never noticed it.'

'Rolled under the chest-of-drawers by the door.'

'Murderer's initials on it?'

'No, sir,' replied Superintendent Phillips gravely. 'Pencil came out of the morning-room. Any number of 'em there. Kept ready for guests who fancy to do a bit of writing.'

'Quite so. Anything else?'

'Well, sir, as no doubt you observed yourself, there was no overturned chair or such-like near the body. Of course, the poor lady might have stepped off that luggage-rest – I believe it is – at the end of the bed. Or even off the bed itself. But they generally use a chair.'

'Yes, we can't press that point much. How about the rope itself?'

'Mrs Restorick says it was cut from a spare length of clothes-line, kept in her store cupboard. This cupboard's in the passage past the small dining-room. Anyone might have taken the rope. I'm following it up of course.'

'In fact, everything points to its being a premeditated crime.'

'That's my opinion, sir,' said the Superintendent, treating

Nigel to one of his widest beams. 'Cutting the rope all ready beforehand, for staging a suicide. Pencil and string to lock the key inside. It looks bad, sir. Cold-blooded, if you see my meaning.'

'I do indeed. I think we can reconstruct the business in its general outline now. At ten o'clock, Milly leaves Miss Restorick. The latter, she says, is in her nightdress, applying cold cream to her face, having removed her make-up. Apparently all ready for bed. But she is excited, and has told the maid she needn't bother to put away her clothes. Which all suggests she was expecting a visitor quite soon. A male visitor, obviously, or she wouldn't have taken the trouble to put Milly off the track by removing the make-up, and wouldn't have made herself up again.'

'The trouble is the "quite soon", isn't it, sir? You suggest that her telling Milly not to put the clothes away means she was expecting a visitor any moment and didn't want the girl to be there when he arrived. But surely he wouldn't come to her so early? There might be people about. Besides, you were all up in the Bishop's room last night till 10.30 or so.'

'Yes. That's a curious point. We'll have to pass it by for the moment. At any rate – by the way, I suppose you've found out when the rest went to bed?'

The superintendent had recourse to his note-book again.

'The party broke up shortly after you left. Mrs Restorick and Miss Ainsley and Mr Andrew Restorick went up to bed at eleven o'clock. Dr Bogan and Mr Dykes about ten minutes after. Mr Restorick stayed downstairs a little later, but was in bed by 11.30, he says. The servants were all in bed by 11.0, except for the butler, who went round the ground floor locking doors and windows at 11.15 and retired at 11.20. We have not been able to cross-check these times yet.'

'So the household was all in bed by 11.30. Theoretically, the murder could have taken place any time between eleven and midnight, allowing the murderer ten minutes to rig up the suicide business. But he'd have to pass Andrew Restorick's room to get to Elizabeth's. He might possibly have done this while Andrew was still awake, but there'd have been a risk. He'd probably leave at least half an hour for Andrew to go to sleep. So he'd be in Elizabeth's room any time from 11.30 till 12.10, when the Special Constable saw the light there put out.'

'I agree, Mr Strangeways, the period from 11.0 to 12.10 is the one we've got to investigate most thoroughly. But we've no proof that the person who turned out the light at 12.10 is the murderer. She might have had a second visitor later.'

'Yes, that's possible, I suppose. It would imply she had two lovers in the house, though. Nobody else would be likely to visit her room at such an unearthly hour.'

'The murderer need not have been a lover of hers, sir. Or he might have been a discarded one.'

'You've been hearing about Mr Dykes?'

The superintendent gave Nigel a shrewd, complacent glance.

'Mr Dykes was engaged to marry her, they tell me. Then she –'

'"*They*" tell you?'

'Miss Ainsley was my informant, sir. Then Miss Restorick broke it off. She said she couldn't go through with it. A possible motive, Mr Strangeways, particularly if Dykes believed it was someone staying in the house who had supplanted him.'

'Well, I suppose that's the sum total of our knowledge, till you get the findings of the post-mortem.'

The superintendent beamed on him again, and rose to take his leave.

Nigel spent the evening reading and playing piquet with Miss Cavendish: they were both of them a little distrait.

Next morning, at eleven o'clock, a familiar voice greeted Nigel on the telephone. It was his old friend, Detective-Inspector Blount of the C.I.D. Scotland Yard had been called in.

'Can you spare me half an hour or so, Strangeways?' said the suave voice with its faint Scots inflexion. Blount never wasted time on preliminaries. 'I'm up at the Manor.'

'It's a royal command. I wondered if they'd send you down. How d'you like this weather? Must make you feel quite at home.'

'Oh, fine,' replied Blount unenthusiastically. 'The post-mortem results have just come in. The deceased was a drug-addict. Cocaine. You can be thinking that over on your way up.'

'Cocaine? Yes, so I imagined. How long has – ?' But Blount had rung off.

As Nigel turned into the village street, the east wind drove at him, drilling into his bones, clamping round his head like an iron cap. It seemed to dry up the very juices of life with its searing breath. Just beyond the village, men were digging a car out of a drift; their breath steamed up into the air. A drug-addict, thought Nigel. Poor Betty. It was obvious enough, though. Everything he had been told of her recent behaviour pointed to it – the edginess, the alternations of exuberance and depression, the violence.

And yet it was odd. It somehow didn't quite fit in with the picture of Elizabeth Restorick that had been forming in his mind's eye – the picture of a woman who retained a kind of innocence at the heart of her experience, who was wanton, yet not vicious. Such a priestess of the body's rapture surely would not need the artificial excitement that drugs give.

Arriving at Easterham Manor, Nigel was shown straight into the morning-room, which the police had taken over as their operational headquarters. In spite of the fire burning in its ample grate, the room looked bleak – too like the writing-room in a station hotel, Nigel thought, with its inadequate tables, sheaves of notepaper, and metal ash-trays. In spite of the fire, too, Inspector Blount was wearing his night-cap. It was an article of attire Nigel had never approved of. The Inspector, he pointed out, had not been formed by nature to represent either a pirate or a character out of the *Rake's Progress*. But Blount insisted that, when you were bald as a coot, the head needed protection during cold weather, even indoors. 'I have to use my head,' he was accustomed to say, 'I can't afford to let it catch cold.'

Superintendent Phillips and a detective sergeant were also in the room when Nigel arrived. Blount, sitting at a writing-desk drawn near to the fire, took off his gold-rimmed pince-nez and motioned with them towards a chair. Nigel obediently took it. As usual, if one could overlook the incongruous and Hogarthian rakishness of the white night-cap, he resembled a bank manager about to interview a client on the subject of his overdraft.

'So you've got yourself mixed up in something again, Strangeways,' he said severely.

Nigel hung his head.

'You'd better tell me about it, in your own words.'

'I am not accustomed to using other people's words,' replied Nigel with dignity, and gave Blount an account of the case from his own angle. The detective-sergeant scribbled industriously.

'Hm,' said Blount when he had finished. 'There are some points of interest there. What – e'eh – interpretation do you put upon the cat incident?'

'I'm inclined to think its milk was drugged. We've got to find out if there's any drug that would have that effect. We know about cocaine jags, but I don't think cocaine would work on animals in the same way. It might have been a practical joke, of course. But, now we know Miss Restorick was a drug addict, we can envisage some relation between the cat episode and the murder. Was it, perhaps, an attempt on someone's part to convey that he knew she was an addict?'

'The first hint of blackmail? Or a warning? But why couldn't this person do it by word of mouth?' asked Blount.

'I can't imagine. Unless, for some reason, he didn't want

her to know that he knew. A blackmailer would always prefer to remain anonymous.'

'It's all theoretical.' Blount dismissed it with a brusque gesture. 'Have you anyone in mind?'

'Miss Cavendish – she's the cousin of my wife's we're staying with – said that, during the cat's exhibition, Andrew Restorick was watching his sister very attentively. She said it was like *Hamlet*. You know the scene where – '

'I have attended performances of the play,' said Blount dryly.

'Suppose Andrew was not sure whether his sister was a drug addict. He might have been flying a kite in that direction.'

'The assumption is hardly tenable, Strangeways. It presupposes first that the deceased would recognize the cat's symptoms as caused by a drug, and second that Andrew – who we're told was exceptionally fond of his sister – didn't dare to mention the thing openly to her. No, we must do better than that. Ask Dr Bogan to step this way, please.'

The sergeant went out. Blount reluctantly removed his night-cap and shifted to a chair farther from the fire, where he would have the light at his back. When the doctor entered, Blount was apparently absorbed in the papers upon his desk. After a considerable pause, which Dr Bogan spent in absently combing his fingers through his beard, Blount blotted a sheet of paper, looked up and said:

'You were treating Miss Restorick for cocaine addiction.'

'That is so.' The doctor's voice was neither startled nor resentful.

'You realized this was bound to come out soon enough. I don't understand why you held it back yesterday.'

'I was doubtful of Mr Strangeways' status, for one thing. And, being a friend of the family, I had personal as well as professional reasons for maintaining secrecy as long as possible.' The doctor spoke with a dignity that impressed Nigel in his favour.

'Your treatment was – e'eh – of a somewhat unconventional character.'

Dr Bogan's white teeth showed in a quick smile. 'Some of my colleagues call me a quack. Pasteur suffered from the same suspicions.'

'Yes, yes,' said Blount a little testily. 'But hypnosis – '

'Cocaine is a habit-forming drug. Habits take root in the unconscious mind. Hypnosis is, I believe, the most effective way of counter-attacking on that front.' Dr Bogan shot a quizzical glance at the inspector. 'I have, of course, a statement signed by Miss Restorick that she was willing to submit herself to such a treatment.'

'I'll be glad to see the statement in due course,' said Blount woodenly. 'Was the treatment successful?'

'I believe we were on the road to success. Miss Restorick was by no means cured yet. But we had already experimented in stopping the doses of the drug altogether.'

'Was any one else in this house aware of her addiction, would you say?'

'Not to my knowledge. But the signs were there to read, for any one who was familiar with them.'

'Quite so. Ye-es.' Blount slapped his bald pate vigorously several times. 'I would like you to tell us the case-history now.'

According to Dr Bogan's account, Elizabeth Restorick had put herself in his hands six months ago. He had met her first some weeks before this, at a party in London. She had begun to take cocaine not long before this first meeting. For the initial stages of the treatment, she had gone to Doctor Bogan's own nursing-home; after a month there, she had been released and kept under observation, the treatment being continued in a less drastic form. She had always refused to tell him who had introduced her to the habit and kept her supplied, and it was not his province to inquire stringently into this. As far as he could tell, she had received no supplies of the drug after his treatment had begun, apart from the diminishing doses he had allowed her. These had been stopped altogether a fortnight ago. It was their cessation which accounted for the patient's recent indisposition.

'Have you any idea why she wished to break herself of the habit? Just when she did, I mean?' asked Nigel when the doctor had finished.

'I have no proof about that. It is possible that her engagement to Mr Dykes had something to do with it. If she was in love with him – '

' "If"?'

'Well, he's not exactly the kind of person one would expect her to fall in love with. He's so different from the folks in her own set.'

'Perhaps that was why,' said Nigel.

There was a pause. The doctor had sounded vaguely embarrassed by Nigel's last question. Still, thought Nigel, his account seemed quite natural and above-board, it can all be verified, and he impresses one favourably – a striking personality.

Blount evidently thought the same. 'I expect you'll be wanting to get back to your practice to-morrow,' he said. 'We'll just keep in touch with you – we've got your address. Your evidence will be required at the inquest.'

As Dr Bogan rose, Superintendent Phillips, who had been called out of the room during this conversation, returned and whispered in Blount's ear. Blount raised a detaining hand.

'Just a minute, Doctor.' His voice had, beneath its suavity, the faint rasp which Nigel knew of old. 'Will you kindly tell us about the papers you burnt in your grate this morning?'

CHAPTER NINE

'A little snow, tumbled about,
Anon becomes a mountain.'
SHAKESPEARE

THERE are moments when time, as they say, stands still. There are also moments when, as though another gear has been silently engaged, time leaps effortlessly ahead or checks to a crawl. It was this last manifestation which Blount's question brought about. For Nigel, everything seemed suddenly to take on the dream-like quality of a slow-motion picture. A kind of deadly deliberation came over the movements of his companions in the room: it was almost as if they had reached the moment in the stalk when the quarry has been sighted, or had at last come to the edge of a skyline swept by the enemy's fire.

If Dr Bogan was the quarry, however, he didn't seem aware of it. A little frown of puzzlement came and went instantaneously upon his forehead. The sallow face seemed to grow a little darker. The piercing eyes lifted themselves deliberately to Blount's, then played that strange trick of losing focus which Nigel had noticed before. His voice was firm, however, as he said:

'The kind of treatment I was giving Miss Restorick has its difficulties. You are aware, probably, of what is called "transference" between a psycho-analyst and a patient. With hypnosis the same danger sometimes arises. To put it bluntly, the patient falls in love with the doctor.'

'You are suggesting,' said Blount, 'that the papers you burnt were – e'eh – love letters from the deceased?'

Bogan's eyes focused again, and shone with peculiar intelligence.

'That you will no doubt discover soon enough for yourselves: I am told that your modern scientific methods can reconstruct burnt paper and bring out the writing on it.'

His remark was made conversationally, to the room at large. Superintendent Phillips blurted out:

'No good. The ashes were swept – '

There was a crack which startled like a pistol-shot. It was the pencil in Blount's hand, snapped in two, and that was the only sign he gave of his anger at Phillips' intervention. Nigel glanced at Bogan with new respect. Was it by accident he had thus neatly elicited the information that the papers were illegible?

'You have not answered my question, Dr Bogan,' said Blount. 'You tell us it was love-letters you burnt?'

'I'm sorry. I'm as interested as you are in the contents of the papers. For, you see, I haven't burnt anything in my grate for days.'

The detective-sergeant goggled. Phillips let out a gasp. But Blount continued imperturbably.

'I see. Can you tell us when you were absent from your bedroom, then?'

'Yesterday or to-day? When were the papers found?'

Blount's eye, flickering, confessed the failure of his little trap.

'The morning of the murder.'

'I came down for breakfast at 8.45. We were still at breakfast when the maid found Miss Restorick's body. Mrs Restorick, her husband and her brother went upstairs at once, leaving Dykes and myself at the table. Miss Ainsley hadn't appeared yet. About five minutes later – say five past nine – they sent for me upstairs. I examined the body. Then I came down again. To the best of my recollection I didn't go into my bedroom again till midday.'

Blount pressed him further. Bogan was sure there had been no burnt paper in the grate before he came down to breakfast. Charlotte and Hereward were already in the dining-room, Andrew and Dykes turned up a moment later. When he returned from examining the body, Dykes was still at the breakfast table and Eunice Ainsley had joined them: this was roughly 9.20. The three of them had sat on at table till quarter to ten.

'We now have evidence from the housemaid who cleans your room that she went up there just before nine o'clock and brushed up a quantity of burnt paper from the grate,' said Blount. 'In the general to-do, she forgot all about this. The paper was put into an ash-bin, and the contents of this were scattered over the rubbish heap later in the day. So the paper ash is dispersed. But it would appear that it must have been planted in your grate between 8.45 and 9 o'clock yesterday morning.'

'I am relieved that you accept my version of the affair,' said Dr Bogan, with the flashing smile which reminded Nigel of his Italian blood.

'We shall go into all that,' replied Blount unresponsively, 'I think that is all for the present, Dr Bogan.' He paused, as though expecting the doctor to say something more, but Bogan just rose and left the room.

'A lot of time on his hands for an eminent specialist,' murmured Nigel.

'Yes. I was expecting him to ask when he could get back to London. Still, the week-end isn't over — if he's the kind that takes long week-ends.'

Blount proceeded to inform Nigel of other matters. Material evidence put the time of death as between ten p.m. and two a.m. The post-mortem had failed to reveal whether Elizabeth was throttled before her neck had been put in the noose. The double coil of rope round her neck had superimposed its own marks on any bruises that might have been made already. The body showed no other signs of violence. But the rope, microscopically examined, proved quite clearly that the body had been hauled up to the position in which they found it.

'So that disposes finally of the idea of suicide,' said Nigel. 'No marks of violence on the body, though?'

'Which tells us something. Only a person intimate with the

deceased could have entered her room in the middle of the night, and put his fingers round her neck, without her raising an alarm and struggling. She was a light sleeper. Besides, we have good reason to think she was expecting someone.'

'Still, one might have expected her to have left some marks on her assailant. None of the people in the house seems to be scratched, as far as I've noticed.'

'If she was throttled from behind, or smothered by a pillow first, her assailant might have been unscathed. You'd expect to find scratches on his hands and wrists, perhaps. But remember, no fingerprints on the light switches, he was maybe wearing gloves.'

'Surely her lover – if that's who you think it was – wouldn't come to her bed in gloves.'

'No. But he could pretend to leave her, put them on, and move back to the bed. All this is petty detail, Strangeways. The important thing is that no one but the woman's lover answers all our requirements.'

'Narrowing it down to Dykes or Bogan, or some unknown X who got into the house that night? It seems reasonable. But there's a bad flaw in your argument.'

'A flaw? I don't see it.'

'A logical flaw. Or a logical-emotional flaw, to be precise. Have you interviewed Dykes yet?'

'No. He's coming next.'

'May I have a quarter of an hour with him first? Alone?'

Blount gave Nigel one of his coldest looks. 'Why?'

'He might tell me things he'd hold back from your official inquiry. You're an intimidating sort of bloke, you know.'

'I may take it you're not acting on any one's behalf in this affair?'

'Not now,' replied Nigel, a sudden vision of Elizabeth Restorick in the outrageous beauty of her death flashing through his mind.

'Very well then. I shall expect you to pass on all relevant information, of course.'

'That's understood.'

Nigel found Will Dykes poking about in the library and brought him out into the garden. The novelist seemed to have taken a grip on himself since yesterday, though his eyes showed he had slept little last night. They walked briskly, for the wind bit hard, towards the sheltered side of the house where stood a coppice of birches holding the snow delicately at their fingertips.

'Are you – spying out the land for the police?' asked Dykes flatly when they had got beyond earshot of the house.

'You don't like the police?'

'People of my class never have liked them. They're the paid guardians of privilege, and every one with any sense knows it.'

'I gathered you'd feel like that. That's why I want a little preliminary talk with you. Blount – that's the C.I.D. chap – is very much the policeman. He's fair enough, and able, but he doesn't allow his heart to interfere with his head.'

'Why should he?'

'He might be a better detective if he did. But that's by the way. My point is – he'd put your back up, put you on the defensive, make you give a far worse impression of yourself than you need.'

Dykes was about to make a truculent reply. But he thought better of it. Nigel's words appealed to the novelist in him – the analytic observer.

'Maybe you're right. Yes. You seem to have got some sense, young man. Though I'm damned if I can see what business it is of yours.'

'Never mind about that. And let's get this clear. I'm not on your side. Not on any one's side. Except perhaps Elizabeth Restorick's. Anything you tell me, which I believe relevant to the inquiry, I shall pass on to the police. I'm talking to you because I believe you'd feel able to say things to me you wouldn't say before a row of policemen.'

'Plain speaking, eh? Well, I reckon it's a tonic after the

milk-and-water of some of those in there.' He jerked a finger towards the house. 'Not that I've anything to conceal.'

'I dare say not. Except, perhaps, your blushes.'

Will Dykes halted and studied him keenly. 'Oh, I see what you mean. The sex side of it. Well, I dare say I used to be a bit of a prude – working-class chaps are foul-mouthed all right, but they don't wear dirty hearts on their sleeves like that Ainsley bitch. Still, after the sort of people Betty ran around with, I'm properly inured.'

'How long had you known her?'

'Six months. No, eight. It was in May. I met her at one of those bloody publishers' parties. You know – I was being shown off. We took to each other, because all the rest of the people in the room looked such a bloodless crew. Talk about ghosts! Betty was no angel. But, my God! she'd got some blood in her.'

'You say she was no angel. Did you know she was a drug-addict?'

The novelist grunted involuntarily, as if he had been struck over the heart. 'Is that true?' he demanded, seizing Nigel by the arms. His tears yesterday, his violence now – there was an easy emotionalism about the man which you might call a flaw of character if you were born to the standards of the Restoricks, thought Nigel.

'I'm afraid so. It came out at the post-mortem. Cocaine.'

'So that's what it was,' muttered Dykes. 'Poor Betty. Oh, the vile, cold devils!'

'You suspected it, then?'

'That Ainsley woman hinted at it. And others of Betty's friends. "Friends"! My God! If only she'd told me! We could have faced it out together. Who – introduced her to the stuff?' Dykes added with murderous rage in his eyes.

'We don't know. I'd like to tell you this, Dykes. Six months ago, Elizabeth put herself under Bogan's treatment. She wanted to be cured of the habit. Has that date any significance for you?'

'Significance? Oh, I get you. Yes, it was about six months ago I asked her to marry me.'

'She agreed?'

'She said I must wait. I see why now. She wanted to be cured first. I remember her saying – it was on top of a bus, we used to go for long bus-rides in London – you know, take a ticket from one end to the other – a new thrill it was for her, I suppose, riding on a bus – she said: "Willie, I love you, God knows why – but I love you too much to let you marry me yet." Now I understand it.'

They were walking on into the birch coppice, struggling through the thick snow. A queer setting for such a tête-à-tête, thought Nigel.

'Pretty, these trees, aren't they? We used to have one in our backyard at home. Always covered with soot. A pretty, black girl.'

'Were you lovers?' asked Nigel.

'No. Betty wanted it. But I wasn't having any of that. Marriage or nowt, I said. And nowt's what I've got.'

Little by little, Nigel reflected, he was realizing the strange attraction Will Dykes must have had for Elizabeth. At first, he'd put it down to sheer perversity on her part. But Will, he could see now, was not just a new thrill for her, he was a new world. He combined imaginative understanding with sturdy common sense and a code of morality she had never met. But it was more than that. It was the impact upon her own of a personality which combined loyalty with lack of illusions. He would treat her neither as a Cleopatra nor a playgirl. The kind of men she had met before would feel for her the awe that precedes a too easy passion and the contempt that follows it. They could at no time, as Dykes did, perceive in her an equal, to be respected. Moreover, the very intensity of Elizabeth's passion, the all-for-love-ness of her life, would deeply shock the ordinary philandering man. Such men, afraid to commit themselves as deeply as Elizabeth, for to do so would be to go right out of their depth, must always have failed her. But

Will Dykes, Nigel fancied, would not be shocked nor afraid: though physically she might enslave him, a part of him would remain not so much her master as out of her control, detached, self-sufficient.

Yes, Will Dykes represented for her that stability and wholesomeness which every rake, at some stage of his progress, yearns for. But this did not necessarily mean he had not murdered her.

'You realize,' said Nigel after a long silence, 'that you'll be suspected by the police?'

'Suspected of killing Betty? I suppose so. Trust them to pick on a working-class chap if they can.'

'It won't be for that reason. They'll say it was a *crime passionel*, that you had been her lover, and killed her from jealousy because she had thrown you over for Dr Bogan. For all I know, they may be right.'

Will Dykes spat. 'What a filthy business! Reckon I'll never get the taste of it out of my mouth. Me kill Betty! Oh well, it should be a lesson to me to stick to my own folk.' They had turned back, by tacit consent, towards the house. 'You think I'm callous, Mr Strangeways? I ought to be saying that my life is finished now Betty's dead? Nay, you can get over anything. I'm lucky. I've got my books to write, and I've got Betty in my heart to keep me going. Chaps like me – we're used to the rough side of things. Not like those sheltered ones in there' – he jerked his thumb at the house – 'who think it's the end of the world if the electric light fails.'

'I wouldn't call Andrew Restorick a sheltered type.'

'Oh, he's not so bad. But he's always had this to fall back upon, if the worst came to the worst. No, they don't get within a hundred miles of life. Look at this stuff – ' Dykes kicked his foot through the snow. 'Where I come from, it means snowballs for the kiddies – with stones in 'em; it means your clothes aren't thick enough and your fire isn't big enough; maybe it means a stoppage of work and less money in the pay-packet on Fridays. Aye, it does so, and we don't make a song about it. But what do these folk here make of it? Just a bit of icing on their cake. Or a damned inconvenience – the pipes burst, and they kick up such a fuss you'd think it was Noah's flood, and then they have to send for one of us to mend them. Or the trains are a bit late, and that silly Ainsley girl won't get up to town in time for her appointment with the beauty specialist, and she'll – '

'Take it out on you?' Nigel suggested.

'On me? Why should she?'

'You two seem to be permanently at loggerheads, judging by your performance the night before last.'

'I didn't like the way she hinted things. I didn't know what she was hinting at, then. I thought it was just plain jealousy.'

Nigel suppressed a smile. The idea of this stumpy little man, with his oiled quiff, his coarse skin and coarser manner, being a battleground for two such elegant females – it was laughable. Disconcertingly, Will Dykes divined his thought.

'Funny, isn't it? You have to laugh. Y'see, in the ordinary way, Miss Ainsley wouldn't look at me twice. A shatteringly common little twirp, my dear' – he mimicked her drawl to the life. 'But she became obsessed by the interest Betty took in me. What could Betty see in me? It began to worry her. After a bit, I've no doubt she was thinking I must be a Great Lover, a sort of Valentino in disguise. And the next step was she wanted me herself. It's a fair knock-out, is female curiosity. That's why she was jealous.'

'Yes, I see. Miss Ainsley was an old friend of Elizabeth?'

'I believe so. One of that click, any road. The trouble with Betty was being so warm-hearted – people like that have no discrimination. Like the sun, shining upon the just and the unjust.'

A good epitaph for Elizabeth Restorick, thought Nigel. Well, we must get on with it.

They entered the house, and Nigel took Dykes along to the writing-room. He had hoped to put a call through to London, but Blount told him the wires were down. That meant an icy, protracted railway journey for him. Still, it was necessary. He had come down to Easterham to see about a cat, and he intended to go through with the mission.

CHAPTER TEN

'How soon prospers the vicious weed!'
PHINEAS FLETCHER

IT was on the afternoon of the same day, while Nigel's train was painfully making its way to London in the face of snow-drifts and iced-up points, that Georgia unwittingly laid her finger upon another of the scattered pieces of the puzzle. With her cousin's consent, she had invited the Restorick children to spend the afternoon at the Dower House. They were a little subdued when they arrived, for that morning they had been told of their Aunt Betty's death, but a protracted snowball fight with Georgia in the garden, which incidentally made John revise his opinion that women could never throw straight, soon restored their spirits.

When it was over, they went indoors. Georgia had been doubtful how to entertain children in a house of which three-quarters was as bare as Mother Hubbard's cupboard and the rest full of priceless and fragile *bric-à-brac*. The problem, however, was resolved by fetching down a number of trunks from the attics into one of the empty rooms and building them up to make an imaginary pirate ship. John, as the pirate captain, made Georgia and Priscilla walk the plank to his heart's content. Georgia, combining the rôles of victim and navigator, forgot for a while the tragedy hanging over Easterham Manor, and Priscilla seemed quite happy in being ordered about by her masterful brother.

During an interval of the game, Georgia lit a cigarette and in fun offered one to John. 'Smoke, captain? Or do you chew your tobacco?' she said.

The effect of this harmless remark was odd. The children exchanged covert glances, whether of guilt or simple embarrassment Georgia could not decide. Perhaps they indulged in an occasional secret smoke at home. But she fancied that

87

John Restorick had momentarily winced away a little from the cigarette case she extended to him.

'No, thanks. We never smoke,' said Priscilla a trifle sanctimoniously.

'Aunt Betty smoked like a chimney,' said John. 'She was an addict.'

'It isn't fair. Why should grown-ups – ? I mean, she got in a frightful flap when we –'

'Oh, shut up, Priscilla. She's dead now. I say, Mrs Strangeways, why are there policemen in the house?'

It was the question Georgia had dreaded. 'Hasn't your mother told you about it?'

'I dunno. She said Aunt Betty wanted to die and go to Heaven, so she did. Do policemen always come into the house when a person dies like that?'

'Yes. There's a law about it.'

'I think it's silly,' said Priscilla. 'Why shouldn't you die if you want to?'

Georgia had no answer to this, and did not feel that the ordinary vague reassurance or changing of the subject would pass with these children. It was they, to her relief, who changed the subject. Swinging his legs over the bulwarks of the pirate ship, John said abruptly:

'Do you believe in ghosts, Mrs Strangeways?'

'Well, I've not seen any,' she replied. 'Have you?'

A cunning, secretive look came into the boy's eyes. 'Oh, our house is full of them,' he boasted.

Georgia had the fancy that, in spite of appearances, he was side-tracking the subject.

'Don't talk bosh, Rat,' said Priscilla. 'You've not seen them, anyway. You wouldn't half whiz away if you did.'

'That's what *you* think, Mouse.'

'Are you talking about the Bishop's room?' Georgia asked.

A faint frown of puzzlement showed on John's face, then it closed down into the stubborn, mock-innocent look which warns the sensitive adult not to press a child's confidence any farther. Georgia let it go, and they resumed their game.

It was not till nearly ten o'clock that Nigel returned from London. He was numb with cold, but experiencing the agreeable light-headedness of the civilized man who has endured a few mild unaccustomed rigours.

'They had to dig the train out of a drift,' he announced proudly, as he gulped down some of Miss Cavendish's whisky – "a glass of spirits" as she described it.

'And did you dig anything out in London?' asked Georgia.

'We are not impressed. We ourself think nothing of walking over the Andes in mid-winter, but – '

'It wasn't mid-winter,' Georgia protested.

' – but here is a person who makes a song about being held up for an hour or two in a drift. Yes, I know. But I believe scientists would concur with me in stating that snow is as cold in England as in South America. This is excellent whisky, Clarissa.'

'I am gratified that you approve it. Pray take another glass.'

'Thank you, I will.'

'So you did find out something in London. Nigel has an irritating weakness for dramatizing his squalid little discoveries,' Georgia explained to Miss Cavendish. 'He holds up the action for his entrance like a spoilt matinée idol.'

'A metaphor from the playhouses,' remarked Miss Cavendish. 'It is apt enough. I believe it may suffice.'

'Well, as you insist on spoiling my entrance, I've a good mind to dry up on you. However, here it is. Uncle John put me on to one of their poison-experts. He recognized Scribbles' symptoms at once. The cat had been dosed with hashish.'

'Hashish? Upon my soul!' exclaimed Miss Cavendish. 'That is the drug, if I am not mistaken, from which we derive the word "assassin".'

Nigel gazed down his nose. His hand, straying to the side-table on which his glass of whisky rested, took up absent-mindedly a very different object. It was a musical box, and it began to play – in tones thin and crystal as an icicle: 'Where'er You Walk.' They heard out the air in silence. Even at that moment they could not interrupt it. Then Georgia said:

'Is there some connexion? I mean, between the "assassin" drug and the murder? It becomes more and more like the play scene in *Hamlet*.'

'Except that in this case the murder was still to come.'

'And, of course, Miss Restorick wasn't killed by a drug.'

'Hashish,' announced Miss Cavendish in her most donnish manner, 'is derived from Indian Hemp. To-day it is used chiefly for the purpose of obtaining sensuous intoxication. But the original "assassins" were members of a Mohammedan sect, headed by a person who earned the sobriquet of "Old Man of the Mountains." This sect was in the habit of employing the drug as a kind of stimulant before murder. Its effects, in the later stages, are conducive to extreme violence and cruelty. I make no doubt that the cat was experiencing hallucinations similar to those felt by the "assassins".'

'Good Lord, cousin Clarissa!' exclaimed Georgia, 'you sound as if you were a devotee of hashish yourself!'

'The facts should be familiar to every schoolgirl,' replied the old lady, austerely.

'Oh, damn!' cried Nigel. 'I'm terribly sorry.' He had dropped the musical box on to the floor, where it tinkled a few bars of Handel and then gave out.

'You're tired, I am sure, Nigel,' Miss Cavendish said. 'No, please, it is of no consequence at all. The instrument is undamaged. But we must not keep you any longer from your well-earned repose.'

The well-earned repose had to be postponed for a little, though. Up in their bedroom, Georgia asked him why he had dropped the musical box.

'No, it wasn't to create a diversion, I swear,' he said. 'I was just startled out of my wits.'

'But why? Clarissa only said the facts should be familiar to every schoolgirl.'

'Exactly. School-*girl*.'

'Well, naturally. She was a schoolmistress. A female don, anyway. It'd be just the phrase she'd use to quell some young upstart at Girton.'

'It's not *that* I'm thinking of. Her words gave me a thought association I've been groping after all the way from London. Listen. Elizabeth Restorick was a schoolgirl in America. She went wrong. Now then. You've heard of marijuana; it's home-grown Indian hemp. Since the last war, there's been growing anxiety in the United States over the practice of dope-pedlars haunting the vicinity of high schools and selling marijuana to the boys and girls in the form of candies or cigarettes. Marijuana creates erotic hallucinations. Hashish or marijuana crops up just before Elizabeth's death. Was it also the original cause of her downfall? Surely there must be a connexion – or why should any one dope the cat with the stuff?'

'You mean, it was a kind of warning?'

'Or of blackmail? Or a symbol of – no, it's no good. I'm too sleepy, and we don't know enough of the facts yet.'

As he composed himself for sleep, Georgia said, 'The stuff is supplied in the form of candies or cigarettes?'

'Yes. A nasty racket. Good-night, my sweet.'

'Good-night.'

Next morning, in obedience to a note received from Blount, Nigel ploughed his way to the village pub where the inspector was staying. He found him, fully dressed to the nightcap, taking porridge: a plate of cold ham stood at his elbow.

'Really, Blount, with the temperature at God knows what below zero, the sight of you preparing to eat cold ham is more than I can bear. For a man who cossets himself with nightcaps, this Spartan diet is not only disgusting but inconsistent.'

'Oh, well now,' replied Blount, slapping his forehead rapidly many times, 'oh, well now. Prime ham. Delicious. Delicious. Mustn't derogate the noble ham. Irreverent. Sacrilege.

Besides, I'm taking parritch first. Warms the cockles.' He slapped a large spoonful into his mouth.

'I often think that porridge explains the Scots,' said Nigel darkly. 'It's as colourless as your kirks, as sloppy as your sentiment, as jejune as your character, as – '

'Did you get anything from them in London?' asked Blount, with one of his disconcerting returns to the business line.

Nigel told him about the explanation of the cat's behaviour, and his own theory that it might link up with Elizabeth Restorick's girlhood aberrations.

'It's a plausible idea,' said Blount slowly. 'But I can't see just now why such a roundabout method was employed. Suppose one of the people up there had the knowledge that Miss Restorick once took marijuana and lost her virtue, and wished to blackmail her on the strength of it. Surely he would communicate this to her secretly, not stage that funny business with the cat. After all, it took an expert to discover what had caused the cat to behave as it did. There's no reason to think Miss Restorick would recognize its symptoms. The same argument holds good against the cat incident being a warning or any kind of symbolic by-play.'

'Yes. That's true enough.'

'I'm inclined myself to put a different interpretation on it. Either it was a practical joke, unconnected with the murder, or it was an attempt by the murderer to concentrate our attention upon the drug-aspect of the whole business.'

'Leading up to what?'

'Well, if the murderer had some motive for his crime quite unrelated to his victim's drug-habit, but he knew of this habit, he might try and call attention to the latter in order to confuse the whole issue.'

'There's something behind all this, I fancy.'

'The murder bears every mark of a sex crime. And the motive for most sex crimes is jealousy.'

'Ah! So you've got your knife into Will Dykes already.'

'Oh now, I don't get my knife into people,' replied Blount, a little shocked. 'I'm not saying, mind you, that I found Dykes a very satisfactory witness. But he's not the only person who could have been motivated by jealousy; there's Miss Ainsley, and Dr Bogan, and Andrew Restorick, even, maybe. But it's unfortunate for the wee man,' he added, spearing a slice of ham, 'that we should have found one of the cords from his dressing-gown tassel in the deceased's room.'

'Dykes' dressing-gown? When?'

'Yesterday afternoon.'

'But the local police had searched the room before that.'

'Local police don't know as much about searching as we do. Not that I blame them in this case. The bit of cord was lying in the fringe of a mat beside the bed, and it's of very much the same colour as the fringe. Anyone might have missed it.'

'Have you taxed Dykes with this?'

'Oh yes. He says it's a plant. In fact, he insinuated that we put it there ourselves, to work up the case against him. He's got an awful dislike for the police.'

'Still, it could be a plant. There's a precedent in this case. Look at those papers in Bogan's grate. Had the bedroom been left unguarded between the time they were told it was murder and the time you made your search?'

'I'm sorry to say, yes. Last forenoon, after I'd interviewed Dr Bogan and while you were walking Dykes around the policies, Robins admits he left his post upstairs for a matter of five minutes. The laird – Mr Hereward Restorick that is – asked him to step downstairs for a snack. Mr Restorick is accustomed to having his own way down here, you see, and Robins – well, he inclines to treat Robins as a family retainer. So there it was. But I shouldn't bank too much on it. In my experience, clues are nearly always straight clues, it's only in books that you get false ones planted all over the place.'

'Have you found out where everyone was during that five minutes?'

'Yes. As a matter of routine. Mrs Restorick was in her boudoir. Andrew Restorick and Miss Ainsley were playing piquet. Dr Bogan was in the lavatory; Dykes out in the garden with you. Mr Restorick in his study.'

'Oh, I thought he was giving the constable his elevenses.'

'No, he told him to go down and get it in the kitchen.'

'And the constable left the bedroom door unlocked?'

'I'm afraid he did. In any case, Mr and Mrs Restorick have pass-keys.'

'Did Robins come down the main stairs for his snack, or by the back stairs?'

'The main stairs, apparently. Mr Restorick walked down with him, and then claims to have gone into his study.'

'Well, no doubt you're looking into that. What lines of investigation are you going to work on now?'

'There's the sex angle and the drug angle. We'll have to put your friend Dykes through it, I'm fearing. Investigate further the relationships of all the people at the Manor with Miss Restorick, go into their antecedents; all the usual routine; that ought to give us something, whether it was sex or drugs behind the affair. What you've told me about the hashish is very interesting, but I doubt if it tells us more at present than that someone in the house was in possession of the drug two to three weeks ago.'

Nigel admitted this to be true, though, as it happened, Georgia was to unearth during the next hour a piece of information which put hashish back in the centre of the stage, and Nigel had already heard something from Miss Cavendish that only needed a correct interpretation to advance him much further towards the solution of the case.

Blount removed his nightcap, clapped on his head an austere bowler, summoned his detective-sergeant, and the three of them sallied out for the short walk to Easterham Manor, followed by the inquisitive or gloating eyes of half the population of the village.

'A dour lot they are, down this way,' remarked Blount. 'Do they talk to you at all in the bar, Lang?'

'No fear, sir,' said the Sergeant. 'The landlord's not so bad, though. He comes from London. He was yarning to me only just now.'

'Uh-huh?'

'All about Mr Restorick. How they respect him in the village, and that. Of course, the Manor gives a good deal of employment, one way and another. But there's a bit of wholesome fear, as you might say, in their respect. Landlord was telling me how Mr Restorick half strangled a man who gave him some lip, a year or two ago. Proper temper the gentleman has.'

CHAPTER ELEVEN

'She dealt her pretty words like blades,
As glittering they shone,
And every one unbared a nerve
Or wantoned with a bone.'

EMILY DICKINSON

GEORGIA admired once again the way Charlotte Restorick, in the midst of the disaster which had fallen upon her home, kept her stately poise and kindliness. When Georgia arrived at the Manor, Charlotte was giving the day's orders to the housekeeper: she greeted Georgia with unruffled charm, apologized for keeping her waiting, and gave Mrs Lake a few more directions. Everything had been thought of – the little fads of her guests, the difficulties of provisioning caused by the snow, even the police; Mrs Lake was to inquire whether Inspector Blount and his colleagues would take lunch at the Manor, what they would like for lunch, what time would be most convenient for them.

'And now, Mrs Strangeways,' she said when the housekeeper had retired, 'I don't believe I ever thanked you for looking after the children yesterday afternoon. It was sweet of you. They came back quite full of it.'

'They're very charming children. I wondered whether you would like me to look after them for a bit this morning.'

'Why, that's too kind of you, my dear. But I'd hate to feel we were imposing on you.'

'I'd like it. If it would take any work off your hands. Things must be terribly difficult just now. But you're such a capable organizer – '

'I know it seems heartless to be worrying about petty little domestic details just now,' said Mrs Restorick with one of her shrewd, steady looks. 'But what else is there for us women to do? Indeed, I think we're lucky having these things to take our minds off – well, it quite wrings my heart to see poor

Hereward moping about. He's taking it very hard. He doesn't know how he'll be able to lift up his head in the county after this.'

Georgia cocked an eye at her. Had there been a note of indulgent satire in that last remark, or was it just the American naiveté? Charlotte Restorick's rather heavy face gave nothing away.

'There is just one thing,' said Georgia. 'I didn't like to press the children about it. But do they know the legend of the Bishop's room?'

'Surely not. I don't think it's wise, especially with highly-strung children, to talk to them about that sort of thing.'

'But the servants might have – '

'They're under strict orders not to repeat the story,' replied Mrs Restorick commandingly. 'Why, what gave you the idea?'

Georgia repeated John's remarks of the previous afternoon. 'I expect he was talking through his hat,' she added mendaciously: 'the male habit of boasting before the female starts early.'

She lit a cigarette, and advanced cautiously towards another objective. 'Tell me, Mrs Restorick, did you happen to be present on an occasion when Elizabeth got very worked up? – it was something to do with the children smoking, I fancy.'

'Gracious! Smoking? What an extraordinary notion! I'm sure they don't smoke.'

'So am I. But I offered John a cigarette yesterday, just in fun. And his reaction was rather peculiar. You know the way children close down on something that frightens them, and they don't understand. John said "Aunt Betty smoked like a chimney." Then Priscilla said something about it's not being fair and Aunt Betty getting "in a frightful flap" – and John shut her up quickly. I got the impression that she was going on to say "when we were caught smoking," and it somehow seems out of character with what I know of your sister-in-law.'

There was a wondering, far-away look in Charlotte's eyes. After a pause, she said, 'I believe I know what – yes, I remember now.'

Prompted by a few questions from Georgia, she came out with the story. A few days before Elizabeth's death, the party were acting charades with the children after tea. During one of these charades, in which the children were playing the Babes in the Wood, and Andrew, in a sinister black beard, the Wicked Uncle, he offered them – in a diabolical manner – cigarettes. Elizabeth, who was sitting next to Charlotte in the audience, had startled everyone by giving a suppressed scream and swaying in her chair as if she were about to faint. Dr Bogan, sitting on her other side, had taken her out of the room and returned later to explain that it was one of her attacks. Everyone had been rather upset.

As well they might be, thought Georgia, for the story had chilled her own blood as if it were an outburst of lunatic talk from a person always believed sane.

'The whole episode sounds so horribly meaningless,' she commented five minutes later when she had passed it on to Nigel.

'Horrible. But not meaningless,' he said, his blue eyes gleaming with sudden intelligence. 'I must go and think this out, darling. See if you can get the children to tell you whether Elizabeth said anything to them about the affair afterwards. It's very important.'

Nigel was pacing to and fro along the terrace at the back of the house, wearing a path in the snow. Cigarettes, he mused. Marijuana is peddled in cigarette form. The cat was doped with the same drug. In each episode, Andrew and Elizabeth play leading parts. Elizabeth was a marijuana addict. She and Andrew were both at school in America. Link all that up, and what have you? Twice a little play was staged in which the drug was implied or implicated. It is conceivable that Elizabeth would have been able to recognize the cause of the cat's demoniac behaviour. She certainly saw some meaning in the offered cigarettes. Andrew offered the cigarettes, and it may well have been Andrew who doped the cat. Why? To frighten Elizabeth? He was watching her reactions attentively that night in the Bishop's room. But why should he want to frighten his best-beloved sister?

To frighten her off something? Ah, that's getting warmer. And frighten her off what else but marijuana? But he could just have had a heart-to-heart with her. And besides, cocaine, not marijuana, was her present fancy. But you're forgetting the children. God! Supposing that's it? Suppose it was Betty that Andrew was talking about when he said there was someone in the house who revelled in evil? Suppose Betty was going to make these children addicts of the drug which had set her off upon her own vicious career? And Andrew somehow knew of her intentions and staged these dramatic episodes to warn her off? Or to discover whether his suspicions were well-founded? Like Hamlet?

Nigel went indoors and communicated these ideas to Inspector Blount, who had been interviewing the butler in the writing-room. Blount heard him out patiently, then said:

'That's very interesting. There may be something in it. But I can't see it's directly relevant to the murder.'

'Oh, damn it, surely – '

'You don't mean to tell me that Andrew Restorick would murder his sister, even to prevent her corrupting the children? Why should he? He'd only to tell his brother what he suspected, and Elizabeth would never have been allowed near the children again. You're letting your imagination run away with you.'

Nigel's imagination was indeed frequently stimulated to frenzy by Blount's stolid common sense.

'Well then, what about this?' he now said. 'Elizabeth is acting under somebody else's influence. X is using her as an instrument to get possession of the children. He realizes that Andrew is wise to her little game, and murders her lest she crack up and implicate him.'

'X being Dr Bogan?' inquired Blount dryly. 'Or have you cast Hereward Restorick for the rôle? I'd not put it past you, in your present frame of mind. Lang, will you ask Miss Ainsley to step this way.'

Presently the detective-sergeant ushered Eunice Ainsley into the room. Nigel, shivering on a window seat, now for the first time studied her closely while Blount ran her through some of her previous evidence.

He put her age round thirty. She had the restlessness and slightly protuberant eyes of the neurotic – the type of woman one sees in residential hotels, living with a mother who would look equally 'well-preserved'. Well-preserved without, ill-conditioned within. Restless, dissatisfied, kittenish in front of men, having an occasional unsatisfactory affair with a man considerably older than herself – a business man or engineer or colonial. She smelt rather stuffily, of powder, not scent. She was a chain-smoker, but not, as far as Nigel could see, a drug-addict. Her voice was husky, drawling, with harsh undertones. She wore a well-tailored, check tweed costume, and her hair – which could have been her best feature – was moulded into a disagreeable, almost metallic neatness.

'– you were a close friend of the deceased?' Blount was asking.

'Yes, I suppose so. We used to share a flat – that was four years ago. But I've told you all this before.'

'And she never hinted to you that she was afraid of – something like this happening to her?'

'Oh, no. Of course a person like Betty was always taking the risk.'

'"Taking the risk"?' prompted Blount, his voice soft as silk.

'Well, you can't expect to play around with men as she did, and get away with it every time.'

'You mean, she created jealousy?'

'I've seen two men fighting like wild beasts over her,' said Miss Ainsley, shivering, and crossing her thin legs.

'Anyone connected with this case?'

'No.' Nigel fancied it came out rather unwillingly. 'Not that it mightn't have happened here. She'd got Mr Dykes and Dr Bogan on a string. Poor Betty – it seems awful to be talking about her like this. She couldn't help it, after all. I mean, she was made like that, wasn't she?'

Blount declined to comment on the matter. He said, 'But I understood she was engaged to marry Mr Dykes?'

'Oh, that? Yes, I suppose so. But she wouldn't have gone through with it. I heard her say as much, not long ago. They were having a bit of a row about it.'

Pressed by Blount, she toned down the last remark. No, it hadn't exactly been a row, but both of them had sounded worked-up.

'You don't like Mr Dykes?' put in Nigel.

'I think he's an insufferable little twirp. He's a pacifist, too.'

'Shocking!' said Nigel solemnly.

'Have you any reason for thinking that Miss Restorick had transferred her affections to Dr Bogan?' asked Blount.

'Well, he's a very charming, interesting-looking man, isn't he? And poor Betty *was* inclined to fall for anything new in trousers.'

'That's hardly evidence.'

'And they were together a great deal. Oh, I know it was supposed to be just professional services, and, of course, Dr Bogan has his reputation to look after – though I can't see he's anything so marvellous – anyway, I knew a girl who went to him and she was supposed to be cured, and a few months later she was taking dope worse than ever. But you can get away with anything in Harley Street.'

Blount brought her firmly back to the point. 'But you have no actual evidence of an improper connexion between Dr Bogan and the deceased?' he asked frigidly.

Eunice Ainsley lit another cigarette, her fingers holding the old stub in a taloned gesture. 'Depends what you mean by evidence.' She puffed out a cloud of smoke. 'I happened to hear him saying to her, about a fortnight ago, "It's no use fighting, Betty, I've got you body and soul now, for ever".'

This statement created a sensation, evidently not displeasing to its maker. Blount had a professional scepticism about statements made by neurotic women, but she persisted, in the face of all his attempts to shake her, that it was true.

'Did anyone else hear this? Did you pass it on to anyone?'

'Nobody else heard it. But I told Mr Dykes – I mean, I don't like him, but it was only fair to let him know how the land lay, don't you think?'

'How did he react?'

'Oh, he didn't believe me.' She crushed out her cigarette angrily on the table-top. 'He wouldn't hear a word against her, the silly little man. He was most offensive.'

'And this took place some days after you'd heard her tell Dykes she couldn't go through with it?'

'Yes.'

Blount tapped his teeth with the edge of his gold-rimmed pince-nez, and raised an eyebrow at Nigel. Uncoiling himself from the window seat, Nigel walked over to Eunice Ainsley.

'Did anyone else in this household know about Elizabeth's drug-taking or the situation between her and Bogan, do you think?'

'I can't say. Of course, they'd only to use their eyes.'

'Or their ears,' put in Nigel, with quiet malice.

Miss Ainsley's voice took on a whining undertone. 'Well, I can't help it if I hear things. Betty was so indiscreet – I often warned her, but she didn't pay any attention.'

'You were just thinking of her best interests. Is that the reason why you have your knife in Will Dykes, too? Or is it just plain jealousy?'

Blount coughed deprecatingly. Eunice Ainsley flushed. 'You can't really imagine that anyone could be jealous over Will? It's fantastic,' she said. 'Why make a dead set at me? I suppose I had a right to try and stop my best friend from making a disastrous marriage.'

'Oh well, let it go. Did Elizabeth ever talk to you about her schooldays?'

'What a curious question! No, she didn't much. I gathered she'd been expelled from some seminary in the States, but I don't know why.' Miss Ainsley's eyes popped hopefully at Nigel, eager for enlightenment.

'She never made a more explicit reference to it?'

'I don't think so. Oh, there was one rather funny thing she said to me once – she was a bit tight at the time, and I thought she was ravers – she said: "I'd be an honest girl to-day, Eunice, if it hadn't been for a stick of tea." Well, I ask you! Stick of tea! But she used to invent the silliest pet names for her men. I suppose some men like that sort of thing. Trust Betty to know what the gentlemen liked, poor sweet.'

'On what terms was Mr Restorick with his sister?'

'He liked her just about as much as a – well, a load of dynamite. I mean, he never knew when she mightn't explode some howling scandal in the ancestral home. Hereward's very kind, of course, in his way, but such a stick-in-the-mud. He'd turn himself inside out to avoid a blot on the family scutcheon. But he couldn't do much about Betty, you see, because she had two thousand a year of her own. Which, incidentally, will help to swell the family coffers now. And do they need it!'

'Why, isn't Hereward well off?'

'Oh dear!' exclaimed Miss Ainsley kittenishly. 'What have I done now! Forget it. Hereward is far too respectable – no, honestly he is, I'm not being cynical – even to think of that. But, of course, the money will come in handy. It takes a packet to keep up a place like this nowadays the way Hereward does, and Charlotte has lost a good deal through the war.'

After a few more questions, Miss Ainsley was dismissed.

'Bloody women,' said Nigel, distastefully sniffing the powder-scented air.

Blount smoothed down imaginary hair on either side of his skull. 'Dear me. Dear me,' he said. 'No, indeed. Not an altogether charming representative of her sex. But useful.

She's helped to establish one of your theories. Mustn't look gift horses in the mouth.'

'One of *my* theories?'

'Yes, sir. "Stick of tea" is American slang for a marijuana cigarette.'

'My goodness, Blount, your general knowledge is breathtaking. Is that really so?'

'It is. But you can't get away from it – things look worse for Mr Dykes. We know now that he had a motive for killing Miss Restorick. He had a better chance of being admitted to her room in the middle of the night than anyone else – '

'Except Dr Bogan.'

' – and a cord from his dressing-gown tassel was found there.'

'No, I still think it's wrong emotionally. You agree the evidence of the rope proves the crime was premeditated. I can see Will Dykes strangling his girl in the heat of the moment, but not planning it all out beforehand.'

'Well, we must agree to differ. You'll have to find me something stronger than an argument based on the character of a man you've only met two-three times.'

'And *you've* got to find something stronger than the cord of a dressing-gown tassel. If Dykes did the murder in the heat of passion, he'd not have cut a length of rope and brought it with him. If he had already planned out a murder, do you seriously think he'd take the risk of walking from one wing of the house to the other, before midnight, when there might still be people moving about the passages or awake in their rooms?'

'You forget the medical evidence, which gave the time of death as between ten p.m. and two a.m. We can't lay too much stress on the Special Constable's seeing the light turned off at 12.10 a.m. She may have turned it off herself, and her lover may have entered the room later. He'd expect to find the house quiet after 12.30 or so, at any rate. But I admit it's a bit of a facer – the way nobody heard any movements that night.'

'All sleeping-dosed?' suggested Nigel.

'No. I inquired.'

'Anything on the Hereward Restorick angle? Is he really hard-up?'

'We're making discreet inquiries about the financial position of everyone concerned in the case. But, as you know, that sort of investigation has to be done pianissimo.'

Blount's fingers played a sprightly little tune on the table in front of him, in odd contrast with the sedateness of his expression.

'But I don't think much of that line,' he went on. 'You may call me a snob. But these old country families have certain traditions – they're used to being hard-up nowadays and they don't murder for money.'

'There's something in that. Though I shouldn't let Will Dykes hear you producing that argument. We've heard about Hereward's violent temper, too; but his having half-strangled a man in rage is irrelevant to a premeditated crime like this. I believe Hereward might plan out a murder if it was the choice between that and family disgrace; but, even if we'd accepted Elizabeth's death as suicide, it would have been almost as bad a scandal as whatever it was meant to cover up. In fact, her violent death was bound to start an investigation and stir up mud, so I can't imagine any set of circumstances which would justify it for Hereward.'

'Well, I must get to work.' Blount rose and shepherded Nigel to the door. 'We've just got to stick at it till there's more evidence – What the devil!'

Blount's exclamation was wrung from him by the pain of his nose, which had collided with Nigel's shoulders. Nigel had stopped dead on his way to the door. He now swung round on Blount, muttering, 'Stick at it. Stick it. Stick it, E. Crikey, Blount, I've remembered something! Miss Cavendish told me that, after the cat episode, she overheard Bogan whispering to Elizabeth, "Stick it, E." But no one here called her "E" – "Betty" was the only abbreviation. See? He was whispering something rather different. He was whispering "Stick o' tea." He recognized that the cat had been doped with marijuana; and he automatically used the American slang for it. Now watch my dust.'

'Hey, where are you off to?' cried Blount. But Nigel was already out of the room.

CHAPTER TWELVE

*'Goin' up State Street, comin' down Main,
Ho, ho, honey, take a whiff on me.'*
ANON.

THE difference between Andrew Restorick and the rest of the people at the Manor – Nigel had noticed it before – was Andrew's capacity for filling in time. 'Filling in' was an accurate enough phrase, since time yawned like a chasm of boredom and uncertainty for the household during these early days of the investigation. The rest of them sat about, fidgeted, started games or bits of work or conversations which they never finished, irritable or lapsing into a fatalistic coma like passengers at a remote junction who have missed their connexion and lost the rhythm of their lives. But Andrew always seemed self-contained and occupied. One might almost have thought he had some sort of command over the situation and was only awaiting the right moment to exercise his authority, seeing him now in Hereward's study with a complicated game of patience spread out before him. Whereas Hereward, gnawing his moustache and looking up eagerly from his account-books as Nigel entered, had evidently only been waiting for someone to come and do something normal, tell him something, ask his advice – anything to restore the impression that one lived in a world where the landowner, the gentleman, the practical man carried some weight.

'Could I have a word with you?' said Nigel to Andrew.

Andrew placed a card in position, gave him a charming smile and said 'Private?'

'I think you could both help. Yes, I'd like to talk to you both. It's rather a difficult subject. You see, I want to know the details of that affair when Miss Restorick was expelled from school in America.'

Hereward's blue eyes went blank for a moment, then kindled with anger. He half-rose from his swivel-chair.

'Really! I know we should be grateful to you for the help you've given, Strangeways, but raking up these wretched things out of the past – I don't see –'

'I wouldn't if it wasn't necessary. It's painful for you both. But Miss Cavendish told me your sister had had a baby when she was a schoolgirl over there –'

'She'd absolutely no business –'

'– and, if we're not careful, there's going to be a grave miscarriage of justice.'

Andrew, with a swordsman's turn of the wrist, flipped over a card. 'Miscarriage of justice?' he asked.

'Yes. The police are, I should say, within distance of arresting Dykes for the murder.' Nigel told them about the clue that had been found and Miss Ainsley's statement.

Andrew was frowning. 'What a woman for making trouble! To think Betty should be pursued by one of her lame dogs even after she's dead. Lame bitches, more likely.'

'I wondered why she was friendly with the Ainsley.'

'Yes. Eunice didn't have much of a chance. Her parents divorced when she was a girl, and she lived a ghastly hotel life with her mother. Betty was sorry for her. And Betty was the kind of person who didn't stop at *feeling* sorry.'

'So I imagined. But we're getting off the point. I've an idea that the solution of the problem lies a good way farther back in her life. Marijuana.'

Andrew's long lashes, which reminded Nigel of the dead woman, concealed the expression in his eyes, but his body betrayed him a little; it did not grow tense, as Nigel might have expected, but seemed to relax, to be relieved of a long tension. He swept the cards into a heap and gave Nigel all his attention.

'Marijuana. You've got something there.'

'What the devil are you two talking about?' exclaimed Hereward. 'Sorry, Strangeways. But this last day or two I've been so utterly in the dark –'

'Like Betty! Like Betty!' murmured Andrew, his voice charged with momentary sadness.

'When your cat behaved in that extraordinary way, it had been doped with marijuana, which is home-grown hashish.'

'Good God! D'you mean the stuff was grown here, on my land?' said Hereward.

'No. Miss Ainsley informed me your sister had once told her that this drug was the original cause of her downfall. It's a vile business. But there are people who peddle it outside high schools in America, in the form of sweets or cigarettes. The drug creates erotic hallucinations.'

'Erotic? Oh, I say, this is too much!' Hereward muttered, flushing with embarrassment.

'My dear Hereward,' said Andrew patiently, 'this is no time for shying away from unpalatable facts.'

'What I want to know first,' Nigel continued, 'is whether either of you knew about this.'

There was a pause. Andrew inclined a little derisively to his brother, as though inviting him to lead the way.

'Obviously, I didn't,' said Hereward at last. 'I mean, I was told about Betty, of course. Didn't see her for some time afterwards, though. In the army then. But I'd never heard of this marijuana stuff.'

'What about you?' Nigel turned to Andrew. 'You were Betty's confidant, weren't you, for a long time?'

'Oh yes, I was at school with her when it happened. It was my last term there. I knew a good deal about it.'

'You'd better tell us then.'

'Yes, I think I'd better.'

Andrew Restorick rose in a single lithe movement, went over and stood by the mantelpiece, looking – with his Savile Row suit and the quick eyes beneath the girlish lashes – even less like a rolling stone and black sheep than his brother.

As Andrew talked, the Elizabeth whom Nigel had seen dangling upstairs in the snow-dazzled room was slowly transformed into a schoolgirl, mischievous, captivating, young, with a red ribbon in her hair. She was wild then, Andrew said, full of vitality, impatient for some experience beyond the chatter of her friends and the four walls of the school. But it was only just outside the school's four walls that it came to her. A knot of them were hanging about there during the recess one morning when a youngish man approached. He fell into conversation with the boys and girls. Presently he produced a cigarette-case and lit up. 'None of you babes smoke, of course.' Well, that was enough for Elizabeth. She never refused a dare, and the rest of the gang were watching. She took a cigarette. She strutted up and down the sidewalk, outside the school gates, puffing away in full view of all the townsfolk passing.

That cigarette, of course, was a perfectly harmless one, as were the candies the stranger distributed to the rest of the gang. But he began to turn up quite often, same place and time, and, after a while, he took a few of the children aside and promised them – if they would swear to tell nobody – something special in the way of smokes and candies. That was the start of it. He was an ingratiating sort of man, treated them as equals, in a pleasant off-hand way. Before long, his victims had developed a taste for these very special luxuries he brought, but their effect was such that no boy or girl dared tell anyone what was happening to him.

And, of course, they had to pay for their pleasure. The stranger was not at all pressing about it, at first. But presently they found they owed him sums of money they couldn't hope to pay. He was nice about it. But he made it quite clear that it would be unfortunate all round if their parents discovered about these debts. Not that his victims would have been likely to tell, in any case. The vice took root and sprouted with atrocious rapidity. They needed the stuff and they had to go on getting it. Then the mild petting-parties in which some of the older ones had indulged changed character. Elizabeth, who had never bothered her head about such things, was drawn into them. And Elizabeth's exceptional vitality, played upon by the drug, could only lead one way.

Andrew himself had never fallen a victim to the stuff. 'I was rather a prig, those days,' he said. 'I even objected to Betty's smoking what I assumed were ordinary cigarettes. But you couldn't be angry with her, she could twist iron bars round her finger, the darling.' But, when the habit got a grip on her, she became sullen and secretive. Everything he was telling them now had been confided to him by her two or three years after the calamity took place.

What she had told him at the time was that she was going to have a baby. He assumed that its father was the cigarette-providing stranger and, meeting him one day outside the school, went for him. There was a stand-up fight, in which the man got considerably knocked about, and after that he was never seen in the town again. But Elizabeth assured her brother soon afterwards that the stranger was not responsible for her condition. 'It might have been anyone,' she had said wearily, 'what does it matter who it was?'

'I was more shocked by her saying that than by anything else,' said Andrew. 'God, what a callow prig I was! I went cold on her. Poor, sweet Betty, poor child, trapped like that – and then to find her best-loved turned against her!'

The scandal soon had to come out. Betty was sent to a nursing home in another State, then brought home to England by her parents. Andrew ran off and got work in a lumber camp: he had been a wanderer ever since.

That was the gist of Andrew Restorick's story. Nigel had heard a good many queer stories in his time, but none in so paradoxically inappropriate a setting – this country gentleman's study with its sporting prints, leather chairs, reference books and trophies of the chase, its smell of tobacco smoke and beeswax, and its view over the uneventful Essex landscape.

Nigel, studying the brothers, noticed that Hereward's face was struggling between incredulity and consternation, and that Andrew was shivering uncontrollably.

'It's the first time I've ever told anyone about this,' said Andrew apologetically. 'Confession has curious physical effects on one.'

'Good God!' sighed Hereward on a released breath. 'What a damnable business! If only I'd known – I'd like ten minutes alone with that fella. Wasn't any attempt made to find him?'

'Oh, yes. But he'd disappeared very successfully. He gave Betty and her friends a false name, of course. Must have made a packet, if he did it regularly. The children had to pay through the nose for the dope he peddled – some had rich parents and plenty of pocket-money, and others stole to get the cash. Even then, he claimed that what they paid him was only on account – that was to get an extra hold over them, as I told you.'

There was a long silence, which Nigel finally broke by saying, 'Isn't it about time you also told us whom you were referring to when you said there was someone in this house who revelled in evil? I suppose you meant Miss Restorick?'

Andrew's fists clenched on the arms of his chair, his face darkened like a thundercloud. 'I don't know. Damn you! Can't you see it's because I didn't know – ' he broke off.

'That you doped the cat's milk and offered John and Priscilla cigarettes during the charade?' insisted Nigel.

Hereward's face was ludicrous with consternation. He turned his head from Nigel to Andrew and back again as though he were watching a game of tennis almost too fast for the eye to follow.

'Yes,' said Andrew. 'You may as well know. Knocking about the world, you develop a sixth sense for danger. I felt there was something wrong as soon as I got down here – something to do with Betty, or Bogan, or both of them. It's funny, I've got the artist's intuitive power, yet I can't write a line of verse or play a bar of music, and old Hereward here, who looks like a bit of Essex clay, plays the piano like nobody's business. Well, anyway, I snuffed danger in the air. I hadn't seen Betty for some time, and I was horrified by the change in her. There was a look on her face of – of – I don't quite know how to – '

'Disgust?' Nigel quoted Miss Cavendish.

Andrew glanced at him strangely. 'Maybe you're right. However. I didn't trust Bogan an inch. Betty refused to talk about him. So I poked around a bit in his room.'

'Dammit, Andrew, wasn't that a bit steep? I mean, the fella's my guest.' Hereward's face was a study of dismay and curiosity.

'Yes, dreadfully bad form, I'm afraid. I even opened a locked cash-box I found there – I'm pretty handy at opening locks. And I found some cigarettes. Well, you don't generally lock up your fags in a cash-box. So, at a venture, I tried one of them on the pussy-cat. With startling results.'

'Why not just smoke it yourself?'

'Because I wanted to observe reactions. You see, I had to give Bogan a fair trial. It was possible that he'd confiscated the marijuana cigarettes from Betty, I didn't know then that he was treating her for cocaine-addiction. Even now, it's conceivable that she couldn't stand being deprived of the cocaine, and had gone back to hashish, and Bogan had got wise to it and taken her cigarettes away.'

'You observed reactions. What were they?'

'Result negative. Bogan has the medical pokerface. Betty seemed more or less apathetic, nothing you could take hold of.'

'What about the charade?'

'It was like this. Finding those cigarettes and discovering what they contained, my mind went back to that business in America. I began to wonder was history being repeated here. John and Priscilla – '

Hereward Restorick groaned and put his head in his hands.

' – so, when I played the charade, I used the same phrase as the stranger used outside the school when he offered the cigarettes. I said, "None of you babes smoke, of course?" It was enough to send Betty off the deep end. Bogan preserved his usual dignified façade. Now, what I ask myself is this –

would Betty have reacted so instantaneously to those words, which she'd originally heard twelve years or so ago, if marijuana wasn't – so to speak – in the air again?'

'That's very sound,' commented Nigel. 'You thought she was intending to get at the children? But didn't you put your suspicions to her openly after that?'

Andrew's eyes looked as if he was in physical agony. 'I wish I had,' he said painfully. 'But don't you understand? She was my sister. We'd been as close as any brother and sister have ever been. I couldn't even hint to her that I suspected her of trying to corrupt the children. I just couldn't. I funked it. Besides, there was another interpretation of the whole affair, and I wanted to look into that first.'

'You mean, Bogan might have been the evil genius at work and Betty an accomplice – willing or unwilling?'

'I say,' remarked Hereward, 'I suppose Bogan isn't the same fella as the one who originally gave this bloody stuff to Elizabeth? I mean, he's been in America. I never did cotton to the fella.'

'I wish I could be certain.' Andrew's voice was a whisper. 'I didn't see much of Engelman – that's what the chap called himself. He had a yellowish face and a thin black moustache, about the same height as Bogan, but the voice was quite different. I just don't know. I told you I had a scrap with the fellow. It was twelve years ago. When I met Bogan down here, I felt a sort of physical reaction – when you've had an all-in scrap with a man, something in you always recognizes him again. But that's not evidence. And I'm not sure my reaction wasn't just a natural antipathy. As he said himself, I was jealous over the influence he had on Betty. She was so different. She seemed to have closed up against me.'

'Quite so,' said Nigel. 'I don't think Bogan's possible identification as Engelman is of primary importance at the moment. The question is, could he have killed your sister, and why should he want to?'

'I'm prejudiced against him, I admit. But let us suppose the worst about him. Let's suppose he's the devil incarnate, and go on from there. He has Betty under his thumb, with the hypnosis.'

Nigel thought, 'It's no use fighting, Betty, I've got you body and soul now, for ever.' Was this the true meaning of what Miss Ainsley had overheard?

'He intends to use her as his means for getting at Hereward's children. He tells her she must entice them to smoke the marijuana cigarettes: he may have some doped sweets as well. Now I don't believe,' Andrew went on with a compelling seriousness, 'I don't believe the human soul may not be utterly damned. But also I don't believe that Betty could have changed so terribly from the girl I knew. Whether Bogan's method of compulsion was hypnotism or withholding from her the cocaine she craved for, I am certain she'd still have a powerful resistance against doing such a thing to John and Priscilla. They were always special favourites of hers, weren't they, Hereward?'

His brother nodded dumbly.

'Now suppose Betty had made up her mind to disobey his orders, at whatever cost to herself. She might even have recognized him as the original Engelman – but that, as you say, is not strictly relevant. What would she do? She'd pretend to fall in with his evil designs. She'd collect all the evidence she could against him – remember, Bogan's an eminent specialist and his reputation is vulnerable. When she'd got her evidence – it'd probably have to be written evidence, for no one would take the word of a neurotic drug-addict against her doctor – she'd force a show-down. Touch those children and I'll expose you. Well, Bogan can't afford to live under a threat like that. Betty knows too much. He's got to get that evidence back, and in the process he kills her.'

The burnt papers in Bogan's grate, thought Nigel. Bogan whispering to Betty 'stick o' tea' after the cat episode, suggesting there was such a conspiracy between them. It all fits in.

'That's remarkably interesting,' he said. 'I can't understand why you haven't put it before the police.'

Andrew eyed him quizzically. 'My dear chap, I have a skin to save too, for what it's worth. My room is nearest to Betty's. If I tell the police I'd grounds for thinking that Betty was after the children, they'd begin to wonder very hard if it wasn't I who killed her.'

CHAPTER THIRTEEN

*'My belly's as cold as if I had swallowed
snowballs for pills.'*

SHAKESPEARE

ONCE again Dr Bogan was on the carpet. Nigel had communicated to Inspector Blount the story which Andrew had told him. Blount was at first sceptical of its value; he had the policeman's dislike for the melodramatic, and Andrew's statement opened up a difficult field of investigation. But he was conscientious: if, to solve the case, it was necessary to research into events that had taken place far back in the past and in a distant country, he would do so.

'Now, doctor,' he was saying in his suavest tones, 'some evidence has come to light I'd like to have a word with you about. You're – e'eh – familiar with the effects of hashish, no doubt?'

Dr Bogan nodded. His eyes, unwinking, gazed back at Blount. The inspector maintained a full minute's silence, which he employed in diligently sharpening a pencil. But his favourite tactic of forcing an opponent out of an entrenched position by offering long silences did not work this time. Bogan's fingers combed his beard absently, his body was relaxed, he had no intention of taking the initiative.

'There,' said Blount, 'that'll do. Very useful these old razor blades are for sharpening pencils.'

'No doubt,' said Bogan satirically, indicating his beard. 'That is one disadvantage of not shaving.'

'Quite so. Now, perhaps, you'll be so good as to tell us how you happened to be in possession of cigarettes containing hashish?'

'Marijuana, to be precise,' replied the doctor, smiling faintly. 'I take it you refer to those I have locked up in my cash-box. You possess a search-warrant, of course?'

'I do. But, as it happens, my information about the

cigarettes comes from elsewhere. I wonder, by the way, that you made no complaint when you found one of them was missing.'

'That was quite out of the question,' said the doctor firmly. 'It was in the nature of a professional secret.'

Blount paused again for some while, and again without effect. At last he said, a little irritably, 'I asked you how you came into possession of –'

'Sure. If I've held it back, it was partly because it would be a confession of failure. The day I got here, I discovered that my patient was using these cigarettes. I had had certain suspicions before. I confiscated the cigarettes. But I said nothing about it, even when I saw the cat going haywire – it had obviously been doped with the drug – because it meant my treatment had not been as successful as I'd thought, and because professional secrecy demanded it.'

'Have you any idea who took the cigarette which was used to dope the cat?'

'No. I assumed at first it was a practical joke of Miss Restorick's and she'd not handed over her whole stock of cigarettes to me. Then, when I examined my cash-box, I found two missing.'

'You asked her if she'd taken them?'

'Yes, immediately after the cat affair. She denied it. But I'm afraid drug-addicts are quite untrustworthy. On the other hand, I can see no reason why she should play such a silly trick.'

'"Immediately after?"' put in Nigel. 'That was where you used the phrase "stick of tea" to her?'

Dr Bogan glanced at him keenly. 'Yes. It was what she called the marijuana cigarette. It's American slang, you know.'

'Was this marijuana-smoking of hers a recent development?' asked Blount.

'To the best of my knowledge.'

'Does the name, Engelman, mean anything to you?'

Dr Bogan's eyes unfocused for a moment, it gave him an expression almost of idiocy.

'Engelman? Engelman? *Mean* anything? I don't follow you. I don't *know* anyone of that name.'

'Were you ever in — ?' Blount mentioned the name of the American town where Elizabeth and Andrew had been at school.

'No, never. I take it what you're suggesting is that, since Miss Restorick used the American slang for a marijuana cigarette, her supplies must have been American? I'm afraid you're leaving me altogether in the dark. Is this Engelman the person who supplied her?'

'You didn't ask her for the name of the purveyor yourself?'

'I did. But she wouldn't tell me. It was the same over the cocaine. I couldn't press her about it, naturally. You lose the confidence of drug-addicts if you give the impression of doing police work on the side.'

Blount took off his pince-nez, breathed on the glasses and rubbed them vigorously against his sleeve.

'Well, thank you, doctor. I think that'll be all for now. The inquest, as you know, is to-morrow. It will no doubt be adjourned pending further inquiry, and you'll be able to get back to your patients.'

At the door, Bogan gave them a sidelong glance.

'You keep your own counsel, I see, Inspector.'

Blount beamed at him. 'Oh yes, we have our professional secrecy, too ... H'm, imposing sort of fellow,' he added, when the doctor had gone out. 'Got his wits about him. Or maybe just telling the truth. You never know with that type. Dear me, dear me. Now we shall have to go farther back still into antecedents. A weary road. Give the American police something to do, anyway.'

'You think there may be something in this Engelman tie-up?'

'I don't know. But I'm a wee bit suspicious when a witness doesn't exhibit some healthy curiosity. I got the idea he was holding himself in hard when I asked about Engelman and America. It'd be the natural thing for him to ask what the hell I was driving at, you'd think.'

The inspector then went off with his sergeant and one of the local men to continue his search of the house. It was not a job Nigel envied, in a place as big and rambling as Easterham Manor. But Blount would go through with it. If there were any clues waiting to be picked up here, he would find them. Nigel grimaced, thinking of Blount's really terrifying patience and thoroughness. Like a human vacuum cleaner, Blount was. Which reminded Nigel that a maid had gone all over Elizabeth Restorick's bedroom with a vacuum cleaner on the morning before she had been killed, so there was no possibility that Will Dykes had shed his dressing-gown tasselcord there on a previous visit. Either he'd been in her room the night she was murdered, or the cord had been planted there.

Nigel still kept an open mind about Dykes. But supposing he had not murdered Elizabeth and the cord had been planted there, then the burnt papers in Bogan's grate looked bad for Bogan. It was improbable that some third party, as the murderer, would attempt to incriminate *two* of the house-party.

Presently Nigel was walking back to the Dower House with Georgia. On the way, she told him the result of the commission he had given her. John and Priscilla had at first been very cagey: their aunt's behaviour over a harmless little charade had evidently alarmed them deeply. However, Georgia at last coaxed out of them the statement that, the morning after the charade, Aunt Betty had come into the nursery where they were alone and made them promise not to accept a cigarette from anyone, ever, till they were much older. She had been 'in such a flap about it', as Priscilla put it, that they had promised without asking any questions.

'I remembered about marijuana being put into sweets also,' said Georgia, 'so I asked them if Betty had said anything about sweets. They said their aunt had asked them to tell her if anyone gave them sweets which made them feel funny. They said, naturally, "You bet we will". John was quite excited and asked her if she meant someone was going to try and poison them, like Snow White.'

'And did anyone?'

'No. No chocolates, no cigarettes.'

'Elizabeth didn't warn them against anyone in particular?'

'No. I think they would have told me if she had. Have you got any further?'

Nigel gave her a brief account of Andrew's statement, which took them to the gate of the Dower House.

'What a horrible, horrible affair!' Georgia murmured. 'I begin to wish we'd never come here. You know, there's one thing you ought to go into. Andrew was obviously hinting that Bogan's behind the whole thing. Well, I like Andrew, and Bogan gives me a touch of the creeps. But you ought to find out whether Andrew has some quite different reason for having his knife in the doctor.'

'How am I to do that?'

'You might ask Bogan. If he offers an explanation, it could easily be verified or disproved.'

After lunch, Nigel strolled back to the Manor alone. As he walked round the curve of the drive which brought the house into view, an animated spectacle met his eyes.

John and Priscilla were rolling a huge snowball, which increased in size with every revolution and left streaks of green grass where it had torn up the snow. Andrew Restorick was urging them on, while Miss Ainsley stood apart in the tentative pose of one who would like to join in the fun but is not sure whether she has received an invitation. Priscilla's royal-blue hooded cloak, Miss Ainsley's scarlet woollen gloves and John's rosy cheeks, Andrew's buff-coloured sheepskin waistcoat – all made a lively play of colour against the snow-tipped face of Easterham Manor. The children shrieked with excitement, and tragedy seemed far away.

As Nigel approached, Andrew went into the house, to

reappear carrying a kitchen chair. He sat Miss Ainsley down on this, rather unceremoniously, saying:

'We shall execute a statue of good Queen Victoria. You are to be the model.'

'Oh, don't mind me,' she replied, laughing defensively. 'I shall just die of cold, that's all.'

'Don't be alarmed. We're not going to wall you up. You just sit there and flap your arms to keep warm, like Queen Victoria.'

'She wasn't a bird, was she? Or was she?'

Eunice Ainsley's remarks never quite came off. She was too eager to make an impression. Andrew entirely ignored this one, and she turned to Nigel.

'Here comes Sherlock. Are you looking for footprints in the snow? You'll find a good assortment.'

'Why do you call him Sherlock?' asked Priscilla.

'Because he's a detective, of course, you half-wit,' said John amiably.

'Quite right, infant chee-ild,' said Miss Ainsley. 'Go to the top of the class.'

John turned away to his snowball, scowling. Andrew was now beginning to fashion it as the base of the statue. Miss Ainsley stuck a cigarette into her mouth and puffed at it nervously. She said:

'I hope brother Hereward doesn't disapprove of all this.'

'Why should he?'

'Well, he's such a stickler for etiquette. And the books of etiquette are very firm about gentlemen not making snowmen when their sisters have just – '

'Shut up, Eunice!' Andrew's tone was level, but remarkably forbidding.

'You look quite handsome when you're sweating,' she tried again presently. 'It makes the Restorick profile look almost human, doesn't it, Mr Strangeways?'

Nigel gave an equivocal murmur. Eunice glanced challengingly at Andrew.

'You can get away with anything, with a face like that.

What a marvellous confidence-trickster Andrew would make! But perhaps he is one already. One never knows, with these dark horses.'

'How you do prattle, Eunice,' said Andrew, busily moulding the snow.

'Well, if I've got to sit here shivering, I suppose I can be permitted to talk. Feel my hands, they're icy.'

'There are plenty of fires indoors.'

Miss Ainsley flushed unbecomingly. She turned to Nigel and said:

'Andrew's a very hard sort of character, don't you think? It must be because he's so self-centred. I mean, things that would appeal to you or me just bounce off him. Betty was quite different. She could never refuse anyone anything.'

There was a vicious little stab of resentment in her last phrase. Andrew, smiling at her gently, walked up, tipped her off the chair, took a handful of snow and rubbed it into her mouth. The children shrieked with delight, and began to pelt everyone indiscriminately with snowballs. Eunice was laughing, too, but in a different manner, as she got to her feet and wiped the snow off her face.

'Oh, you beast!' she exclaimed. 'You just wait!' She threw a snowball, in a half-hearted manner, at Andrew. Something about her manner, or her voice, or the smouldering look of her eyes, stopped the children ragging.

Andrew said equably:

'Now you're warmer, aren't you, Eunice? You ought to take more exercise.' His mild mercilessness gave Nigel a disagreeable sensation. 'I think we'd better use this chair for Queen Victoria,' Andrew went on. 'She needs a throne.' He took the chair, and began building up the snow around it, quite, impervious apparently to Eunice Ainsley's black looks.

The snowman grew apace. Andrew was extraordinarily skilful with his fingers, and soon a recognizable figure was taking shape beneath them. Miss Ainsley recovered her form sufficiently to remark that the Good Queen would get piles from sitting on a cold, wet chair. When Andrew was giving the snowman its finishing touches, she went into the house and reappeared carrying a widow's bonnet with flowing black streamers, which she had unearthed from the acting-cupboard.

She placed this upon the effigy's head, and they all stood back to admire their handiwork. The dumpy snow-figure sat there, larger than life, regally surveying the façade of Easterham Manor, the crêpe streamers of its bonnet fluttering in the east wind. Andrew gave John and Priscilla a halfpenny each, to insert in the blank eye-sockets. It was at this moment that Hereward Restorick, emerging from the house, strode towards them.

'Hallo, children. Been making a snowman?'

'Yes, daddy. It's a super one, isn't it? Bet you can't guess who it is.'

'Well now, let's see. Is it cook?'

'Oh no,' cried Priscilla. 'It's Queen Victoria.'

'Queen Victoria? H'm, I see.' Hereward's tone had frosted up quite perceptibly.

'Oh, dear,' murmured Eunice. 'We've committed *lèse majesté!*'

Hereward tugged at his moustache. 'Sorry,' he said abruptly. 'I don't much like that bonnet. John, be a good chap and put it back where you found it.'

'Poor little me! Guilty again! It was I, sir, who bonneted the Queen. But don't you like it really? I think it's the making of her. So artistic.'

Andrew was glancing quizzically at the two of them. His brother said:

'I wasn't talking about artistic effect, Eunice.'

'Oh, don't be an old curmudgeon.' Miss Ainsley tried hard, but she was incapable of the light touch. Hereward frowned.

'If I must speak plainly, I don't think that bonnet is very good form – under present circumstances.'

'It *is* a little *démodé*, perhaps,' said Eunice, flushing angrily.

Hereward removed the offending article and tossed it to his son.

'Take it in, old man. Run along with him, Priscilla, there's a good girl.' When the children were out of earshot, he said to Eunice, 'I think you're deliberately misunderstanding me. No doubt I'm old-fashioned, but I call it rank bad taste to use that bonnet when Betty's lying in there dead. Now have I made myself clear?'

'Yes, indeed, Hereward.' Eunice was lighting a cigarette with shaky fingers, but her voice had taken on an unwonted firmness. 'Your feelings do you justice. *De mortuis nil nisi bonnet*. I say, that's rather bright, isn't it? Eunice is coming on. But you forget Betty was a friend of mine. And *I* wasn't ashamed of her when she was alive. *I* didn't go about trying to hush her up. Aren't you forgetting, too, *how* she died?'

'Really, Eunice, I fail to see – '

'Betty was murdered. I know it was rank bad taste for someone to murder her in *Easterham Manor*. But there it is.'

'I must remind you that you're a guest of mine here.'

Miss Ainsley removed a shred of tobacco from her tongue. 'Yes,' she said. 'And so was Betty.'

A long pause followed. Hereward's blue eyes flinched away from her. 'I really can't conceive what you're driving at.'

'No?' she said sweetly. 'We must have another little chat about it some time, then. In private.'

She walked off towards the house, a queer sort of triumph in her gait, her fur boots stepping delicately through the snow.

CHAPTER FOURTEEN

> *'And when I found the door was shut*
> *I tried to turn the handle, but –'*
> LEWIS CARROLL

THERE is something particularly sinister, reflected Nigel as he paced up and down the snow-laden terrace, about the turning of a worm. It has a nightmare quality, both in its reversal of natural law and in the impression it gives of some puny object swelling to grotesque proportions. Not that I believe a worm ever does turn. Has anyone seen a worm rearing up and biting its oppressors? I doubt it. Unless 'worm' means 'snake' in this context. Eunice Ainsley is a bit of a snake, no doubt about that. Her little scene with Andrew can probably be disregarded. She is attracted to him, her rather gauche advances are not so much repulsed as ignored, and she naturally tries to get her own back for this public humiliation by striking at his weakest point – Betty. She reminds Andrew, by innuendo, that his beloved sister was a promiscuous bitch, and very properly gets her mouth filled with snow. All O.K. Nothing unnatural about that. Though *n.b.* that Andrew has not altogether lost the priggish, puritanical, idealist – call it what you will – streak, which estranged him from Betty when the scandal broke in America.

But the Eunice-Hereward barney was quite a different kettle of fish. Eunice, for once, knew she had the upper hand, and she couldn't resist demonstrating it, which was unfortunate for them both, since she was hinting plainly that Hereward knows more about the murder than he has admitted, and that she herself is in a position to make things very awkward for him. What other interpretation can one give to her remark about Betty having been a guest of his too, and her 'we must have *another* little chat about it some time?' Has she got as far as actual blackmail yet, I wonder.

At any rate, we see now why Hereward has been looking

so worried. I shouldn't like to have Eunice on my track. That's the trouble about the worm turning. When the strong cut up rough, we can be pretty sure – if we know them at all – what lines they'll work on. But when the weak become aggressive, there's hell to pay: it's like being suddenly attacked by a lunatic, a blind man, or a total stranger – one simply can't plot out their course or anticipate their next move; they probably don't know it themselves. I think I'd better have a word with Hereward before anything else happens.

It was a good notion. But Nigel, as it happened, had been forestalled. When he entered the house and inquired for Mr Restorick, the butler returned with a message from Mrs Restorick asking him to defer the interview for half an hour. Nigel decided to improve this shining half-hour by a showdown with Eunice Ainsley.

At first she was inclined to be defiant or sullen. But Nigel's patience, his calmness, the air of expert and unshockable impartiality which was his professional manner, soon broke down her resistance. He realized what an unhappy woman she was, and she sensed a certain sympathy behind his impersonal approach to her.

'I thought I'd better see you at once,' he was saying. 'I was interested by your remarks to Hereward.'

'Oh?' She scrutinized him warily.

'Yes. You gave me the impression of having something up your sleeve – about him and Betty.'

'I was very fond of Betty,' Eunice said tonelessly.

'I believe you were. Now don't get the idea that every man's hand is against you. Mine isn't. But I don't think Betty would like you to be doing to Hereward – what I think you're doing.'

'And what am I supposed to be doing to Hereward?'

'Blackmailing him.' Nigel's pale blue eyes opened at her in mild astonishment. 'That was obvious, wasn't it?'

'I must say you do get queer ideas. Just because I said – '

'My dear girl, don't let's start a fencing-match. I'll put it this way, if you like. *If* you have some information which makes you suspect that Hereward knows more about Betty's death than he's told the police, you should come out with it. Suppose,' he continued, in his flattest voice, 'suppose Hereward did murder Betty – ' Miss Ainsley gasped, and fingered her lip ' – it would be extraordinarily dangerous for you to keep your information to yourself. If, on the other hand, you are acting under a misconception or malice, you're also in danger. Hereward will go to the police and you'll get a stretch for blackmail.'

Miss Ainsley's answer to this well-meant, if laborious advice, was to burst into tears. She was not a woman who wept gracefully: she gulped and sniffled peevishly, as if resenting the weakness that made her do it. At last, controlling her voice, she said:

'Oh, damn and blast it all! I lose, as usual. It isn't fair. It was my money, really.'

'Your money?' Patiently questioning her, Nigel elicited the statement that Betty had recently promised to leave Eunice her money if she died, and had for some time been helping her with generous sums. But Betty had put off making a will till it was too late; now, since she had died intestate, her capital would go to her next of kin. After Betty's death, Eunice had approached Hereward and told him of Betty's promise, but he had refused to admit it. Eunice's own small income having considerably diminished as a result of the war, she was desperate.

'So you put the screw on Hereward? Well, don't let's worry about that any more. But you must tell me *how*.'

'No. Please, I can't. You wouldn't understand. Ask him yourself first, anyway, and, if he won't tell you, come back to me again.'

'Very well. Just one thing. Did Hereward know, before Betty's death, of her intention to leave you her money? Did she ever tell you she'd mentioned it to him?'

'No. Not as far as I know. After all, why should she? She wasn't expecting to die.'

Nigel believed Eunice to be telling the truth now, but she was an unreliable witness at the best of times, and he could not forget how, during the interview with Blount, she had seemed to hint at Betty's money as a possible motive for the crime.

It was now time for his talk with Hereward. Entering the study, he was rather nonplussed to find Charlotte Restorick there as well as her husband. In her black mourning-robe she looked more impressive than ever, her figure and assurance both dwarfing the thin and uneasy Hereward. With one of her impresario gestures, she motioned Nigel to a chair and made a brief announcement.

'I hope you don't mind my being here, Mr Strangeways. Hereward has been telling me about what happened just now – and other things. He wants to make a clean breast of it.'

Hereward's expression was a comical blend of the guilty schoolboy and the man who deprecates female interference.

'Yes. Quite so. H'm, 'm,' he said. 'Afraid I rather put Miss Ainsley's back up just now. Nervy sort of woman.' He glanced at Nigel, with a mute appeal for sympathy. Nigel's face, however, was at its most non-committal. 'Fact is,' Hereward floundered on, 'fact is, as I dare say you gathered, she's got the edge on me. Nothing discreditable, of course. Total misunderstanding. But looks bad. What I mean – '

Charlotte Restorick, like a ship of the line, bore down to his rescue. 'What Hereward wants to tell you is that Miss Ainsley is in possession of certain facts which she has misinterpreted. On the night poor Betty died – '

'All right, Charlotte. I can speak for myself,' interrupted Hereward irritably. 'I'm afraid I slightly misled the police about my movements that night. I told them I went up to bed at 11.30. So I did. But, when I got to my dressing-room, I thought I'd go along and say good-night to Betty. As you know, her room is in the opposite wing. To get there, I had to pass Miss Ainsley's door, and apparently she heard me, looked out, and saw me walking towards the opposite wing.'

'Why?'

'Eh? What?'

'Why did she look out of her room? Does she peer out whenever anyone passes her door?'

'Blessed if I know. Does sound a bit odd, now you mention it. Just a coincidence, I dare say.'

'Nothing of the sort, Hereward,' interposed Charlotte. 'I hate to say anything against Eunice, Mr Strangeways, but she does suffer from morbid curiosity.' (True enough, thought Nigel, considering the number of things she has 'overheard' already in this case.) 'She was genuinely fond of Betty, but terribly jealous of Betty's men friends. That was why she and Mr Dykes didn't get on. Now, Mr Dykes' room is next to Hereward's dressing-room. Eunice may easily have thought it was Mr Dykes going along to the other wing.'

'I see. Yes, that's possible. Did all of you make a habit of going to say good-night to Elizabeth?'

'Oh no,' said Hereward. 'Fact is, I'd had a bit of a row with her earlier that day – afraid I spoke rather sharply – wanted to make it up, you know.'

'A row? What about?'

'Oh, nothing really, storm in a tea-cup, nothing to do with –'

'The police will want to know.'

Hereward tugged his moustache, visibly ill at ease. 'Well, I disapproved of her language in front of the children. Poor Betty – swore like a trooper – I'm not a prude, I hope, but I don't like to hear a lady swearing; couldn't have it with my children, anyway – you know the way they pick things up. Wish I hadn't parted from Betty that way, though.'

'You went to say good-night to her and make up the quarrel, and Miss Ainsley saw you pass into the west wing,' prompted Nigel. 'You went straight to her room?'

'Yes.'

'So you'd get there between 11.30 and 11.35?'

'About that.'

'Didn't see anyone else on your way?'

'No. I prowled along quietly, you know – didn't want to wake people up – I dare say, that's what put it into Miss Ainsley's head that – ' Hereward broke off in some confusion.

'Leave it a moment. You got to her room. What happened then?'

'Well, the door was locked. I tapped gently and called her name, very quietly, once or twice. There was no reply, so I assumed she was asleep and returned to my own room.'

'How long did all this take?'

'My husband was not gone more than three minutes when I heard him come back into the dressing-room,' said Mrs Restorick.

'I take it you would have seen a light under the door if the light had still been on in Miss Restorick's room.'

'Yes. Her light was out. No question about that. She generally read in bed till midnight, but of course she'd been out of sorts lately.'

'Did anyone else but your wife hear you return to your room?'

'Couldn't say, I'm sure.'

'Miss Ainsley's curiosity didn't extend as far as watching for you to come back?'

'Apparently not. Wish it had, in a way. Devilish awkward – you see, she's got the impression that – well, that, in the light of what did happen that night, there was something suspicious about my movements.'

'Why didn't you tell this to the police?'

'That is scarcely an ingenuous question, Mr Strangeways,' said Charlotte. Her smile was friendly enough, but there was a touch of haughtiness in her voice. Nigel shrugged.

'You didn't want to be mixed up in the affair?' he said.

'Afraid that was it. Feel a bit ashamed of myself now. But, honestly, I couldn't conceive that the information could get the police any forrarder. After all, I didn't hear anything in her room, or see anyone about. So I just kept mum.'

Charlotte, who had been watching her husband with the fond anxiety of an impresario watching an infant prodigy at his first public début, leant back with a sigh.

'And where does Miss Ainsley come into this?' asked Nigel.

'Why, damn it, I've just told you. She saw me going along –'

'What was she talking about this afternoon, then?'

Nigel interrupted a glance from Hereward to Charlotte that said S.O.S. as plain as a pikestaff. But Charlotte remained silent. Finally, Hereward mumbled:

'Oh, that didn't mean anything. You know how it is with these nervy women. I mean –'

'No, Hereward.' Mrs Restorick had merely been holding her fire till he was in the most favourable position. 'You Englishmen are so absurdly chivalrous, Mr Strangeways. Hereward would rather cut off his hand than say anything bad about a lady.'

'Eh? Oh, come, my dear!'

'It's true, and you know it. I shall have to explain for him. After poor Betty was killed, Eunice came to my husband, told him she'd seen him going stealthily to Betty's room just before she was murdered, and promised to say nothing about it if he'd hand over Betty's income to her. It was downright blackmail, of course, and I told Hereward he mustn't let himself be intimidated.'

'When did you first hear of this, Mrs Restorick?'

'My husband came in just now, half an hour ago, and asked my advice. I'd seen he was badly worried before this, of course, but I'd no idea Eunice was back of it.'

Nigel contemplated the two of them for a moment. 'Why should Miss Ainsley ask you to hand over Betty's income? I mean, why should she blackmail you in those particular terms? I'd have expected her just to ask for a given sum of money – and then probably come back for more.'

'Surely, the best person to ask about that would be Miss –'

Charlotte began to say, but Hereward, with unusual firmness, broke in on her.

'No. Must give Strangeways all the facts now. According to Eunice, Betty had promised to leave her the money in her will, so she thought she had a claim to it.'

'That was the first you'd heard of Betty's intentions?'

'Oh, yes. Yes. Rather.' said Hereward, with a certain overacted negligence, as though he had been asked in the witness-box a question whose crucial nature he must not appear to recognize.

'I don't understand,' said Nigel. 'How did Miss Ainsley know that your sister had not carried out her promise? Nothing has been said in this house to suggest that she died intestate, has it?'

'Well, as a matter of fact it has. A few days before Betty died, we were all talking about the war. At lunch it was. I happened to say that, with air-raids likely to occur any time now, everyone ought to make a will. Betty agreed – said she'd see her solicitors about it when she returned to London. You remember, Charlotte?'

'Yes. Mr Dykes made rather a harangue about private property and how immoral it was for people to inherit money they'd never worked for.'

'Fellow's a bit of a Bolshie,' said Hereward apologetically. 'But not a bad sort when you get to know him.'

'I wonder did it occur to anyone,' remarked Nigel, staring at his toes, 'that Betty might make a will in Mr Dykes' favour. After all, they were engaged, more or less.'

The Restoricks made no comment on this, so Nigel added, 'I take it, since she died intestate, her property will be divided equally between you and Andrew?'

'That's so, I believe,' replied Hereward. 'Wish I knew what to do about it. I mean, if Betty really did promise it to Eunice, I feel I ought to hand it over. But, tell you the truth, I need it myself. The way securities are depreciating, it's a job to keep up a place like this.'

'I tell Hereward he should offer Easterham to the government for a hospital,' said Charlotte. 'But, of course, they don't seem to need hospitals yet. I wonder when the war is really going to start in earnest.'

Hereward grinned. 'Charlotte fancies herself as a Matron. She'd keep 'em in order all right, eh?'

'Don't be absurd, Hereward.'

On this playful note, Nigel left them. The last glimpse, as he closed the door, of Charlotte queenly and capable in her black dress and Hereward with his drooping moustache that might have graced the Thane of Cawdor, made Nigel contemplate even more seriously the possibility that the drama being enacted here might resemble *Macbeth* rather than *Hamlet*.

The Restoricks had been remarkably candid with him, but that might have been because Miss Ainsley had forced their hand. Hereward's evidence had seemed ingenuous enough, but maybe his wife had coached him in it. It was difficult to believe that, however precarious his financial affairs, Hereward would murder his sister for a half-share in property which only brought her two thousand pounds a year. On the other hand, if Hereward had had some other motive, his wife might attempt to distract attention from it by stressing the inadequate motive of the inheritance. If so, she was playing an audacious game. But Nigel fancied she was an audacious as well as a clever woman.

Something else in Hereward's statement, however, was nagging at him. As he walked towards the drawing-room, he was trying to assess the significance of Betty's door being locked at 11.30 that night. Deep in thought, he bumped into Andrew, who emerged suddenly from the drawing-room.

'What the —? Oh, it's you,' exclaimed Andrew. 'Where's the inspector? Some — has just tried to poison me.'

CHAPTER FIFTEEN

*'Revolving in his altered soul
The various turns of chance below.'*
DRYDEN

As if it had been a signal, Andrew's remark released a babble of voices within the drawing-room.

'In my milk,' he jerked out to Nigel. 'Scribbles wouldn't take it. Smell of bitter almonds. I'll fetch Blount.'

He ran upstairs. As Nigel turned the knob of the door, it was opened from inside, and Will Dykes and Miss Ainsley appeared. Eunice, deathly white, clutched Nigel's sleeve.

'I can't stand any more of this!' she cried. 'You've got to stop it.'

'It's a queer do, I must say,' murmured Dykes.

Dr Bogan was standing in the middle of the room, looking mightily perplexed, and shaken out of his normal calm. Nigel's eye took in the tea-table, with a glass half-full of milk on it in addition to the tea-things, a saucer of milk on the floor, and the cat Scribbles gazing at it resentfully from the hearthrug.

'What's happened?' he asked.

All three of them started speaking at once, then stopped. Dr Bogan took an authoritative step forward.

'Restorick poured a little milk from his glass into a saucer for the cat. The cat sniffed at it and backed away. Dykes made some remark about Scribbles being wary of saucers of milk nowadays. Restorick took up the saucer and smelt it. "Bitter almonds," he said, "that's some kind of poison, isn't it?" I told him potassium cyanide. We kind of hadn't taken it in yet. Then I took up his glass and smelt that. It's potassium cyanide all right.'

'Oh God!' exclaimed Eunice. 'We might all have been poisoned.'

She ran over to the hearthrug, plumped down beside

Scribbles with an ungainly movement, and snatched him to her breast, babbling stupidly.

'I don't think there was any fear of that,' said Bogan. 'It looks as if this was aimed at Restorick alone. He never took tea – always had a glass of milk brought in specially for him, you see. Unless – '

He broke off. As if by common consent, he and Nigel moved quickly to the tea-table. With a gesture, Bogan left it to Nigel, who bent over the delicate milk-jug and delicately sniffed it. Then he sniffed at the cat's saucer.

'Yes. I'm afraid so. In both of them. The jug smells less strongly than the saucer. More diluted there, of course.'

At this moment Hereward and Charlotte came in, and the incident had to be narrated over again. Hereward's expression changed from bewilderment to outrage. He cleared his throat once or twice, but before he could get any words out Andrew returned with Blount and the detective-sergeant.

His eyes glittering frostily, Blount at once assumed control, his presence seemed to pull the unnerved company together.

'Mr Restorick has put me in possession of the facts,' he snapped out. 'Please sit down, all of you. Those of you who were in the room, sit where you were when Mr Restorick poured out the milk.'

Eunice and Bogan moved to a sofa near the tea-table, Dykes to a chair on their left, while Andrew sat down on the opposite side of the table. Blount gingerly sniffed at the saucer and the glass.

'The milk jug, too,' murmured Nigel.

'What's that?' exclaimed Andrew, so fiercely that Eunice gave a little cry.

'Yes. The milk in the jug is poisoned too,' said Blount, wrinkling his nose over it.

'Good Christmas!' Andrew said. 'D'you mean to say – ? It's mass-murder. Why, I assumed – '

'No, you were not specially favoured, Mr Restorick,' Blount commented dryly. He gazed round the company, with a slow, formidable look that made even Nigel curl up a little inside. 'This is a stupid job. Untidy. Botched-up on the spur of the moment. Someone's hand has lost its cunning. Anyone could smell this stuff through milk and tea. All the chances were against your drinking it. And we shall soon find out who was in a position to tamper with the milk. Hadn't you better confess now, and save trouble?'

Dead silence, broken by Hereward, who had found his voice at last.

'I – this is outrageous! Are you suggesting that one of my guests – ? These are all friends of mine. What about the servants? Didn't they have access to – ?'

'Aye. Shuffle it off on them,' muttered Will Dykes. 'Ladies and gentlemen don't poison each other. It's not done.'

'Oh, shut up, Dykes,' Andrew exclaimed angrily. 'This is no time for your ridiculous class-consciousness.'

They all stared at him. It was a strange outburst from the usually equable Andrew.

'I'll attend to that,' Blount said to Hereward. 'Now will you four just go through the several actions you performed when Mr Restorick poured out the milk.'

Bogan, Dykes, and Eunice sat still. Andrew, who had recovered himself, said:

'Cue please, Eunice.'

'What? Oh, I see,' she said faintly. 'Hallo, pussy-cat.'

Dykes said, 'I'm glad I haven't got nine lives. One's enough for me on this bloody planet.'

Andrew said: 'I wonder is he a bit more cautious of saucers of milk nowadays.' He lifted the glass, and pretended to tip some milk into an imaginary saucer. A pause.

Dykes said: 'Nay. He looks gift saucers in the mouth. Sensible cat.'

'That's funny,' remarked Andrew. They had been re-enacting the episode in stiff, self-conscious voices; but Andrew's tone had suddenly, alarmingly altered. 'That *is* funny,' he said. 'There's not so much milk in my glass.'

'Of course there isn't,' said Dykes. 'Some of it's in the cat's saucer.'

'No, I don't mean that. There's less milk in my glass now than there was when I left the room to fetch Blount. I'm certain there is. What do you say, Bogan?'

He lifted the tumbler and held it out to the doctor, balanced on his palm.

'I couldn't say. I didn't notice the level particularly before.'

Blount had already rung the bell. A maid appeared.

'Did you bring in these tea-things?'

'Yes, sir.'

'Just take a look at the milk jug. Did you fill it to the top?'

'Oh no, sir. Not right up. It might spill over, you see. It's fuller now than when I brought it in.'

'You're sure of that?'

'Yes, sir.'

Blount dismissed her for the present. 'You see what that means?' he said. 'Somebody poured some milk from the glass into the milk jug, presumably between Mr Restorick's finding his milk was poisoned and Mr Strangeways' entering the room. Why? The only possible reason is to give the impression that both lots of milk had been poisoned. The attempt to poison Mr Restorick had failed. The criminal hoped to confuse the issue by making it seem that the attempt had been directed against anyone or everyone who would be sitting down to tea. And the criminal – ' Blount gazed at them coldly through his pince-nez ' – must be one of you three in the room, Miss Ainsley, Mr Dykes, Dr Bogan.'

Dykes grunted. Eunice cowered back against the sofa. The doctor remarked, 'Your argument is *logically* correct. But – '

'Of course it is. Now, did any of you three see it happen?'

But, hard as Blount tried, he could not establish anything. In the short interval during which the milk jug could have been touched, they had all – apparently – been upset and moving about every whither. None of them could vouch for having had any other one under his observation all the time. They had been too bemused by the unexpected shock. Nigel privately was inclined to put his money on Bogan. When he entered the room, Eunice and Dykes had been at the door, facing him, their back to Bogan, who was standing near the table. They would presumably have gone out of the room, if they hadn't met Nigel, and this would give Bogan a better chance than anyone had had while all three were still there.

'Did you make a habit of giving the cat milk, Mr Restorick?' Blount was asking.

'No. Never did. It sort of arose out of that conversation we were having. Lucky for me, too.'

'Chance has played an – e'eh – capricious rôle in this episode,' remarked Blount rather pedantically. 'Now then, does anyone know of the existence of any potassium cyanide in this house?'

'Yes,' said Hereward. 'Yes. I have some. Use it for photography, y'know.'

'Will you be so good as to see if it's still where you keep it, sir?' Blount signed the sergeant to accompany Hereward. It was less than two minutes – and seemed hours – before they returned.

'The bottle's gone,' announced Hereward, almost wildly. 'Kept it in that cupboard on my study wall. It's not there any more.'

'When did you see it last?'

'Eh? Oh, see it last. Let me think. Why, only this morning. Opened the cupboard to get a packet of pipe cleaners.'

'You keep the cupboard locked, I presume?'

'No. As a matter of fact I don't.'

'You ought to. Potassium cyanide's dangerous stuff to leave about.'

'But, damn it, the bottle had POISON on it. Red label. Anyone could see – '

'Exactly,' said Blount, with the faintest twinkle of amusement in his eyes. 'Well, we've got to find that bottle and find out when there were opportunities to poison Mr Restorick's glass of milk. I must ask you all to stay here. Sergeant Phillips, don't leave this door and don't take your eyes off them.'

'Damn it!' exclaimed Hereward heatedly. 'You're treating us all like criminals.'

His wife said: 'My dear, I'm afraid someone here *is* a criminal. I suppose you will want to have us searched, Inspector?'

'If I don't find the bottle elsewhere,' Blount replied.

'Then – you will want someone to search Miss Ainsley and myself – I suggest asking my housekeeper.'

Blount stared at her dourly. He did not approve of people taking control over his head. But Mrs Restorick's charming smile softened him a little.

'Thank you, ma'am. I'll bear it in mind. Mr Strangeways, I'd like you to come with me.'

Nigel followed him out, and along the hall towards the servants' quarters. Blount was muttering, 'Preposterous! Wouldn't deceive a bairn! Lost his grip. Or – ' He jerked out over his shoulder to Nigel: 'D'you suppose it was another practical joke?'

'With potassium cyanide? This is England, not North Britain. We like our practical jokes to have a lighter touch this side of the border.'

'T'chah!' said Blount. He was the only person Nigel had ever met who pronounced this precisely as it is spelt in works of fiction. 'T'chah! That Andrew had a nasty little twinkle in his eye. Probably put the stuff in the glass himself. Just to make things more difficult for me. Scoundrel. Coincidence. Chance. Just happened to pick on the one afternoon he had poison in his milk to offer some to the cat. No animal lover. Oh well now, oh well now.'

Blount employed the figure of asyndeton only when he was in a cheerful mood. Rubbing his hands briskly, he marched into the housekeeper's room, where she was having tea with the butler: their scandalized looks at this intrusion quite failed to deter him.

'Aha! Having tea? Splendid. Delicious. Now, Mr Butler, sir, if I may take you away a wee while from your cookies – I'm sure Mrs, er-um, Lake will excuse you – I want your co-operation.'

The butler, gaping fishily, seemed to be dragged in his wake like one of those celluloid fish that follow a magnet. Presently they were in the pantry, at the back of the hall, where the tea-things had been put ready. The maid who had brought in the tea was summoned again, and the following facts came to light. At 3.45 she had begun to prepare the tray. The milk had been taken from a refrigerator in the kitchen: several of the servants had milk from the same source for their tea, so it could not have been tampered with at that end. The tray, with the milk jug and Andrew's glass of milk, had been left unattended in the pantry between 3.50, roughly, and 4.15 when the maid carried the tray into the drawing-room. This, she stated, was her normal routine.

Nigel made a mental note that, between 3.50 and 4.15, he had been talking to Hereward and Charlotte in the study. They, at any rate, could not have tampered with the milk.

The butler deposed that he had entered the pantry just after four o'clock, to run his eye over the tea-tray.

'You're an – e'eh – observant man?' asked Blount. Nigel stiffened. When that Glasgow accent took command over Blount's voice, it meant that he was hot on the track of something.

'I hope so, sir. My duties –'

'When you entered this pantry just after four o'clock, was that bottle there?'

He wiggled his pince-nez at a small bottle, standing with little attempt at concealment in a deep bowl above the shelf where the tray had rested.

'Good gracious!' exclaimed the butler. He might well do so, for the bottle had a red label marked POISON. 'No, sir, that bottle wasn't there when I –'

'You're sure?'

'Absolutely certain,' replied the man, in a tone of austere rebuke like that of a cathedral verger defending the authenticity of his medieval glass.

Blount took up the bottle gingerly in a handkerchief, removed the cork, and sniffed very cautiously.

'Yes. This is it. Seen it before?'

The butler, after some humming and hawing, admitted that he had seen a bottle of similar appearance in a cupboard in the master's study.

Half an hour later, Nigel was summoned to the writing-room. Blount had interviewed the house-party in the meanwhile, with the following results. Between four and four-fifteen, Mr and Mrs Restorick had been in the study with Nigel, Dykes and Eunice in the drawing-room; at about five past four Andrew Restorick entered the drawing-room, and was there till the tea-things were brought in. Dr Bogan was the only member of the party whose movements during this period were uncorroborated. He claimed to have been upstairs in his room till about 4.10, when he had come downstairs, washed his hands in the hall lavatory, and entered the drawing-room just before the maid brought in the tea-tray. Blount summed it up.

'If the butler is correct in stating that the poison bottle was not in the pantry just after four o'clock – and chaps like that instinctively notice anything that's out of place – the only people who could have poisoned the milk are Andrew Restorick and Dr Bogan. I can imagine no reason why Andrew should poison his own milk and then give it to the cat. So –'

'Q.E.D.? I wonder. It sounds almost too easy. If Bogan did it, he'd surely have given himself some sort of alibi. And why leave the bottle in such a conspicuous place? It looked as if we were meant to find it.'

'He'd not have much time to hide it anywhere. And I don't expect to find fingerprints on it, no doubt he held it in a handkerchief.'

'I believe you're making a mistake in concentrating on the

four to four-fifteen period. The butler may be wrong, which'd give us 3.50 to four to play about in. Or the criminal might have doped the milk earlier and planted the bottle after 4.15, to throw suspicion on Bogan.'

'No, that won't do. They were all under somebody's eye then. Dykes, Bogan, Andrew, and Miss Ainsley in the drawing-room, Mr and Mrs Restorick with you.'

'Not quite accurate. There were a few minutes between the time I left the Restoricks in the study and the time they entered the drawing-room. They –'

'Oh, come now! You're not suggesting –?' Blount looked really shocked.

'I didn't go to the study for my talk with them till four o'clock. One of them could have poisoned the milk before that, then popped into the pantry after the interview was over, on the way to the drawing-room, and planted the bottle. They knew better than anyone else here the household routine. They'd know that the butler always went to inspect the tea-tray ten or fifteen minutes before it was brought in. They could rely on us believing his evidence that the bottle was not there at four o'clock, thus providing themselves with a good but not too perfect alibi.'

'But why on earth should they want to poison Andrew?'

Nigel related the substance of his interviews with Eunice Ainsley and the Restoricks.

'You see how it is?' he concluded. 'If the Restoricks really are hard up, they've got a remarkably solid motive for murdering both Elizabeth and Andrew. Elizabeth's money would be divided equally between Andrew and themselves. Now suppose Andrew dies intestate, or has made a will in their favour, all his money plus his share of Elizabeth's would come to them also. It'd make a tidy sum. You'll have to ask Andrew about his will.'

'Restorick's no poisoner,' said Blount irritably. 'A man with a temper like that is the wrong type.'

'Macbeth, I fancy, had a temper, too.'

Blount scrutinized him keenly. 'H'm. So that's your line. Will you tell me, then, how Mr and Mrs Restorick managed to put some of the milk from Andrew's glass into the milk jug when they weren't in the drawing-room at all?'

'Oh, they didn't do that, of course. That was Bogan's work, I imagine. He's getting a bit rattled, I expect you've noticed. If those burnt papers really were planted in his grate, he'd act quickly to diffuse any further suspicions that might be coming his way.'

'I can't see how pouring poisoned milk from a glass to a jug could distract suspicion from him. It'd merely make it look as if he'd intended to poison the whole company and not Andrew alone.'

'I said, "diffuse" suspicion, not "distract". We know – and he must realize it – that there's some sort of private duel going on between him and Andrew. Whether it has anything to do with the murder isn't established yet. But it's imperative now for him to cover up anything which might suggest that he's out for Andrew's blood in particular.'

'All this is very fanciful, Strangeways. And it doesn't help you to pin anything on the Restoricks.'

'I don't want to pin anything on them. But I'm worried about that locked door.'

'Locked door?'

'Yes. As I told you, Hereward states that, when he went to Betty's room at about 11.30 on the night she died, he found the door locked. Don't you see the contradiction? We have been assuming that she was expecting a visit that night – from a lover or someone else. If she was expecting a visitor, she would not leave the door locked. If the door *was* locked, she wasn't expecting a visitor and no one could get in without a pass-key. Hereward has a pass-key. On the other hand, if the door *wasn't* locked, Hereward for some reason is lying.'

'You do get tangled up in your logic,' said Blount, beaming at him mildly. 'Why shouldn't her lover be already in the room when Hereward came along? That'd account for the locked door.'

'Yes. I hadn't thought of that,' replied Nigel disconsolately. 'But I still feel in my bones there's something odd about that door being locked.'

In which he was later to be proved, if illogical, highly correct.

CHAPTER SIXTEEN

*'She who, wise as she was fair,
For subtle doubts had simple clues.'*
COVENTRY PATMORE

Now that the Macbeth motif had entered his head, Nigel's position as a sort of unofficial investigator for the Restoricks had become impossible. Not liking to declare this openly to them, for it would put them on their guard if they were guilty, he pleaded business in London. Some loose ends, too, might be tidied up if he went there, he told the Restoricks.

Loose ends, he was thinking as the train took Georgia and himself through the snow-bound landscape, was an understatement. The whole case had become a tangle of loose ends; it was almost impossible to find the real thread in the midst of them all. For Blount, of course, it was worse still. His job was to make an arrest, and it seemed as though, whenever he was ready to pounce on one player in this grim game, another player jumped up and attracted his notice. Besides, as Blount remarked just before Nigel left, you can't make bricks without straw. He couldn't arrest Will Dykes on the strength of one cord out of a dressing-gown tassel and a broken engagement. He couldn't arrest Bogan just for being a sinister character who might or might not have supplied Elizabeth with marijuana fifteen years before, and who might or might not have burned papers in his grate on the morning after the murder. Nor, again, could he have arrested Hereward because of a locked door, or Eunice Ainsley because she had as good as blackmailed Hereward, or Andrew because he had talked about people who revel in evil.

No motives had come to light which, unsupported by really damaging material evidence, a defending counsel couldn't tear to shreds; and not enough material evidence even to make shreds of. The inquest had been adjourned, and Blount could not keep his suspects at Easterham any longer.

Indeed, he did not want to. He knew that time was always the police's long suit: sooner or later something would come to light, someone would grow impatient or careless and give himself away. He had hopes of the unobtrusive watch which had been set on Elizabeth's flat in town: nothing material to the case had been discovered there, but there was still a chance that the criminal, who seemed to have a penchant for planting false clues, might try something on at the flat.

Seated in front of their own fire that evening, the sound of London's traffic beating like a distant surf into the Bloomsbury square below them, Nigel and Georgia were both thinking of the events into which Miss Cavendish's invitation had plunged them. Easterham Manor and its occupants seemed remote already, and Nigel felt he might at last be able to get things into perspective.

'It's the loose ends that bother me,' he said after a long silence, absently watching the flames gesticulate in the hearth. 'The loose ends. The cross currents. How many plots *are* there in the story?'

'Ignore them,' replied Georgia crisply.

'It's all very well to say, "ignore them". They're like a scaffolding in this case, which looks as if it ought to contain a finished building, but take it away and there's nothing there at all.'

'Not nothing. The body of Elizabeth. Why not start again from that – start at the beginning?'

'Very well. But –'

'Why did Elizabeth die?'

'Sex. Money. Drugs. Take your choice.'

'All right. Sex. That means jealousy, a brainstorm by someone.'

'Dykes or Bogan. More likely, Dykes.'

'Or Andrew. You mustn't leave him out.'

'In some respects, Andrew qualifies better than any of them. His room is nearest to Elizabeth's, and I still think it odd that he shouldn't have heard Hereward knocking at her door, or the actual murderer turning up a little later – after all, he didn't go to bed himself till eleven. The morning the burnt papers were found in Bogan's grate, Andrew came down to breakfast a few minutes after him, so he could have planted them there. But what could have been his motive for killing Elizabeth? And where did his motive-*power* come from? – that's even more important – we know he was exceedingly fond of her.'

'Motive-*power*? Oh, that's not so difficult. Just think of his past. An intelligent, charming, versatile young man, with good traditions behind him and a bright future before him, falls right away. When did it happen? In America, after his sister was disgraced. He ran away and got work in a lumber camp, he told us. Ever since, he's been knocking round the world at a loose end. He admitted he behaved like a prig and a prude on that occasion. He must have been wrapped up in sexual idealism, to have treated his beloved sister so harshly. Well, then –'

'I see what you mean. That tragedy perverted his idealism, left him with a hatred for sex? The idealism, having nothing positive to build on, has turned bad. He found out his sister was having a liaison with Bogan, killed her, and tried to pin the crime on her lover. It's possible. But she's had so many lovers. Surely Andrew hasn't disposed of them all. Why pick on Bogan?'

'Because, I suggest, he recognized Bogan as Engelman, the original cause of her downfall. For him, Bogan would represent not only that, but also the agency which killed his youthful idealism, his faith in humanity, and made him throw up a potential career of success.'

'I must say, that sounds very plausible.'

'Here's another point. If we assume it was a sex crime, and line up Andrew, Bogan, and Will Dykes as suspects, Andrew is the only one who really fits such a crime. If Bogan *was* her lover, he'd have no reason to kill her; if he wasn't, he surely wouldn't dare to do it, because even to be touched with a breath of the ensuing scandal would damage his professional reputation. He knows which side his bread is buttered on, all right: he'd never lose his head through jealousy of a successful lover.'

'Yes. I agree to that. What about Dykes?'

'Dykes is a realist. His upbringing made him one. Now a man like him might do murder in the heat of the moment. But this was a premeditated crime. Sane, realistic people don't commit *premeditated* sex crimes. His reactions after the event prove he's that sort of person. He was terribly distressed. But it was not the end of the world for him – he admitted that to you himself. He's a well-balanced type psychologically, don't you see? He has his creative work to compensate for anything the world can do to him. He's not all for love. If he'd found Betty playing about with another man, he'd have taken a stick to her, not staged a melodramatic, Othello sort of murder.'

'You're very good, Georgia. I find all this quite convincing. But what about the cord from his dressing-gown tassel?'

'During the five minutes it could have been done – let's see,' Nigel flipped through some scraps of paper he took from his pocket. 'Andrew and Eunice were playing picquet, Hereward, Charlotte, and Bogan have no alibis, Dykes was with me in the garden. It was Hereward who invited the constable to a snack downstairs, and took him away from the door of the room.'

'My money's on Bogan, then.'

'Why Bogan, rather than the Restoricks?'

'Because at that point the Restoricks had not yet come under suspicion, whereas Bogan had – the papers had been found in his grate. Where does he claim to have been during the five minutes in question?'

'In the lavatory. Just to the right of the stairhead on the first floor.'

'Did Hereward bring the constable downstairs that way?'

'Yes.'

'So Bogan could have heard them talking, and known the coast was clear for a little. Did Dykes leave his door unlocked?'

'He says so.'

'Right. Then it was possible for Bogan to have planted that clue. He was already rattled by the burnt paper episode, and he'd be looking out for an opportunity to distribute the suspicion a bit. Dykes would be his choice, because the thing looked like a sex crime and Dykes' secret engagement to Betty had already come out.'

'D'you think the potassium cyanide business was another attempt to throw suspicion, then?'

'I shouldn't be surprised.'

'Andrew staged it himself, you mean?'

'Why not? It fits in with the theory that he hates Bogan inveterately and wants him incriminated.'

'That's true. And Andrew was unduly startled, and rather bad-tempered, when he returned to find that the milk-jug was poisoned as well as his own glass.'

Nigel rose and walked over to the mantelpiece, where he absent-mindedly patted the head of an Etruscan dog. He glanced at Georgia, curled up in an armchair, looking as wise as Baviaan.

'Things are sorting themselves out,' he said. 'You ought to be running this case, not me. It looks as if we could leave Bogan out of it, if it's a sex crime.'

'I think so. After all, Bogan's a doctor. Surely he'd have thought of some neater, more professional way of killing Betty than that rope trick. An overdose of cocaine would have been the obvious thing, under the circumstances. And given himself some sort of alibi for the poisoning of Andrew's milk.'

'Yes. He seems to spend all the crucial times in lavatories. Not very adroit. Well then, if it was a sex crime, Andrew is our man. And if Bogan is Engelman, it would answer the question why Andrew has been making such a dead set at him. Now, what about the money motive?'

'I give it a poor third. We can't tell till we know the exact state of the Restorick finances. By the way, did you find out about Andrew's will?'

'M'm. Left two thousand pounds a year by his parents, like Elizabeth. His will leaves this to Hereward in trust for John and Priscilla.'

'So, if the Restoricks killed Betty and tried to poison Andrew, they were doing it on the strength of Betty's capital and the interest on Andrew's. Well, let's suppose they were nearly broke, which I somehow doubt. Can you see them contemplating a couple of murders?'

'Charlotte, perhaps. She's an able woman, and one always wonders what's going on behind imposing façades like hers. I mean, when a façade is so elaborate, has grown so much part of the personality, its upkeep may become the most important thing in life for that person. If she lost the means of preserving it, to all intents and purposes she'd cease to exist. The very fear of poverty – comparative poverty – will often terrify the rich so much that the whole world turns unreal for them, if they've been accustomed to wealth all their life, that is to say. And when the future becomes unreal, it infects the present. And that nightmare sense of unreality can be the starting point of crime.'

'That's all very well,' said Georgia. 'But the few thousands a year she'd get out of the deaths of Elizabeth and Andrew wouldn't seem much better than poverty to a woman of that sort. And what about Hereward? All the facts go to suggest that there must have been collusion between them if either of them is concerned in the crimes at all. Now can you see Hereward in the part of second murderer? I can't.'

'Superficially, no. But we don't know enough about the relations between them to dogmatize. How far could ancestor-worship carry an inoffensive, conventional English country-gentleman? Easterham Manor has been in the family for centuries. He might weigh those two not very creditable Restoricks in the balance against it, and find them wanting.

Moreover, Clarissa told us the family is badly inbred. How do we know Hereward hasn't got the bug too, as well as Betty and Andrew? And d'you suppose he doesn't feel the way his wife overshadows him? I fancy Lady Macbeth had put in a good deal of quiet work before the play opens, telling her husband what a worm he was.'

'Grooming him for evil stardom?' Georgia laughed. 'No. It won't do. Charlotte isn't like that. You might as well say Eunice Ainsley did it.'

'Eunice? If Betty hadn't just disclosed to them all that she'd not yet made a will, Eunice would have to come in on the money motive. But she'd hardly kill Betty on the strength of a hope that Hereward would honour Betty's promise to her.'

'All right. That brings us to drugs. Did Betty die because of drugs?'

Nigel stretched his long legs, and regarded the frayed toes of his carpet slippers.

'If drugs were behind it, these were the alternatives: *either* Betty was murdered to prevent her revealing something dangerous to the murderer – probably that he trafficked in drugs, or to prevent her contaminating someone else with the drug-habit. You agree so far?'

Georgia cocked her head on one side, considering. 'Yes, I think so. And you can cut out the second alternative straight away.'

'Oh?'

'The only possible victims she could have in the house – victims who couldn't defend themselves, so to speak – were the children. Everyone tells us she was devoted to them, and we know she warned them against accepting cigarettes or candies. Obviously she was scared stiff of someone else doing it.'

'Unless her potential victim was someone not in the house party at all.'

'We can't start worrying about that now. It's up to Blount.'

'O.K. Then she was murdered because she knew something dangerous to the murderer. Who does that give us?'

'It gives us a drug-trafficker,' replied Georgia. 'Maybe the person, probably, who threatened to corrupt the children if Betty didn't keep her mouth shut. A person with some sort of hold over her, other than the drug-habit, or Betty would have exposed him before – as soon as she decided to try and get cured of the habit.'

'Yes. Another thing suggesting this person had some hold over her is that she warned the children in such general terms. Otherwise, why not tell them "Don't take any cigarettes from X"? Why not, in fact, blow the gaff to Hereward and have X turned out of the house? The next question is, why did X murder her when he did? What had just happened to make it urgently imperative?'

'It was the night you reconstructed the Scribbles episode. Apart from the maid and the murderer, Bogan was the last person to see her alive. He was in her room just before dinner.'

'Suggesting that something came out, either during my reconstruction or Bogan's visit to her room, which decided X to kill her? It's possible. But it doesn't give X much time to have worked out the crime and cut off a length of rope, does it? Remember, they were all under each other's eye from dinner-time till the party broke up for the evening.'

Georgia, lying back in her chair, pressed her fingers against her eyes. 'I'm trying to remember,' she said. 'No, I can't think of anything that happened at your séance which could have – unless it somehow gave away to X that you're a detective.'

'He waits till a detective is in the house before committing his murder?'

'Yes. That won't do. Forget it. Could she have been murdered because she took drugs, then, and X had just discovered it?'

'That would point to Hereward or Andrew? To save the

family name from dishonour? No, I don't think that's possible. Andrew doesn't worry about the family name. Hereward does, but the scandal of her death, even if it had been accepted as suicide, would seem to him just as bad as the scandal of drug-taking.'

'I agree. That brings us back to the first idea. X killed her to prevent her giving away their complicity over drugs. Is there any one of the house party who could have been her supplier?'

'Eunice or Bogan. Dykes very unlikely. Hereward or Charlotte more unlikely still. Andrew impossible – he was out of the country when she started the habit.'

'Take Eunice, then.'

'Blount is checking up on her. He should be able to find out whether she's a purveyor of the stuff. But I doubt if she'd have the resolution for a murder of this sort. And she'd not have enough to lose by exposure – she's no special reputation, for instance. Besides, why should Betty want to give her away to the police? If Eunice had been supplying her, and Betty was now being cured of the habit, she'd just say: "No thanks, I don't want any more of the stuff." If Eunice then threatened to corrupt the children, Betty could have her chucked out of the house. No, Eunice wouldn't risk being hung, just to stop Betty's mouth. It doesn't make sense.'

'So we come back to Bogan?'

'Now *he's* a much sounder proposition. He's got a tremendous reputation to preserve, and his large income depends on that reputation. It's easy to construct a hypothetical case against him. Betty goes to him to be cured of the cocaine habit. He falls in love with her. She rejects his advances. He then turns on the heat. Several levers he could use against her. Threaten to expose her addiction to Dykes or her family; threaten the children; and, of course, if he's devilish enough, he could have used the hypnosis treatment for the opposite of what it was intended for, or pretend he had done so – yes, that would explain his remark, "I've got you body and soul now, for ever." And it'd explain the look of disgust your cousin noticed on her face.'

'But why couldn't Betty just refuse to have anything more to do with him, when he'd come out in his true colours?'

'It mightn't be so easy. Maybe she had to fight against the influence of the hypnosis. And there's no doubt she was terrified by his threats against the children. It'd be no good just breaking off with him, if he's as bad as we're painting him, he'd bide his time and get the children later. So she'd need time to collect evidence damning enough to render him absolutely powerless. This is all very much on the line of Andrew's theory, by the way. Now supposing she'd got her evidence and confronted him with it, a man in his position couldn't afford to let her live, not an unstable character like Betty who might blow up on him at any moment.'

'Well then,' said Georgia. 'It looks like Bogan if drugs were behind the murder, and Andrew if it was a sex crime. The Restoricks come in a bad third on the money motif.'

'You don't sound very enthusiastic.'

'I'm not. I'm sure there's a hopeless flaw in all this, something we've missed. I can't see Andrew murdering his sister, in spite of all the plausible arguments we've trotted out in its favour. Can you?'

'It's difficult, certainly. What about Bogan, then?'

'I wonder. He's so correct, and impressive, and essentially colourless. We ought to know more about him. If he's really our X, then he qualifies for Andrew's description of a person who is absolutely evil. But —'

'Funny. Those are just my reactions, too,' Nigel interrupted. 'I mean, his odd colourlessness. Opacity. Like a jelly fish. He's obviously extremely able. He has personality, when he cares to switch it on. But what you remember about him is —'

'He's like a mansion with a caretaker in it. The caretaker shows you over. You see the family treasures, the portraits, the public rooms, and perhaps some of the private ones.

Everything is spotlessly kept, in perfect order. But your attention wanders. You become insatiably curious about the family who inhabit it. The mansion gives you no clues to them –'

'And then you hear the sound of wheels on the gravel drive, and you look out of a window and see seven devils rolling up in a barouche.'

Georgia laughed, a little uncertainly. Nigel went on:

'But all these similitudes don't tell us whether Bogan committed the crime. You were going to say –?'

'Three things. If Bogan did it, why did he do it like that? Why not a more professional touch? He's a doctor, isn't he?'

'Yes. That's been worrying me too.'

'Second, if he did it, how did the burnt papers come to be in his grate? You suggest Andrew planted them there, meaning us to think they were the written evidence against Bogan for which he killed Betty. O.K. But if Andrew planted them there, it implies he knew Bogan had done the murder. Why didn't he just simply denounce Bogan?'

'No. It doesn't imply he knew Bogan had done the murder. Not necessarily. It could mean simply that he hated Bogan, knew Bogan had things he might wish to conceal, and wanted him arrested for the murder.'

'All right. I give you that. My third point is this – if Bogan is the devil Andrew wants us to think he is, his diabolic career doesn't begin and end with Elizabeth. The link between him and Betty – the only one we're certain of – is cocaine. Look for other cocaine links, find some of the other people he's treated –'

Nigel, snapping his fingers, jumped to his feet, went to the telephone and looked up a number.

'I've just remembered,' he said. 'Eunice mentioned a girl who went to him for a cure and was worse than ever in a few months. Hallo. Can I speak to Miss Eunice Ainsley? This is Mr Nigel Strangeways. Good evening, I wonder could you tell me the name and address of . . .'

A short conversation followed. Nigel put down the receiver, turned, made a face at Georgia.

'Did you get it?' she asked.

'Yes. Oh yes, I got it.'

'Don't tell me *she's* been murdered too.'

'No. But Eunice says Blount asked her for the same information several days ago.'

CHAPTER SEVENTEEN

*'Be a physician, Faustus: heap up gold,
And be eternis'd for some wondrous cure.'*
MARLOWE

It was not till a week later that Nigel heard the result of Blount's investigations. During this period, he gave his mind a vacation from the case, he was convinced that the next step forward could not be taken till more evidence had been accumulated about Dr Bogan and Elizabeth, and he himself would only be wasting time on investigations for which Blount had far better facilities. A telephone conversation with the inspector assured him that the police were steadily raking over Elizabeth's associations and Bogan's practice.

Then, one morning when Georgia had just gone out to work on her refugees committee and Nigel was writing up his war diary, the telephone bell rang. It was Inspector Blount. He wanted Nigel to invite Andrew Restorick and Will Dykes to dinner that evening – he himself would turn up later.

'So I'm to be your stool pigeon,' said Nigel. 'Your decoy duck. Your stalking horse. Do I get expenses from the C.I.D.?'

'I just thought it'd be – e'eh – cosier at your flat,' said Blount and, laconic as ever, rang off.

Dykes and Andrew were both free that night, so Nigel was able to give Blount the all-clear. At 7.30 Andrew Restorick turned up. A few minutes later, an altercation in the street below announced the arrival of Will Dykes.

'These damned popinjays!' he exclaimed, after greeting the three of them. 'How they love the war!'

'Been getting into trouble with the police again?' asked Nigel.

'A special. I just shone my torch on the door to see if I'd got the right number, and some young busybody in uniform as good as told me I was Hitler in person. "Young man," I said to him, "I was an anti-Fascist," I said, "when you were cutting your wisdom teeth, if any, which I very much doubt."'

Georgia giggled. 'That didn't go down too well, I expect.'

'He said he was only doing his duty. I told him straight, "You can do your duty without losing your manners, my young cock," I said. But there it is, give a petty bourgeois a little power and the next thing he's throwing his weight about as if he was Goering. Yes, thank you, I don't mind a glass of sherry. It's bitter cold outside still.'

'You'll have another brush with the police soon,' said Nigel. 'Inspector Blount's coming round after dinner.'

'Oh, him. I don't mind him. Getting used to the chap. We've been seeing quite a lot of each other lately.'

'Have you? Did he tell you anything? How's he getting on?' asked Andrew.

'He doesn't give away information, he asks for it. Wanted a list of all the people I'd met in Betty's company — that sort of thing. Well, I admire a chap that's good at his job. Blount's all right. But I wish he'd make up his mind to arrest me or call it off. It's not nice having plain-clothes men hanging around your house. The neighbours talk, you see.'

Andrew's eyes twinkled. 'That's a highly petty-bourgeois reaction on your part, Will.'

The novelist's under-lip jutted out pugnaciously. His alert, intelligent eyes fastened upon Andrew. 'Time you learnt the facts of life, Restorick,' he said, 'and one of them is that you need a lot of money before you can afford not to be respectable.'

'That's one in the plexus for me.'

'Where I come from, the moral code's simple enough — crude, I daresay, you'd call it — but it's bound up integrally with the kind of life we have to live; it's not artificially imposed and just formally accepted, like yours.'

'If any, which I very much doubt,' murmured Andrew.

'There you are, you see? You can afford to be flippant at its expense. I don't blame you. In a way you're lucky. What I'm saying is, where I come from, you can keep the moral code or you can break it, but you can't afford to laugh at it. Either you're a wrong 'un or you're not. And respectability's a thing you fight to keep because you've had to fight to achieve it. But I'm afraid I'm talking too much,' he said, with a pleasant grin at Georgia. He got up and walked over to the bookcases. 'Some lovely books you've got here. Hallo, what's this? Henry James' prefaces. Can I borrow it?'

'Of course. You admire James?'

'Yes, I suppose I do. Like a Tyneside dockie might admire the Taj Mahal. He'd hardly believe anything so elaborate could be real. All those elaborate states of mind and superfine relationships James describes – well, to me, it's like conjuring drama out of thin air. Yes, I respect him for that. He makes so much out of such tenuous material. I like a chap who knows his job.'

At dinner, the talk was of books and the war. They kept off the subject of Elizabeth Restorick, but, as the meal was ending, Dykes' growing distraitness and a sort of controlled excitement which made Andrew's voice even quieter and his movements more leisurely, showed how important to them was Blount's coming visit.

The inspector, when he arrived, was at his most genial. He smacked his lips over Nigel's brandy, patted his bald head vigorously, warmed his ample bottom at the fire, and in general gave a lively representation of Father Christmas in mufti, which was, under the circumstances, a little sinister.

'Aha. Brandy. Noble liquor, noble liquor. H'mm'ff! What bouquet! Eh, well. I hope my men have not been giving you any trouble, Mr Dykes.'

'He's just been telling us they've ruined his reputation with his neighbours,' said Georgia.

'Och, that's too bad, too bad. Have to tell 'em to go away. Must look after all you good people, though.'

'D'you mean you expect the murderer will have a shot at one of us?' asked Andrew.

Will Dykes laughed harshly. 'When he says "look after", he means "keep an eye on!"'

'Oh, well now. Not always. An innocent man doesn't mind a little inconvenience of that sort. *Integer vitae, scelerisque purus*, as the old tag has it.'

Nigel ostentatiously removed the brandy bottle from Blount's reach. 'When you start quoting the classics, it's generally time to break up the party. I suppose you didn't come here just to soak my brandy?'

'No, indeed. Scandalous suggestion. I thought you'd be interested maybe to hear what we've been doing. Quite a lot of information came in this last week. By Mr Dykes' good offices, and Miss Ainsley's, I've been able to get in touch with most of Miss Restorick's friends. We've also made inquiries into Dr Bogan's affairs.' Blount took off his pince-nez, polished them, gazed keenly round the company, and resumed. 'I've asked for Mr Restorick and Mr Dykes to be here tonight, because they were both closely involved with the – e'eh – with Miss Restorick. I may need their co-operation later. You all realize, of course, that what I'm going to tell you is for your ears alone. And you mustn't assume that it's necessarily relevant to the murder.'

They all nodded seriously. Will Dykes was fidgeting with a cigarette-rolling gadget. Andrew sat in the quivering, intent trance of a terrier watching a rat-hole. Puffing noisily at one of Nigel's cigars, Blount took up his tale. He first mentioned that Hereward's own account of the Restorick finances had, after tactful inquiry elsewhere, been proved correct. A considerable percentage of Charlotte's capital had been sunk in Polish holdings, so the invasion of that country had struck them very hard. Hereward's own income, apart from the increased drain of income-tax upon it, had suffered little; but the estate, owing to his generosity rather than any inefficiency as a landlord, had been run at a loss for some time.

'Your brother and sister-in-law had no objection, I should add, to my making these affairs public, Mr Restorick.'

Possibly not, thought Nigel, but why come out with the information now, in front of us all?

'You didn't seriously think Hereward and Charlotte could have killed Betty? For her bit of income?' asked Andrew.

'We have to explore every avenue. And there's your money, too.'

'*My* money?'

'Well, someone tried to poison you, you'll not be denying that, Mr Restorick?'

The blandness of Blount's tone brought Nigel to attention. So that's why –

'It can't be denied they had a strong motive for getting rid of you and your sister. We also know that Hereward went to your sister's room the night she was murdered. And further, they had an opportunity for poisoning the milk, and the poison used belonged to your brother.'

Andrew's thin, bronzed face took on a horrified expression.

'My dear Inspector,' he began, 'surely you don't really suppose my brother – '

'You're a light sleeper, Mr Restorick.'

'I don't see – '

'Most people are who've knocked about the world and lived in dangerous places. I verified that, of course. I've also verified your own statement that you were out of England at the time when your sister began to develop the cocaine habit. What I'm getting at is this – how did it happen that a light sleeper like yourself wasn't awakened by the sound of Mr Restorick knocking at his sister's door and calling her name? Even suppose you *had* gone to sleep at all – it was only half an hour after you went to bed.'

'You're suggesting that I've been trying to shield Hereward?'

'Possibly. At any rate, I'd be glad of any information you could give me that would clear Mr and Mrs Restorick of the suspicion of having killed your sister – and attempted to kill you.' Blount paused. 'If they could be cleared of the attempt upon you, even, it would diminish the possibility that they murdered your sister.'

The firelight, gleaming on Blount's bald pate, furrowed Andrew's face with shadows. He looked both worried and perplexed.

'I wish I could give you some information about it,' he said at last. 'But I didn't hear Hereward that night, and I can't tell you any more about who put the poison in my milk. I presume Charlotte or Hereward aren't the only people who could have done it.'

'No. Dr Bogan could have. But why should Dr Bogan want to get rid of *you*?'

'I don't know,' said Andrew slowly. 'Unless he thinks I'm in possession of evidence which would incriminate him over Betty's death.'

'And why should he think that,' Blount's voice flashed out smoothly as a cat's paw, 'when you claim to have been asleep at the time of the murder?'

Andrew laughed, the light, excited laugh of a fencer admitting a touch. 'Search me. Maybe it's just his guilty conscience. Maybe I have evidence without being aware of it. I've given you my reasoned grounds for thinking Bogan did it; if I had proof, I'd certainly not keep it back.'

'Oh well, we shall have to leave it at that, then. And now I'm going to tell you a few things about this – e'eh – *bête noir* of yours. About Dr Bogan.'

Nigel stared at his toes, puzzled. It was both unusual and unprofessional of Blount to be so confidential among suspects, but the inspector, like a canny Scot, seldom gave things away without the prospect of a good return. When he cast his bread on the waters, it was always well baited. He was attempting now, Nigel surmised, to push Andrew Restorick into further disclosures.

Dr Denis Bogan (said Blount) had come to England ten

years before, with good medical degrees from the Johns Hopkins University. The American police had nothing against him, and certainly no proof of any connexion between him and the mysterious Engelman who peddled marijuana. They were now investigating Bogan's own statement of his activities during the period Engelman had met Elizabeth Restorick. The only suspicious fact unearthed up to date was that, though as a student in America he had been a comparatively poor man, when he arrived in England there were indications that he possessed ample means. His own explanation of this, freely given to Blount, sounded plausible enough. Soon after he had begun to practise in the States, he had been left a legacy by a woman patient and had plunged successfully with it on Wall Street. After his acquisition of wealth, he had travelled about America for some while – this was the period when Engelman had been at work – and then come to England. The American police were working on all this part of his story, but Blount was not sanguine as to their chances of following a scent that had grown so cold.

After coming to England, Bogan studied for a while at Edinburgh, was naturalized, and presently placed upon the Medical Register. His reputation in medical circles was still very fair, though the unorthodox methods he adopted did not endear him to his more conservative colleagues. His professional success, however, particularly with rich female patients, was resounding. He had the luck, or the opportunism, to start a new fashion amongst a clientele to whom new fashions were life itself. In the early 1930's the craze for psycho-analysis was beginning to ebb, and rich neurotics were ready to jump at a new craze. Not that, apart from his fairly regular use of hypnosis, there was anything very revolutionary in his methods: it was the man, more than the work, they fell for. A less impressive personality could have specialized in the nervous diseases of women and used similar treatment till all was blue. As one of Bogan's wealthy hypochondriacs told Blount, it was like being treated by St Luke and Rasputin rolled into one. They certainly got their money's worth of sensation – and quite often of cure as well.

So much (said Blount) for Dr Bogan's background. Nor was there anything necessarily suspicious in the fact that many of his patients were drug addicts. But drugs loomed so large in the Restorick case that Blount had decided to follow up a statement made by Eunice Ainsley. He accordingly got in touch with the girl whom Nigel had later inquired about. Blending persuasion with official firmness, Blount, after a great deal of reluctance on her part, got at the facts about 'Miss A', as he called her.

'Miss A' was the daughter of a rich industrialist, in the social swim, a cocaine addict – her parents were unaware of her addiction. As the habit grew upon her, she feared its effects would become manifest to her parents. The consequences would be disastrous, for her father was a strait-laced, unforgiving sort of man. She had therefore, like several of her acquaintances, put herself in Dr Bogan's hands for a cure. The cure was apparently successful, but, a few months after the treatment ended, the girl relapsed. And that was not the worst of it. She began to receive letters threatening to inform her parents of her cocaine habit unless she paid a large sum of money through certain channels. She obeyed. But the demands of the blackmailer became so exorbitant that she could no longer meet them. In an agony of fear and desperation, she wrote a letter imploring the blackmailer to give her an interview. A rendezvous was fixed, at night, outside one of the gates of Regent's Park. The blackmailer, to Miss A's surprise, turned out to be a woman. She was heavily muffled-up, smartly dressed, and entirely merciless. Miss A's entreaties had not the least effect upon her.

Miss A, faced with a hopeless situation, did what she should have done all along. She confessed to her parents. There was a terrible scene with her father, but in the end he relented and she was sent to another doctor, who succeeded in effecting an absolute cure.

Before this, however, something had occurred which seemed of peculiar significance to Blount. Immediately after her interview with the blackmailer, Miss A had decided on an impulse to go to Dr Bogan and ask for his help. She walked to his private house. When about fifty yards away from it, she saw by the light of a street lamp a woman emerge and hurry away from her down the street. It was the woman whom, an hour before, she had met outside Regent's Park.

Of course, she could have no logical proof of this. But, as far as she was concerned, there was no mistake about the recognition. She had been so shocked by the sight of that horrible creature that she abandoned her project and took a taxi home – so shocked, too, that at first she did not ask herself what the woman had been doing there. The thought then passed through her mind that Dr Bogan must be another of the blackmailer's victims, and she reasoned that he therefore could be of no help to her. But later she remembered that, during their interview, the mysterious woman had mentioned something connected with the relationship between Miss A and her father which she could not possibly have known, *unless she had heard it from Dr Bogan*, for, during the course of his treatment, the doctor had required her to give him the fullest, most intimate details of this relationship.

'So, you see,' Blount concluded, 'if Miss A's evidence is to be trusted – and I believe it is over this – we have established a connexion between Bogan and a blackmailer. As it stands, it wouldn't hold water for a moment in a court of law, and I doubt if Miss A would be able to recognize the woman again, after so long an interval, even if we could find her and bring them face to face. The point is, what Bogan did in one case he may have done in many others. If he was behind the blackmailing of Miss A, there may have been blackmail of some kind in the case of Elizabeth Restorick.'

Andrew's breath came hissing through his teeth. 'God, what a foul racket!'

'Clever, if it's true,' said Will Dykes. 'A man of that sort'd be able to worm out any woman's secrets. But Bogan could do it under a cloak of perfect professional respectability. D'you suppose he deliberately engineered it so that Miss A's cure shouldn't be complete?'

'That's impossible to say. There's no question that he has effected many bona-fide cures. We're in a position, now, to investigate his private nursing-home and his practice very thoroughly. We'll know soon enough. He's been in an extraordinarily strong position, just because many people who come for that kind of cure want it hushed up.'

'When I think of poor Betty in that swine's hands, I could break his neck,' cried Andrew.

Nigel reflected, not for the first time, on the way genuine emotions call up the most theatrical clichés.

'Betty could look after herself, I reckon,' said Will Dykes.

'And who knows he didn't start some of them on their drug-habits?' Andrew went on. 'Neurasthenic patients. He admitted he gave Betty sedative drugs. He could create morphia addicts that way, then have them blackmailed for it – and I'd not put it past him to supply the drugs, too, through some go-between. A goldmine out of a cesspool.'

'We're looking into all that.'

'Looking into it!' exclaimed Andrew. 'You've got to stop it now, before he does any more damage. Haven't you arrested him yet?'

'The drug side of the case is being taken over by our experts in that branch. It's the murder I'm investigating, Mr Restorick.'

'Of course. But good heavens, surely – '

'No.' Blount's mild yet almost inhumanly penetrating gaze was fastened upon Andrew. 'No, I see no special reason yet to think Bogan is a murderer.'

CHAPTER EIGHTEEN

'The wicked flee when no man pursueth.'
PROVERBS

LYING in bed next morning, Nigel had to admit that Blount's reasoning was sound. Bogan might be seven kinds of devil, but that did not prove him a murderer. He reviewed Blount's logic. First, if Bogan wanted to get rid of Elizabeth, why do it in such a manner and amongst her own family, where the risk would be so great? How much easier to give the impression that she had committed suicide if he had killed her in his own nursing-home or in her London flat – an overdose of cocaine. Second, why should he want to kill her? Certainly not, had he been successfully blackmailing her. But, as Blount told them, there was no evidence of this. Inquiries at her bank had not shown any large withdrawals from her account which could not be explained otherwise. The only possibility was that she had been collecting evidence against him. Blount's recent investigations had proved there was plenty of evidence to be collected. On the other hand, after exhaustive inquiries among her friends and Bogan's patients, he had not discovered a single fact to suggest that Betty had been trying to collect this evidence. She had not even mentioned Bogan to one of them, except as a friend and her doctor.

So there we are, thought Nigel, back at the beginning again. As far as means and opportunity went, anyone at Easterham Manor might have killed Betty, and they all had motives of a sort, but no one had a motive which could be called really adequate, and premeditated murders are not committed on flimsy motivation. For an hour, while his coffee grew cold and the bitter wind tormented the branches of the trees in the square, he racked his brains and ransacked his memory for some new light on the tragedy. He then reached for the telephone.

Four hours later, he was sitting at a secluded table in the Poisson d'Or. Dr Bogan faced him, diligently plying a toothpick. They had talked on neutral subjects during lunch, and Nigel had been reminded more than once of Georgia's description of Bogan – a mansion you're being shown over by a caretaker. What thoughts, what secrets or iniquities lay behind that strangely opaque personality, in rooms which the master of the house had told the caretaker to keep locked? There was something else Georgia had said, at Easterham. Remembering it, Nigel asked abruptly:

'Why has Andrew Restorick got his knife into you?'

The doctor set down his toothpick amid the remains of his chocolate cake.

'A fixation on his sister, perhaps, as I originally suggested. Perhaps some other, equally irrational antipathy.'

'Yes, I can see that. But such antipathies don't usually push people into incriminating the object of them for murder.'

'Oh dear, has he been trying to do that?'

'You should know.'

Dr Bogan's long fingers combed his beard. He gazed contemplatively at Nigel, as though debating what kind of treatment this patient would best respond to.

'That stupid trick of the burnt paper, you mean?'

'Not only that.' Nigel was determined that Bogan should make his own running.

'You figure it was he who put the potassium cyanide in the milk?'

'That's what you think, isn't it?'

'There's no evidence for it, surely?'

'The question of evidence is irrelevant. If you hadn't believed he'd poisoned his own glass of milk, in order to incriminate you, you'd not have poured some of it into the milk jug.'

'Why now, Strangeways, you know as well as I do that's a gross *petitio principii*,' replied Bogan with a sudden, almost falsetto chuckle. He seemed perfectly in command of the situation. The wicked, reflected Nigel, flourish as the bay-tree.

'I'm not going to chop logic with you, doctor,' he said. 'A girl, one of your patients, has been murdered. Attempts have been made to incriminate you. These attempts have at least been successful enough to compel the police into a most stringent inquiry about your private affairs. As a result of them, you may for all I know be ruined professionally and suffer a long term of imprisonment. I'm not interested in that, however. The question is, whether you wish to be hung. You're going the right way about it, certainly, if you do.'

Dr Bogan's liquid brown eyes became unfocused. It was the only reaction he gave to Nigel's blitzkreig.

'For a celebrated investigator, you're extraordinarily ingenuous,' he said. 'However, I'll humour you. My professional reputation will look after itself. But I certainly don't want to be hung. I take it what you're after is this – if the incidents of the poison and the burnt paper were attempts to incriminate me, they must have been made by the murderer: if they weren't, I must be the murderer?'

'That seems to be a basis for discussion, at any rate,' replied Nigel, his pale blue eyes non-committally scrutinizing the doctor.

'Well, if it's any help to you, and since there are no witnesses present, I don't mind telling you that it was I who poured the poisoned milk from the glass into the jug.'

'So I imagined,' said Nigel briskly. 'Why?'

'Your active imagination should give you the answer.'

'Because you lost your head for a moment. You suspected the poison might be another attempt to incriminate you, and you felt it would create more confusion if it seemed that the poisoning had not been directed against Andrew Restorick alone. You also had a pretty good notion that it was Andrew who had poisoned the milk.'

Dr Bogan gave Nigel a quizzical glance. 'I congratulate you.

That was really most plausible. But I don't lose my head. What actually happened was that I acted purely on impulse – it was a piece of mischief – I just wanted to see how everyone would behave. That is the truth, but, naturally, I don't expect you to believe it.'

'Since we seem to be playing the truth game,' Nigel said, to the intense astonishment of a waiter who was passing, 'did you kill Elizabeth Restorick?'

'Since there are no witnesses present – all right, waiter, you needn't listen – or rather, in spite of that fact, I can assure you that I didn't.'

'Did Andrew, then?'

Dr Bogan's shrug reminded one of his Latin blood. 'Who knows? A puritan. Repressed. An embittered man, for all his surface charm and insouciance. It is not impossible. But why ask me?'

'We agreed that, if you aren't the murderer, the man who tried to incriminate you *is*. We agree that Andrew is very likely this planter of incriminating evidence.'

'Oh no, that won't do. Not so fast, my dear young man. If Andrew is the would-be incriminator, as I dare say he may be, that doesn't make him the murderer. Logically, it means nothing more than that he is using the murder situation to get me into trouble. He hates me. Admitted. He would like me to be the murderer. And from that it's a short step for one of his temperament to believing he's justified in *making* me the murderer.'

'You and Andrew are at great pains to be fair to each other,' remarked Nigel sardonically, 'in spite of your deadly enmity.'

Dr Bogan took a lump of sugar on his spoon, soaked it in his coffee and crunched it vigorously. His white teeth were excellently preserved.

'But the vendetta seems rather one-sided,' Nigel went on. 'I mean, you let him get away with some pretty outrageous insinuations against you at the Manor.'

'I am well accustomed to the irresponsible behaviour of

neurotics,' replied the doctor, with a return to his professional dignity.

'No doubt,' said Nigel. 'But you normally take precautions against it, I presume?'

'I don't quite follow you.'

'Whether Andrew is or isn't the murderer, he's exceedingly dangerous to you. I shouldn't underestimate him. He's still hard at work trying to pin this crime on you – this crime or some other crimes. I'm certain of that.'

'You chill my blood, sir.'

'And I fancy he may still be keeping back certain knowledge of his till he has a complete case. He's hinted that to us often enough, anyway.'

'Thank you for your solicitude, Strangeways. But I'm sure the police will give me adequate protection.'

Dr Bogan, gracefully thanking Nigel for the lunch, rose to go. No, one gets no change out of him, thought Nigel, watching the bearded, stooping figure, reflected in many mirrors, make its way out of the restaurant. What had impressed him most was not Bogan's handling of the murder discussion, but the absolute calmness with which he had received Nigel's hint that the police were investigating his professional affairs. Only an innocent man, or a past master of villainy, could have refrained from asking more details of this. Here was a man who, unless Blount's deductions were hopelessly at fault, used his professional position as a cloak and an instrument for the most abominable iniquities. Yet, when told the police were investigating it, he never turned a hair. Nigel half-raised his hand in a sardonic salute to Bogan's receding figure.

A few minutes later he was in a public call-box. Having dialled a number, he stared out absently into the street, thinking how little the war had changed London – yet.

'Hallo. I want to speak to Inspector Blount ... Yes, the Restorick case. This is Mr Strangeways ... Oh, hallo, Blount. Strangeways here. I've just been lunching with Dr Bogan. He says he did not commit murder ... Yes, you've heard that one before, and no doubt you'll hear it again. Look, I've got an idea ... '

Involuntarily, Nigel lowered his voice. When he had finished, protesting squeaks came from the other end.

'No, no,' said Blount. 'No, no, no. I couldn't possibly do that. It's asking for trouble. They'd take the hide off me.'

'It's the only way I can see. You've got to force his hand, however it is. Nothing else – '

'No,' Blount reiterated. 'It's too irregular. Nothing doing.'

'Well, d'you mind if I work it myself?'

'You'll have to take full responsibility. I know nothing about it, you understand?'

'O.K. I'll report developments, if any. You've got tabs on all the parties involved? ... Right. Take them off where he lives. I'll be responsible for him.'

'You'd better,' Blount replied grimly. 'So long.'

Nigel hurried home to make plans and do some more telephoning.

Events were to tread fast upon the heels of his action: his plan produced only too quickly results which he had hardly expected and could not control. The next morning Andrew Restorick, arriving at the Strangeways' flat in answer to an urgent summons, found Nigel and Georgia in a state of utter consternation.

'Blount's arrested Will Dykes,' said Nigel flatly.

Andrew's face went still. 'Dykes? But that's – what on earth was he playing at here the other night, then? I assumed Dykes must be out of suspicion.'

'I don't know. Blount's infernally cagey. You never know what's going on in his head.'

'Surely *you* don't think – '

'I can't believe Dykes is the murderer. I simply can't. But the police never arrest till they're sure of their ground. Blount must have got hold of some evidence we don't know about.'

Andrew fingered uncertainly a book lying on the table beside him.

'Look here. He's not well off. I'd like to pay any expenses – solicitors, you know. Shall I get mine to visit him and – ?'

'He's called in his own already, to prepare his defence. But I'm sure he'd be grateful for your financial help. I'll let him know.'

Nigel had at all costs to prevent Andrew from attempting to visit Will Dykes, for the novelist, so far from languishing in jail, was at this moment scribbling happily away at his new novel in another room of the Strangeways' flat.

'Well, if there's anything else I can do,' said Andrew. 'Are you prepared to take up the case on Dykes' behalf?'

'Certainly.'

Andrew pondered for a moment. 'I've an idea. If you could come down to Easterham this week-end, I'll get Charlotte to invite Eunice and Dr Bogan. I'm certain there must be some vital clue the police have missed. If we could all get together, I've a notion – only of course Dykes won't be there. Still –'

He petered out rather indefinitely – a contrast with his usual decisive manner, but Nigel took up the suggestion at once. It would be satisfactory to have them all away from London, where there would be no danger of their discovering the truth about Will Dykes. Moreover, he had been convinced for some time that Andrew knew more about the case than he cared to admit, and his project of gathering the suspects at the Manor looked as if he intended an *éclaircissement*.

The same evening, Andrew rang him up to say that the party was arranged. Nigel himself would be staying at the Manor this time, too. Georgia excused herself on the grounds of business: actually, she had to stay behind to look after Will Dykes. Blount also intended that he should be well looked after: plain-clothes men were detailed to watch the flat. Blount, in addition, had notified Superintendent Phillips of the house-party at Easterham, so that arrangements could be made by the local police to keep it under observation. It was all he could do till the C.I.D.'s own investigations had got to the bottom of Bogan's activities, and till further evidence about the murder came to light.

On the Friday night they were all assembled at the Manor. Andrew had gone down the day before. Dr Bogan, who had been detained in town, arrived late, after dinner. The general drowsiness of the party precluded any discussion of the case that night. If Andrew intended to spring a mine, he would have to wait till the next morning.

And, next morning, the mine was duly sprung – its explosion far more devastating than Nigel had expected. He was awoken by a knocking at the door, which competed – not altogether successfully – with the atrocious hammering in his own head. It was the father and mother of all headaches.

'Come in,' he said painfully.

It was the maid bringing his tea. He looked at his watch, whose hands and numerals seemed to be floating all over the watch face. Nine o'clock, he pinned them down to, after laborious concentration. Well, it was the Restoricks' custom to let their guests sleep late. But not, surely, to give them stiff doses of sleeping-draught. Sleeping-draught! The idea penetrated his fuddled senses. He leapt out of bed – a sudden movement that nearly tore off the top of his head. The maid had drawn back the curtains. He noticed vaguely, as he dressed, that there had been a fresh fall of snow during the night.

The faces he met at the breakfast table looked as blurred as his own. But two of them were missing.

'Where's Andrew? And Dr Bogan?' he asked.

'They're not down yet,' replied Charlotte, passing her hand over her forehead.

'Have we all got headaches?' asked Nigel sharply.

Hereward, Charlotte, and Eunice Ainsley nodded.

'Must have had something that disagreed with us. Dinner. Better talk to the cook, my dear.'

'But Bogan didn't have dinner here. Restorick, you've got your pass-key? I think we'd better just go and –'

'Oh, God! Not again. Not again, please,' Mrs Restorick was on her feet, swaying at the end of the table. Her voice sounded far away and childish.

'Now, now, my dear,' said Hereward. 'Nothing to be alarmed about. Take it easy. Two people late for breakfast, why –'

'Betty was late for breakfast that morning,' Charlotte's eyes followed them out of the room. She did not seem to notice Eunice Ainsley, who was ineffectually stroking her hands and murmuring reassurance.

Upstairs, looking over Hereward's shoulder, Nigel saw that Bogan's bedroom was quite empty. It was not merely that Bogan wasn't there: even his clothes, his belongings, his suitcase seemed to have disappeared. A clean sweep.

'I suppose this *is* the right room.'

'Of course it is,' replied Hereward irritably. 'I simply can't understand –'

'Let's try Andrew's,' said Nigel, setting his teeth. Better know the worst. He had failed hideously, unforgivably. Hereward inserted his key in the next door. Andrew's room was not empty: clothes, books, shoes, bedding were all over the place. Everything, as far as one could tell, was still there. Everything except Andrew himself. Ridiculously, Hereward began to peer under the bed, in the wardrobe; he even lifted a pillow off the floor, as though Andrew's body might be concealed beneath it.

'No. It's no good. They're gone,' said Nigel.

'Nonsense. It's – it's downright absurd. We – you must be dreaming.'

'I wish I was.'

They searched the bathrooms, the lavatories, every room in the house. But Bogan and Andrew – that strange pair of duellists – were utterly vanished.

CHAPTER NINETEEN

'All in all he's a problem must puzzle the devil.'
BURNS

THE shock of the discovery cleared Nigel's brain like magic. His head still ached, but the other effects of the sleeping-draught had gone like mist blown off a mountainside. It was not time yet, though, to consider this new development in the light of what had already happened at the Manor. He must act. And the first thing to do was to find out why Robins, the local constable, who was supposed to be keeping an eye on the house, had given no alarm.

It did not take long. Nigel rang up Superintendent Phillips and told him what had occurred. Phillips assured him that Robins should have been on duty at the Manor last night. He would get in touch with Blount immediately, and then drive over to Easterham. Nigel next sent for the butler, who informed him that Robins had been entertained in the servants' hall on the previous evening. When they all went to bed, the butler had left him there, understanding that he would be staying downstairs all night, with an occasional turn round the garden, till the superintendent sent him a relief the next morning.

Nigel at once instituted a search of the outbuildings and servants' quarters. He and Hereward soon ran the missing constable to earth. They found him tucked away out of sight in the boiler-room. He was gagged, and efficiently tied up with a length of what looked like the same cord as had been used to hang Elizabeth Restorick. He was also, to all appearances, dead. But, when they touched his face to remove the gag, it felt warm and breathing. Constable Robins was fast asleep. The fumes of the coke had kept him quiet all night, so that he had not stirred and betrayed his presence even when the odd-job man had come in to replenish the boilers earlier that morning.

Nigel shook the man hard. He came awake, yawned, looked comically incredulous as he began to take in his surroundings, then winced at the pain of his wrists and ankles from which the bonds had just been removed. Hereward hurried out to fetch some coffee. Nigel told Robins what had happened. The constable was still very dazed, and his hand went out tenderly to the side of his head.

'Knocked me out,' he said stupidly. 'I'll get into trouble for this.'

'Take it easy a minute. Not your fault,' said Nigel, examining the bruise on the man's head. No bones broken. He had been black-jacked with the same neat efficiency as he had been tied up and disposed of. His assailant, indeed, seemed to have shown a certain solicitude in putting him in the boiler-room, where he would not suffer from the effects of the bitter night. For Robins made it clear, when the coffee restored him to full consciousness, that it was not here he had been attacked.

At five minutes past one he had come indoors from a brief tour of the house. He was sitting down by the fire in the servants' hall, when a noise excited his attention. It seemed to come from the direction of the main hall, and he went to investigate. He had taken off his helmet. It was as he passed through the swing door from the kitchen passage into the main hall that it happened. Someone must have been hiding behind this door – someone, Nigel fancied, who had deliberately made the noise to lure the constable into a vulnerable position. At any rate, just as Robins was pressing the button of his electric torch, a movement beside and a little behind him made him throw up an arm in self-defence. It was too late. He was struck down, and could remember nothing more till he had woken up in the boiler-room with Nigel and Hereward bending over him.

'You didn't catch sight of the chap at all, then?'

'No, sir. Wait a minute, though. That Dr Bogan's made off, you say? It was him must have hit me, sir. I remember now. When I put out my arm to defend myself, my hand brushed against his beard. Ar, that's right. Funny the way you forget things.'

Leaving the constable in Hereward's care, Nigel ran out of doors. As he had expected, the recent heavy fall of snow had made the recognition of footprints impossible, but it had not quite obliterated the track of a car curving away down the drive. Hurrying round to the back of the house, he found Hereward's chauffeur. Together, they entered the garage. Andrew Restorick's car was missing.

'I can't think – didn't you hear it go out last night?'

'No, sir. I'm sleeping in the house just now, while the master's having the rooms above the garage done up.'

'What's the registration number of the car?'

The chauffeur gave him its number and description, which Nigel telephoned through to Phillips' station-sergeant. The superintendent himself was already on his way to Easterham. Nigel then returned to the garage. He wished to satisfy himself on one point. It was Bogan who had attacked the constable. Bogan and Andrew had disappeared. Either they had run away together then, or Bogan had killed Andrew and dumped his body somewhere. If the latter was true, why hadn't Bogan gone off in his own car? Looking at its petrol gauge now, Nigel saw that there were only a couple of gallons left in the tank.

Robins' relief had not arrived. Nigel suggested he should go off again on his bike to try and follow up the tracks of Restorick's car. If Bogan had killed Andrew and taken the body off in the car, he might well have dumped it not very far away. But the man preferred to wait for orders from Superintendent Phillips.

A quarter of an hour later, the superintendent himself turned up. Neither the intense cold nor the disappearance of two suspects seemed to affect his geniality. Blowing out a frosty breath and beaming at Nigel, he said:

'Here we are again, sir. Funny business this, isn't it?

Inspector Blount sounded a bit old-fashioned when I rang him up.'

'I'm quite sure he did.'

'He's on his way down here. Now, sir, if you'll tell me just what's happened, we'll see what we can do. You don't look quite up to the mark yourself, sir.'

'Nor would you, if you'd had an outsize dose of sleeping-draught.'

'T'ch, t'ch!' clucked the superintendent sympathetically.

Nigel informed him of the most recent developments, whereupon Phillips gave some orders to the men he had brought with him and applied himself for a little to the telephone. He then came into the writing-room, where Nigel was trying to assemble his ideas, rubbed his hands before the fire, and remarked cosily:

'Well now, Mr Strangeways, time for a nice little chat. Suppose you tell me all about it. Maybe we can work it out between us and give the inspector a surprise when he comes.'

'It'll have to be a hell of a nice surprise, or he'll cart me for six. You see, this bright idea of getting the suspects together again was mine. I thought, by giving it out that Mr Dykes had been arrested for the murder, we'd force Andrew Restorick's hand. I was convinced all along that for some reason of his own he's been keeping things back. Well, damn it, I didn't expect they'd stage a vanishing trick the very first night –'

'"They"? You think they were in it together, sir?'

'No. I was speaking loosely. I can't somehow see – anyway, this is what happened. Andrew turned up the day before yesterday, Miss Ainsley and myself yesterday afternoon, Dr Bogan after dinner. Dinner was at 7-30. If the sleeping-draught had been given us then, we'd have felt sleepy much sooner than we did – granted the big dose that must have been used. When Bogan turned up, Mrs Restorick offered him a hot drink. We all decided to have one – Ovaltine. Now, while the stuff was being made, we were a bit dispersed. Hereward took Bogan up to his room, Andrew went out to put Bogan's car into the garage, Mrs Restorick was in the kitchen – she made the Ovaltine herself, Miss Ainsley and I stayed in the drawing-room. In a couple of minutes Hereward returned to the drawing-room, and Andrew shortly after him; then Bogan; then Mrs Restorick and the butler with the tray.'

'You mean, anyone could have doped the stuff?'

'No. That's the trouble. Mrs Restorick swears that there was no one but herself and the butler in the kitchen – the maids had all gone to bed – and that she had the stuff under her eye all the time. Now, if she doped it herself, that's the last thing she'd say, you'd think. If she didn't, it must have been done after the tray was brought into the drawing-room. But it was all ready made in the cups and – Christmas! what a fool I am – I'd forgotten the sugar. Soft sugar. You could sprinkle sleeping-powders over it thick. But we were all moving about and talking, and I've no idea who had a chance to do it.'

'Did they all take sugar in their drink?'

'I didn't *notice* anyone refuse it. Andrew was handing it round.'

'So *that* looks like a dead end, unless we get some more evidence.'

'I don't think we will. After Andrew's glass of milk, if anyone saw a lady or gentleman shovelling white powders into our sugar, he'd have piped up at once. But the point is this – it could hardly have been done on the spur of the moment. Whoever wanted to ensure that none of us would wake up last night wouldn't just carry sleeping-powders about in the hope that a suitable opportunity would arise for administering them, would he?'

'Not unless he was m.d.,' said the superintendent.

'Which disposes of the possibility that Bogan did it. On the other hand, it was Bogan who conked Constable Robins, and Bogan has indubitably disappeared. So what? So we look for an accomplice for Bogan – someone who was already in the house and had had plenty of time for making preparations to put us to sleep.'

'Andrew Restorick, then, obviously, since he's done a bunk too.'

'It looks like it. That would explain why he and Bogan have been at such pains all along to give the impression that they were deadly enemies. Andrew rather overdid it, as a matter of fact. But they certainly contrived to prevent anyone suspecting for a moment that they might be accomplices.'

Superintendent Phillips scratched his head. 'Yes, sir. Maybe. But what were they accomplices *in*? Murdering Miss Restorick? Why should they do that?'

'Blount has discovered that Bogan was probably running a cocaine-racket under cover. But we don't yet know where he got his supplies from or who was his distributor. Suppose Andrew was in it too? And Elizabeth found this out? Andrew spent a good deal of his time abroad, which may be significant.'

'There's something in that, I dare say, sir. But why should Bogan and Andrew Restorick flit just when and where they did?'

'In London, they knew they were being tailed, it'd be difficult and dangerous to shake off the C.I.D. chaps. But down here escape would be relatively easier. Why they did it *when* they did is much harder to understand. Perhaps they had some reason for believing that Will Dykes' "arrest" was dangerous to them.'

'I should have thought they'd feel much safer after an arrest had been made.'

'Yes. Unless they saw through my little stratagem.'

'Well, sir. I'd better go and see how my men are getting on upstairs. I told 'em to give Andrew Restorick's room a thorough search.'

The superintendent went out, and Nigel began to realize how thin his own theory sounded. The next hour he spent in talking to members of the household. Charlotte Restorick seemed to have recovered from the shock she had received, but she was still bewildered and uneasy at the turn of events. Nigel questioned her closely about Andrew's behaviour since his recent arrival. He had been very distressed by the news of Dykes' arrest, she said, as indeed they all were, but he had given no indication of being able to do anything about it. In fact, he had spent a good deal of his first afternoon at Easterham teaching John to shoot with an airgun he had brought down from London for him. Charlotte assured him again that the hot drinks she had prepared on the previous night could not possibly have been tampered with in the kitchen.

Hereward Restorick was no more informative, except for saying that his brother had seemed rather 'keyed-up' yesterday. Nothing of significance had been said by Bogan when he had shown the doctor to his room on the previous night. It was Eunice Ainsley who gave Nigel the first hint of the truth, though at first he did not realize it. They were talking about Will Dykes, she told Nigel; she had said she knew all along he must be the murderer – he was insanely jealous about Elizabeth – those quiet, dim little men always turned out the criminals – look at Crippen. And so on. Andrew, she went on, had not been very forthcoming. At last, however (goaded out of his reticence by this rather tiresome female, thought Nigel), Andrew had said, 'Don't you be so cocksure, my dear Eunice. I'm afraid you'll be disappointed this time if you think Dykes is going to be hung.'

'As though I wanted the poor little man hung,' added Eunice in a tone of grievance.

Nigel disengaged himself from her as quickly as politeness allowed, and went outside the house. Marching up and down the snow-covered terrace, quite unconscious of his surroundings, he meditated this new development.

It suggested what he had believed all along – that Andrew had been withholding some vital information about the murder. Dykes was not going to be hung, declared Andrew, that must surely mean he knew who the real murderer was. Nigel's stratagem *had* worked, then. But why had Andrew disappeared? The only reasonable answer seemed to be that, after they had all gone to bed last night, he had taxed X with the crime, that X had killed him and made away with the body.

But why has Bogan skipped too? Easy. Any schoolboy could tell you. Because Bogan is X, the murderer. But, for once, any schoolboy would be wrong. The sleeping-draughts muck up that theory altogether. Even supposing Bogan could have doped the Ovaltine, why should he? He'd only just that minute arrived in the house. Andrew'd had no time for a show-down.

No. That doesn't follow. Andrew might have hinted his knowledge of Bogan's guilty secret while they were both still in London, when he invited Bogan down for the week-end, perhaps. You'd better come down to the Manor, or I shall reveal all. It's been fun blackmailing you, but now the party's over. I can't let the wrong man be hung. Yes, blackmail might possibly be the explanation of Andrew's secretive behaviour. A new experience for Bogan – being at the wrong end of the blackmail. He might well decide that Andrew must be removed, and lay his plans accordingly.

Well then, if this theory's on the right lines and Bogan took advantage of the Ovaltine to put the household to sleep, what follows? Obviously, he refuses to take any sugar himself (*mem.:* find out if anyone noticed his refusal). He goes to Andrew's room, kills him while he is asleep, comes downstairs to eliminate the constable and give himself a clear run, carries Andrew's body out to the garage, and away to Buenos Aires, dropping the body into a nice deep snowdrift *en route*.

O.K., O.K., said Nigel's imaginary interlocutor. You're marvellous. But if Bogan killed Andrew while he was asleep, why did Andrew's room look as if a dozen all-in wrestlers had been holding a jam session in it?

That's simple, replied Nigel. Bogan turned the room upside down to make sure that Andrew had not left any damning evidence against him in writing.

How very eccentric! He moves heaven and earth to destroy

any possible evidence of his first murder, and then runs off in such a manner as to convict him of a second one.

But he never meant us to take it like that. He expects us to believe that he and Andrew have skipped together, both alive-oh.

Thereby tacitly admitting they were accomplices in the first murder?

Oh, don't be so difficult!

Nigel addressed his devil's advocate with a question of such violence that the odd-job man, passing below the terrace, stopped dead and inquired if the gentleman wanted anything.

'Yes, I do,' said Nigel. 'I want just one straightforward clue. It isn't much to ask, I should have thought. But no one ever gives it me.'

The odd-job man shook his head sympathetically, and started to move away, back bent and covered with sacking. As he did so, John Restorick came skirmishing round the corner of the house with his air-gun.

'Hey, Master John! Hev 'ee pinched my shovel? Out of the boiler-room? Hev 'ee seen it anywhere?' bellowed the odd-job man.

'No. I don't know where it is. Watch me shoot that blackbird!'

'Varmints,' muttered the man. 'That wur a good shovel. Don't understand what's going on round here. They puts Mr Robins behind my boiler, and they takes my shovel. Sodding Hitler!'

Nigel gazed affectionately at the man's retreating back. An answer to prayer, at last. Must make certain that the shovel really has been taken, though.

CHAPTER TWENTY

*'Earth could not hold us both, nor can one Heaven
Contain my deadliest enemy and me!'*
SOUTHEY

'WELL, Strangeways, you've put your foot in it this time. I said it was a wild-cat scheme, and I was right. Two of our suspects gone, and nothing to show for it.'

Blount was in his dourest temper. The eyes behind the gold-rimmed pince-nez glared stonily at Nigel.

'I wouldn't say there was nothing to show for it. We've pushed 'em out into the open. And you'll find them soon enough: it's extremely difficult to get out of the country nowadays. You've circulated their descriptions by now, I expect?'

'Uh-huh. Making more work for me. Next week we'll be getting reports in from all over the country from people who claim to have seen a man with a beard. I know.'

'It'll take your mind off the war. Anyway, that's what you're paid for, isn't it?'

'There are times when I'd like to have you poisoned. Just quietly put out of the way.'

'Well, if that's how you feel, I shall refuse to co-operate. I shall refrain from telling you where to look for the body of Andrew Restorick.'

'Is this a confession? Would you like a stenographer in the room?' inquired Blount sourly. He played for a few moments with his gold pencil. 'The *body* of Andrew Restorick, you said?'

'Yes. The body.'

'H'mphm! Well then, where is it?'

'Buried in a snowdrift.'

'That's – e'eh – very helpful. *Which* snowdrift? It may have escaped your notice that there's more than one of them lying about the countryside.'

'Don't be flippant. A shovel is missing from the boiler-room here. The odd-job man swears he used it yesterday evening. The local constable was put away in the boiler-room. Just before being knocked out, he felt his assailant's beard. There's only one way to reconstruct this. Bogan killed Andrew, and took the shovel so that he could bury the body. But the ground is frozen hard. Therefore he could not dig a proper grave. Therefore, he used the shovel to dig a hole in a snowdrift. The snow that was falling would help to smooth over his work. I shall never love the snow again since Maurice died.'

'That may be so,' commented Blount, relenting a little. 'But it doesn't get us much nearer the body.'

'You'll have to wait till you find the car he went away in. If there's blood or hairs or anything in it, you'll know Bogan didn't bury Andrew in the grounds here. Your chaps who are following up the tyre-tracks will give you some idea of the direction he went in.'

'It'd not be surprising to find Andrew's hairs in the car, considering that it's his car,' Blount remarked.

'Well, you can't have everything. I'm just trying to be helpful. I know I'm only a half-witted Oxford graduate.'

'Quite so. Perhaps you can tell me why Bogan killed Andrew, then?'

'With pleasure. Because the supposed arrest of Will Dykes made Andrew come out into the open with Bogan.'

'If Andrew really had some damning evidence against him, and wanted to free Dykes, why on earth didn't he tell it to the police?'

'I don't know yet. It's worrying me. That, and how Bogan managed to introduce the sleeping-draught into our Ovaltine. I've asked Eunice and the Restoricks, but none of them noticed any hanky-panky on his part.'

Blount took an elaborate apparatus out of his pocket and began rolling himself a cigarette. When he had lit it, and removed several shreds of tobacco from his tongue, he said:

'The sleeping-draught is an interesting point. You've satisfied me that it could only have been administered through the Ovaltine. And the one person who could have safely doped that or the sugar, at leisure, was Mrs Restorick.'

'Ah, ha!'

'Well, now. You could construct a theory on that. The Restoricks have failed at their first attempt to murder Andrew. They seize the opportunity of the party's reassembling to try again. But suspicion must be directed elsewhere. So they kill Bogan as well as Andrew, carry their bodies out to the car – incidentally, the garage was locked last night after Bogan's car was put away, so I don't quite see how *he* could have opened it again – where was I? – oh yes, Hereward drives the bodies away, digs a common grave for them, abandons the car, and walks home, while Mrs Restorick is mauling Andrew's room about to make it look as if a struggle had taken place. She and her husband would, of course, have already removed and hidden Dr Bogan's belongings, to subserve the illusion that Bogan had disappeared of his own free will. The Restoricks will now inherit Andrew's money as well as Elizabeth's.'

Nigel stared Blount full in the eyes. 'I do believe,' he said at last, 'I really do believe that you are trying to pull my leg. Inspector Blount brings off a joke. Is this a record? Well, well, well. And, oddly enough, this ill-timed pleasantry of yours has rung the bell. You've set a very interesting train of thought going in my head.'

Hurrying round to the back of the house, Nigel found the chauffeur leaning, in the *dégagé* manner of his kind, against the Restoricks' Daimler. A few questions elicited the information that there were three keys to the garage: one of these the chauffeur kept, and he stated it had been in his pocket last night; a second was in the possession of Mr Restorick; the third was normally kept on a hook just inside the back door. Nigel asked the man to show him this hook. They went indoors.

'That's funny,' said the chauffeur. 'It isn't there.'

'Mr Andrew didn't borrow your key when he put away Dr Bogan's car last night?'

'No, sir.'

Nigel sought out Hereward and asked him the same question. The answer again was 'no'. Andrew must, then, have used the third key.

'How long has your chauffeur been with you?'

'Eh? Oh, three years. Very reliable fellow. Not getting ideas about him, I hope,' replied Hereward.

Nigel had no time to reply, for there was a tap at the door of the study and Blount entered.

'I thought you had better know, Mr Restorick. Your brother's car has just been found, abandoned, three miles away from here, on the Chelmsford road.'

Hereward's brow creased. 'They don't seem to have got very far, then,' he said. 'I simply can't make head or tail of the business.'

'The car was run into a drift.' Blount watched Hereward attentively.

'What? Run into – you mean, it was done on purpose?'

'Maybe. Maybe an accident.'

'Very likely, if Bogan was driving. Rotten bad driver, y'know. Always had to get Howells or Andrew to put his car away in our garage for him and take it out. Bit tricky, of course, manoeuvring it in there. I ought to have the yard widened.'

'I see. Well, we're having the car taken into Chelmsford, and we'll run over it there. It may give us a line.'

'Was it – er – empty when they found it?'

'Yes. No suitcases or anything, that is to say.'

'You going into Chelmsford now?' Hereward, tugging his flaxen moustache, stared at Blount ruminatively. 'Run you in, if you like.'

'That'd be very kind of you.'

Sitting in the front seat of the Daimler beside Hereward,

as they moved cautiously along the winding, snow-deep lanes, the chains on the tyres clinking, Nigel pondered. Suppose Blount's little *jeu d'esprit* turned out to be a correct interpretation of the facts. Andrew's car abandoned only three miles away. That'd give Hereward quite a short walk back to the house, if it was he who – Glancing covertly at the stiff, correct figure beside him, wrapped in a horsey check tweed coat, Nigel tried to envisage Hereward driving a couple of corpses through the snowstorm in the small hours.

'Difficult road this in the dark, I imagine, with the present lighting restrictions,' he remarked mildly.

'Yes. Don't wonder Bogan piled up. It surprises me he managed to get to us at all, in fact.'

Hereward's eyes were screwed up, there was a tight frown on his forehead. Well, thought Nigel, that doesn't mean anything. It might be the dazzle of the snow added to the effect of an overdose of sleeping-draught, or he may just be putting it on; or, for that matter, he could easily have taken the sleeping-draught after returning from a little jaunt with two corpses last night.

'Didn't he run a chauffeur?' Nigel asked.

'Oh yes, I believe so. Didn't bring him down here though. Tell you what's puzzling me,' Hereward continued, recovering from a skid that sent Nigel's stomach under the floor-boards: 'Your asking me about the garage keys made me think of it. How did Bogan open the garage last night?'

'Used the third key, presumably. The one Andrew had locked it up with.'

'But that's the whole point. He'd never put away his car or taken it out while he was staying with us. How could he know where this key was kept?'

'If he'd planned for a getaway last night, he'd make it his business to find out,' replied Nigel perfunctorily. He wasn't thinking about keys any longer. He was wondering why Hereward had let the car get into a skid just now, whether it had been caused by Hereward's involuntarily starting at his question about the chauffeur. But why should Hereward be alarmed at being asked if Bogan kept a chauffeur?

Fantastic as the snow-patterns on the willows they were passing, a theory crystallized in his head. Suppose Bogan's chauffeur had in fact driven him down. If Bogan was the chief victim in last night's proceedings, the criminal would want his chauffeur well out of the way. Andrew 'putting the car away'; did Andrew put the chauffeur away too? Were he and Hereward accomplices? Once again the pattern of the *dramatis personae* changed. No, it was impossible. A dozen objections. The sketchiest inquiry would be enough to reveal that the chauffeur had come down to Easterham with his master – and then where would Andrew and Hereward be?

They arrived at a bend of the road, where an A.A. man was signalling them to slow down. Just round the corner there was a car deeply imbedded in a drift at the side of the road. Andrew Restorick's car. A sergeant and a constable, standing by it, saluted Blount.

'Not much doubt about it,' said Blount after a brief inspection. 'Look at the depth it's pushed its way into the drift. It was run into it, by accident or on purpose, before it was abandoned.'

And an escaping criminal, thought Nigel, wouldn't do it on purpose – not with several miles to walk to the nearest station. At a word from Blount, the police and the garage-men from the relief car started to dig the snow away from the vehicle. Presently it would be towed into Chelmsford, where the experts could get to work on it.

Meanwhile, all the men that Phillips could spare were prodding with sticks and poles and spades into the snow-drifts around, working outwards in a loose semi-circle from the stranded car in the direction from which it had come. Unless the driver had made a wide detour to bury the body or had carried it far away from the lane – a course which the darkness and his natural desire for haste made unlikely – they should find it before long.

Hereward was staring expressionlessly at the abandoned car, tugging his moustache. He looked oddly helpless, as though it were his own car stranded there and no one around to help him out.

'Don't worry too much, Mr Restorick,' said Blount. 'We've not got to the bottom of this yet. There may be some other explanation. Will we be getting along now?'

When they arrived at the police station, there was news for Blount. Phillips' men had been making inquiries at the railway stations in the vicinity. No one answering to Bogan's or Andrew's description had been noticed boarding a train in the early hours of the morning. But a phone call had just come through from Scotland Yard. A ticket-collector at the London terminus of the line, questioned by a C.I.D. man, had recognized the description of Dr Bogan offered to him as that of a passenger who had passed through the barrier off the 5-20 slow train. A bearded man, of sallow complexion, with a stoop. He had particularly noticed this passenger, because he had paid for his ticket at the barrier, saying he'd not had time to buy one at Chelmsford. There had been few passengers on this train, and the ticket-collector, given a description of Andrew Restorick, was prepared to swear that he was not one of them.

Blount gave Nigel a significant glance as he turned to the telephone.

'It doesn't necessarily follow,' said Nigel, more out of mere obstinacy than conviction. 'Andrew might have got out at another station. He might not have taken a train at all, for that matter. If they were accomplices, the last thing they'd do would be to turn up at London together.'

'No. It won't wash. The obvious interpretation is the right one. Bogan killed Andrew Restorick. And he'll not get away with it – not this time.'

Dialling New Scotland Yard, Blount gave his orders. The

search for Dr Dennis Bogan was to be intensified. Every port and landing-ground would be watched. It was only a matter of time now...

But day after day passed, a week went by, and still no sign was found of the live Bogan or the dead Andrew Restorick. They had both disappeared as thoroughly as if they had melted into the snow which masked the whole countryside.

CHAPTER TWENTY-ONE

> *'Our hearts, my love were form'd to be*
> *The genuine twins of Sympathy,*
> *They live with one sensation.'*
> THOMAS MOORE

NIGEL was extremely susceptible to weather. Afterwards, he pleaded that the palsying cold of those two winter months had prevented his brain from functioning properly. Even when large segments of the truth had been hurled in his face, they made no impression upon his numbed intelligence. Whatever credence one may give to this, there is no doubt that his solution of the Restorick case began on an evening ten days after the disappearance of Andrew and Bogan, when Superintendent Phillips had remarked, with the countryman's slight, ritual upturning of the eyes to the sky, 'We're going to have a change in the weather soon, Mr Strangeways.'

A series of images flashed across Nigel's mind. Their first arrival at Easterham. The Dower House delicately befurred with snow. Clarissa Cavendish's snowy hair piled above her brilliantly painted face. Will Dykes and himself strolling in the little birch copse. Andrew building the snowman, while Eunice Ainsley tried to be playful. John Restorick prowling round the garden with his air-gun. Hereward staring out of the window at the level, dreary white landscape, and turning round to protest mildly at a wrong note Priscilla had played upon the piano. Charlotte, in Wellingtons, a basket on her arm, setting off down the drive to play Lady Bountiful in the village, as to the manner born. Dr Bogan brushing the snow off his collar as he entered the hall on his last visit.

'Snow had fallen, snow on snow, snow on snow.' It had veiled the whole case, drifted into every corner of it. And not only snow, but 'snow'. During the last week, if they had done nothing else, Blount's investigations had revealed the full depravity of Dennis Bogan's character. There was no doubt now that Bogan had been for years, and with a criminal subtlety and opportunism that amounted to genius, using his professional position as a cover for cocaine-distribution and blackmail. The C.I.D. drug squad had at last tracked down his distributors and the source of their supplies. Blount, interviewing one after another of Bogan's long list of patients, had discovered in detail the methods by which he worked. Perhaps the most formidable thing about Bogan was his flair for choosing the right victims. A high proportion of his cures were genuine – so high a proportion that no suspicion had ever touched him on this score. But even with these, the intimate knowledge revealed to him in the course of treatment was frequently used as a means for blackmail. The woman whom Eunice's friend had interviewed was only one of several agents whom Bogan had working at this branch of the racket. His drug victims – the 'unsuccessful' cures – were chosen with equal skill. They were always people who would particularly fear the exposure of their addiction – young women generally, daughters of rich parents.

But the most sinister aspect of Bogan's activities was their apparently wanton malice. His ordinary fees for professional treatment were high enough to make him a rich man without any need for illegal side-lines. Blount's investigation made it abundantly evident that Bogan really did answer to Andrew's description of a person who revelled in evil, for its own sake. It was not wealth or position, but the horrible satisfaction of destroying people body and soul, which appealed to him. Behind that opaque personality, that distinguished, self-contained manner, there lay a dreadful relish for power, a genius so perverted that it could feel this relish only in corruption.

And so, thought Nigel, we come back to Elizabeth Restorick – to that body hanging naked in the sandalwood-scented room, dazzling the eye, the body of a woman who had been lustful, erratic, vain, shameless, but never ungenerous and never a coward. The long talks he had been having with Miss

Cavendish made that quite plain. They had assured him too that, whatever else there had been between Elizabeth and Bogan, there could not have been blackmail; he couldn't blackmail a woman who no longer had a shred of reputation to lose and who had never run away from anything in life.

'We shan't be long finding him once the thaw sets in,' said the superintendent.

'No. But it's queer. Your chaps have been going over the ground for days. Bogan must have found out some extraordinarily ingenious place to hide the body. I suppose it's definitely established that he couldn't have buried it miles away and then ditched the car near Easterham to throw us off the track.'

'Oh yes, sir. No doubt of that. He hadn't time for it. The constable was knocked out just after one o'clock. The cook, you remember, testified to having heard a car being driven out of the garage at a quarter to two. It'd be at least 1·50 before he reached the corner where the car went into the drift. Chelmsford, the nearest railway station to that point, is seven miles away, which'd take him two hours walking at least in the deep snow. Three-fifty. And the train he arrived by in London left Chelmsford at four-five. That gives him a maximum of fifteen minutes for burying the body. He couldn't even have taken it far off the direct route between Easterham and the station.'

'It does leave a long gap of time between knocking out the constable and driving off in Andrew's car.'

'We've been into all that, sir. He had to kill Mr Restorick in the interval and search his room – and you saw yourself how thoroughly it had been searched.'

'Yes. That's true.'

Another long silence fell between them. They were drinking in the pub at Easterham. It was barely half past six, and the little private bar was still empty but for themselves.

Yes, that's all very reasonable, Nigel began to argue with himself. But why should Bogan skip at all? Presumably because he failed to find the evidence against himself in Andrew's room. Andrew, no doubt, had told him that such written evidence existed, and he would now assume that Andrew had put it in safe keeping somewhere else, to be produced if anything happened to himself. But it never had been produced. Neither Andrew's bank nor his solicitors nor his London flat had revealed anything of the sort.

The police theory was that Bogan had found and removed this evidence from Andrew's room. O.K. But, if so, why should he confess to the murder of Andrew by running away and taking the body with him? He had several hours to fake it up into another apparent suicide. The police said it was because he lost his nerve. Bogan was a vile creature: he did not lose his nerve, though. Even at his luncheon with Nigel in the London restaurant, even when he must have realized from Nigel's remarks that the police were investigating his professional life and might any day discover the iniquitous things that were going on behind it – even then, he had shown no signs of discomposure.

No doubt, like other criminals on the grand scale, he had a crazy belief in his own infallibility. But that did not weaken Nigel's argument. Bogan was not a man who lost his nerve. He had not run away after killing Elizabeth Restorick, far from it, his composure had been almost flawless.

Well then, why had he killed Andrew at all? Not, surely, because Andrew had evidence of his drug and blackmail activities; the police would almost certainly turn that up sooner or later. No, it must have been because Andrew could convict him of Elizabeth's murder. Why had Andrew held back from doing it, though, for so long? Was it just a kind of cat-and-mouse game? A revenge?

Revenge! Now he was getting warmer. Had Bogan killed Andrew just to suppress his knowledge about Elizabeth's murder, in the belief that Andrew's knowledge would die with him, he would not have run away. But, if he knew the game was up anyway and believed that it was Andrew who had defeated him, he *would* disappear after killing him. This theory would fit in with Bogan's having waited till the invitation to Easterham gave him an opportunity both to commit the murder and escape afterwards. In London, with all the suspects being closely watched, the chance of escaping would be far smaller.

But there remained a few very awkward obstacles. How had Bogan introduced the sleeping-powders into the Ovaltine or the bowl of sugar? Why, if the murder was purely for revenge and there had been no necessity to search Andrew's room for incriminating evidence against himself, did Bogan delay so long before leaving the house? Why, indeed, was Andrew's room left in disorder at all? There could not have been a struggle, for Andrew had presumably been doped like the others. And if Bogan had somehow failed to dope Andrew and there *was* a struggle, why didn't the maid hear it?

Nigel groaned aloud. The superintendent glanced at him sympathetically over the top of his beer-mug.

'Feeling poorly, sir?'

'I'm feeling like Laocoon. I'm feeling like a professional contortionist who's tied himself into seventy knots and forgotten how to undo them.'

They rose to go. Out in the village street, Phillips again remarked that the weather was going to change. Nigel could not honestly say he noticed any alteration in the prevailing and seemingly eternal bleakness, but a faint sensation of excitement stirred in the pit of his stomach, a feeling of anticipation, like that of a poet in whom a poem is beginning to move.

Taking his leave of the superintendent, he walked across to the Dower House, where he had gone to stay after the disappearance of Andrew Restorick. When dinner was over, he encouraged Clarissa Cavendish to talk once again about Elizabeth and Andrew. They had become firm friends during this last week. The long talks in Clarissa's exquisite drawing-room had bound them together, for Miss Cavendish revealed to him the full extent of her love for the young Restoricks.

Through their lives, warped and shattered as they had been, the tragedy of her own was sublimated. She had never infringed their privacy or taken advantage of their intimacy. They had remained her 'dream children', quite unaware of Clarissa's love for their father. But throughout their childhood, and during their visits to Easterham after they had grown up, she had studied them with the passionate absorption of a mother and the detachment of a keen intelligence.

Now, sitting upright in the straight-backed chair, her hands resting on the ivory stick, she returned once again to her favourite subject.

'Poor Betty. She was born two hundred years too late. In my day' – she raised a deprecating finger and smiled ruefully – 'in the days I like to call mine, her vitality would have been recognized. The history books say that we found enthusiasm odious. But, at least, we were not ashamed of our feelings. Love made us swoon away. We gave sorrow its full measure of tears, and death an elegant epitaph. When we drank, we finished under the table, not in the confessional or the chemist's shop. Betty might have been a king's mistress. You recall, no doubt, the anecdote about the Duchess of Marlborough' – her bright black eyes shot a naughty glance at Nigel – 'how she told a friend, "To-day the Duke returned from the wars and pleasured me twice in his top-boots." I find such behaviour vastly agreeable – and, I suspect, far beyond the capacity of the public figures of our own time. We may say, I think, without impropriety, that such heroic impulsiveness is a thing of the past. Men, in the cant phrase, are no longer men.'

'Which is why Betty turned to Will Dykes?'

'A sagacious observation, my dear Nigel. Mr Dykes' breeding leaves much to be desired, but at least he retains the virility of the class from which he has risen. He would treat a woman, I fancy, neither as an angel, a dictator, nor a sow. The more I see of Hereward and Charlotte, the more I am led to think that calling in the New World has upset the balance of the old. A female may wish her husband to be a mere sleeping partner in a business conducted by herself, but 'tis unnatural and soon enough she will find it so. Will Dykes would have taken a stick to Betty – and she'd have vastly preferred that to all those young men of hers who behaved like carpets. I protest this modern kowtowing to womanhood is hideous immoral. A man of firm character was what Betty needed – one who would both support and direct her own exuberance.'

'And do you think Andrew was an anachronism too?'

Clarissa gazed sadly into the flickering fire. Tears came to her eyes.

'Andrew's is the real tragedy. Betty had, at least, lived some kind of life, even if it was a fruitless flowering. Andrew's never began. You may say he had everything – charm, money, leisure, wit; but with all that, he was sterile, utterly sterile. I am not in the way of exaggerating. Ever since that thing happened to Betty in America, he has been driven by the Furies.'

'He has never forgiven himself for failing his sister then, you mean?'

'That, and more. Consider, I beg you, the shock poor Betty's scandal must have given to a youth who had never before been confronted by real evil. Andrew – I must allow even my favourite *some* failings – was a thought priggish. By which I mean that his ideals – and they were very high – had been inherited, not quarried out of experience. But even *that* signified less than the fact of their extraordinary identity. As I have told you, they were like twins. I recollect how, in their childhood, when Betty had a nightmare, Andrew used to come into her room to comfort her. He told me once that he often knew when she was having a nightmare. It would awake him, with all the sensations of having woken from a nightmare himself. So, you see, when Betty went through that dreadful agony of experience out there, Andrew, I am convinced, felt it far more deeply – more physically and directly, shall I say? – than would the normal devoted brother.'

'Would you say his sanity, in the broadest sense, had been affected by it?'

'Sanity?' A touch of the old crispness came into her tone. 'That is an excessively vague word. Sanity, like some other qualities, lies in the eye – and the prejudices – of the beholder. You yourself, for instance, when you first came down here, thought that *I* was mentally deranged. Did you not?'

Nigel grinned at her. 'Like Justice with her scales,' he replied, 'I suspended my judgement.'

'La! You are a sad prevaricator!' said the old lady, keenly delighted. 'No. I am not speaking of sanity. Let us say that what happened to Betty was, for him, the rape of his own innocence. It is a wound from which the heart never recovers. Nor had he the powers of resistance which would have fortified a coarser nature. His whole life since that day' – Clarissa's voice fell to a brittle whisper – 'has been a penance for the sin which, through Betty, was committed against him. He was like a man who goes through life impotent.'

Nigel felt strangely stirred, a little frightened almost, by the intensity of meaning which Clarissa's fragile voice gave to her words. Her eyes shone, in the gleams of firelight, like blackberries. The hands, folded over her ivory stick, were as placid as cream.

'I remember once, when Betty was ten years old . . .' she began again.

Lying in bed an hour later, Nigel lit another cigarette and made a deliberate effort to empty his mind of all the theories and perplexities which had grown up round the death of Elizabeth Restorick, like the thorn thickets round the Sleeping Beauty. Gradually they lapsed away. A confusion of images took their place, and amongst them, moving forward with the assurance of a conductor, something Clarissa Cavendish had told him this evening came to the front of the stage. As if of its own volition, while he lay back and quietly looked on, it called for silence, beckoned the instruments and began. Everything fell into place: each image struck its true note in the symphony, answered its lead, contributed to the inevitable theme that was being built up. The burning cigarette scorched his lips. Absently he ground it out and took another. It might have been a cigarette of marijuana, for all he knew and tasted of it ...

Next morning he was awoken by the sound of water. Water was chuckling in the gutters, dripping from the eaves, singing everywhere. Superintendent Phillips was right. The weather had changed.

Immediately after breakfast, Nigel sloshed his way through the melting snow up to the Manor. There he talked with Hereward Restorick, interviewed the servants, had a word with John and Priscilla, and inspected the acting cupboard. In the early afternoon he reached London and went to see Chief-Inspector Blount.

'You're looking horribly satisfied with yourself. Solved the case, I suppose?'

'Yes. As a matter of fact I have, up to a point. I don't take any credit, though. It just came to me. Last night.'

'I'm extremely busy just now, Strangeways –'

'It's all right. Honestly. No joking. I had a talk with the Restorick kid this morning – the boy. He had the key to the problem all along, without knowing it.'

Very deliberately, Chief-Inspector Blount pushed aside the papers on his desk, polished his pince-nez as if to get a clearer view of Nigel, and remarked sardonically:

'Who am I supposed to arrest?'

Nigel spoke a name. Blount's smooth features were violently agitated. His pince-nez wobbled.

'Why, man, what are you talking about? That's impossible. We've already –'

Perched on the corner of Blount's desk, Nigel began to talk.

CHAPTER TWENTY-TWO

*'If I can catch him once upon the hip,
I will feed fat the ancient grudge I bear him.'*
SHAKESPEARE

As Nigel walked up to the Manor next morning, with Will Dykes and Miss Cavendish, they could hear the sound of the piano mingled with the slurred water music of melting snow. A phrase was played over, rather laboriously, twice, then a pause. Then the phrase rippled forth perfectly.

'Hereward is giving Priscilla her music lesson,' said Clarissa.

'He plays very nicely, doesn't he?' Will Dykes said. 'Funny he should, when you come to think of it.'

'You would allow us no accomplishments?'

Dykes did not answer. Gazing at the façade of the Manor, the high-pitched roof from which the snow had peeled away in long strips, he said:

'I never thought I'd come back to this house. And I hope I never see it again. There's a curse on it.'

A few minutes later the party from the Dower House were sitting in the drawing-room, together with the Restoricks and Miss Ainsley. Priscilla's music lesson had been cut short.

Nigel gazed round at the company. Hereward's fingers were still unconsciously playing a phrase on the arm of his chair. Charlotte had forgotten to take off her Wellingtons when she came in from the garden – snow was melting off them on to the carpet. Eunice stared back at Nigel rather defiantly. Will Dykes was fidgeting with a waistcoat button. Only Clarissa Cavendish, her delicate, brilliant head looking small as a cameo above the bulky clothing in which she had swathed herself, seemed perfectly composed.

Nigel went to stand with his back against the french windows that opened on the terrace.

'One way or another,' he said, 'you're all interested in what's been happening at the Manor. So I thought it'd be only fair to let you all hear the explanation. It's difficult to know where to begin.'

He paused. There was a painful constraint all round him, reflected in his own expression.

'I'd better tell you first how I hit on the truth. John told me.'

Charlotte's hand made a movement towards her lips, instantly checked.

'It's all right,' said Nigel. 'He didn't know the meaning of it, and he never need know. I had a talk with him yesterday morning. For reasons I'll come to, I believed he might be able to tell me something of vital importance. He did. He said that, on the night Elizabeth died, her ghost came into his room.'

'Ghosts?' said Miss Cavendish testily. 'Surely we are not to fiddle with the supernatural at this juncture?'

'No. He assumed it was her ghost because next morning he heard she was dead, and because – mark this well – "her face was white as death". Those are his own words. I want you to get this clear in your minds. At the time, it never occurred to John that his visitor wasn't the flesh-and-blood Elizabeth. He wasn't frightened. She just came into his room, looking very sad, bent over his bed – he was pretending to be asleep – and then went out again. Now the normal thing for a boy to have done under the circumstances would have been to speak to her. I asked him why he hadn't done so. He couldn't explain it properly, but I got the impression that her appearance overawed him – you know how children react to a violent emotional conflict in an adult: they draw in their horns and go still as mice. That's why he pretended to be asleep.'

'But why didn't the boy tell the police about this. I simply can't understand,' said Hereward.

'They asked him had he heard anyone passing his door that night. You know what literal minds children have. He hadn't heard anyone *passing the door*. Besides, as I say, that midnight visitation was something he'd naturally close up about. I'd never have dreamt of it myself, but for something my wife said. The children were talking about ghosts to her. Priscilla had somehow got to hear of the Bishop's room and the Scribbles episode. But Georgia got the impression that John, who was edgy on the subject, knew nothing about this – that he had some other "ghost" on his mind. So, after something Miss Cavendish told me the other night, I managed to draw it out of him.'

'Something *I* told you?' Clarissa's black eyes looked startled.

'Yes. We were talking about the sympathy that existed between Andrew and Betty. As if they were twins. You told me how, as children, when Betty had a nightmare, it used to awake Andrew and he would come into her room to comfort her.'

A sudden exclamation broke from Charlotte.

'Yes?' asked Nigel encouragingly.

'What you're suggesting is that Betty's agony, when she was murdered, communicated itself to Andrew. He went in and found her – like that.'

'But, damn it, the door was locked,' said Hereward obstinately.

'Yes, the door *was* locked. At 11-30, at any rate. But Andrew admitted to us, rather incautiously, that he was good at opening locks. Go on, Mrs Restorick.'

Her shrewd eyes held Nigel's. 'It's been worrying me ever since. When we found Betty that morning, Andrew was so cool and competent. He took charge of everything. I wondered then how he managed to do it, when he was so devoted to Betty. You'd have thought the shock – but, of course, if he'd already been into her room during the night and seen – I was afraid,' she went on, unsteadily, 'afraid it was he who had – but now you've explained it differently, why he went to her room.'

'You've hit on a great part of the truth. But not all of it. I should have seen, much earlier, that odd point about Andrew's having been in control of the situation, but –'

'Not *all* the truth?' exclaimed Charlotte, her eyes pleading with him. 'Surely you don't still mean that Andrew –?'

Nigel had opened his mouth to reply, when they were all startled by a cry from overhead and feet tumbling down the stairs.

'Daddy! Daddy!' John was yelling. 'Come quick! There's someone inside the snowman.'

'Damn!' exclaimed Nigel loudly. 'So that's where he was put. What a fool I am! Under our noses.'

Hereward was outside the door, ordering the children not to leave the house. Eunice Ainsley, her lips quivering, whispered:

'Oh God! Poor Andrew! And I was there when he built it. I can't bear any more of this.'

Nigel, at the door, turned back to her. 'It's not Andrew in the snowman. It's Dr Bogan' ...

After lunch they collected in the drawing-room again. The police had come and gone, the body had been taken away. The face of the iniquitous doctor staring blankly out of the snowman, the draggled beard hiding the rope round its neck, haunted Nigel unpleasantly.

'Yes,' he said, 'Andrew killed Bogan. I might have known where he'd hidden him too. The murder was planned, and the receptacle decided on. That's why Andrew brought John an air-gun from London. The snowman stood below the nursery window. John would take potshots at the birds from that window. The birds were very hungry during the great frost – Andrew wanted them chivvied away from what was inside the snowman.'

Charlotte Restorick shuddered. Her heavy, handsome face was darkened with horror.

'Andrew,' she whispered. 'But why –?'

'Andrew put Bogan in the snowman simply to gain time. He wanted to get out of the country, and he cleverly arranged things so that we should think it was he himself who had been murdered, and would concentrate the search upon Bogan.'

'How long have you known this?' asked Will Dykes.

'It forced itself upon me gradually. So many things were wrong with the idea of Bogan's having killed Andrew. How could Bogan have doped the Ovaltine? Why was Andrew's room so disordered? Andrew did it himself, of course, to throw more suspicion on Bogan. How could Bogan have known about the third garage key? The one that's hung up by the back door? You, Mr Restorick, told me he was a bad driver, always got somebody else to put his car into your garage and take it out, because manoeuvring's tricky there. I asked the servants yesterday morning. They and the chauffeur were quite definite Bogan had never made any inquiries about this key. How could he have unlocked the garage door, then, since the other two keys were in the possession of yourself and your chauffeur? Another point. Why should Bogan have delayed so long between the time the constable was knocked out and the car driven away –?'

'But Robins told us Bogan was the man who knocked him out,' objected Hereward.

'No, he didn't. He said he felt his assailant's beard. That beard, which – by the way – is missing from your acting cupboard, is the one Andrew wore as the Wicked Uncle when you did that charade. A thick, formidable black beard, which could easily be trimmed to resemble Bogan's.'

'So Andrew spent that time dismantling the snowman and building it up again round – round the man he'd murdered,' said Eunice. 'Oh, I can't believe it! I don't know how he could force himself to do it.'

'Andrew was extraordinarily sensitive and skilful with his hands. It would not be so difficult for him. It had already begun to snow again when Bogan arrived, and this would with luck obliterate the tracks he made round the snowman. Whether he'd planned out beforehand to use the snowman, I can't say, John's air-gun suggests that he did. Even if a fresh fall of snow hadn't come to help him, the snow all over that bit of lawn was covered with tracks.'

'I can't think why we didn't notice the new snowman was bigger than the old,' said Charlotte. 'It'd be bound to be bigger, wouldn't it?'

'The snowman had been there so long, it was a familiar figure. Even the children had stopped playing with it. And the fresh fall of snow would account for its looking bulkier and more shapeless. So we can reconstruct Andrew's movements that night. He has already doped the Ovaltine or the sugar, so that no one on the first floor would awake, and disordered his bedroom. He puts on the beard, neatly puts the constable out and tucks him away in the boiler-room, enters Bogan's room, strangles him in his sleep, packs Bogan's things up in his suitcase, builds the body into the snowman, and departs.'

'Why did he drive his car into that drift?' interrupted Hereward. 'Good driver, Andrew. Can't see him doing that.'

'It was another subtle touch to build up a picture of Bogan as the fugitive – Bogan who was a bad driver. Well, the next we hear of this fugitive is at the London terminus. He buys a ticket. Well, I ask you, if it had been Bogan, can we imagine him calling attention to himself in such a flagrant manner? But Andrew would. And, with his beard, his bronze complexion which, in a dimly-lighted station, would look sallow, and an assumed stoop, he could easily answer the description of Bogan which the police gave the ticket-collector. It was this business that first made me wonder whether somebody hadn't been impersonating Bogan.'

Will Dykes' forehead was creased in a frown. 'Is your theory that the pretended arrest of myself forced Andrew to take action? But why? I can't connect it up. Why should it make him have to get rid of Bogan?'

'That is a highly significant point. You see, Andrew must

have known before he killed Bogan that your "arrest" was not genuine.'

'But I thought the whole thing depended –'

'If the police had really arrested you, it'd have been in the papers the next morning. The Restorick case has had plenty of publicity, in spite of the war. Andrew read the papers, presumably?'

'Why, yes,' said Charlotte.

'It wasn't in the papers. Therefore, Dykes hadn't been arrested. But Andrew went through with his plan for killing Bogan. His motive, therefore, could have had nothing to do with the saving of an innocent man from trial. You see, what misled us all along was our assumption that Andrew had evidence against Bogan for Elizabeth's murder. In fact –'

Charlotte Restorick's voice broke in, hoarse and unsteady, she was making a desperate effort to control it, to control her hands and features. Now she voiced what they were all thinking.

'Please, Mr Strangeways. I beg of you, don't keep us in this suspense any longer. What you are trying to tell us is that it was the other way round. Isn't it? – that it was Bogan who had evidence against Andrew and therefore had to die? That it was Andrew who killed Betty?'

The whole room went still. They stared at him with the most painful anxiety, as if he had come to tell them the result of a major operation upon someone dear to them. Nigel gazed long and seriously at Charlotte Restorick.

'No,' he said at last. 'No, Mrs Restorick, Andrew didn't kill Elizabeth.'

Will Dykes broke the bewildered silence. 'But this is fantastic. Are you telling us there's no connexion between Bogan's death and Betty's?'

'No. There is a connexion. Let me remind you of what John told me – about Elizabeth coming into his room that night. About her pallor and her sadness. She was pale as death, in the moonlight, he said. I questioned him very closely, and he stuck to that. But when we found her, her face was made up. Don't you see it?'

They glanced at each other, shaking their heads.

'I'll give you another hint, then. When the maid left her that night, Betty was removing her make-up, and she seemed "excited". This, and subsequent events, led us to believe that she was expecting a lover in her room; that she began removing her make-up in order to hoodwink the maid. But – don't you see? – if she was expecting a lover, the last thing she'd do would be to go into the children's room in the middle of the night, looking so sad, looking as if –'

'As if –' Will Dykes' words seemed to be dragged, against his will, out of the depth of his heart – 'as if she was saying good-bye to them.'

'Saying good-bye to them,' echoed Nigel. 'Yes. That is what she *was* doing. *It was the last thing she did before she hung herself.*'

They sat in a stunned silence. At last Hereward found his voice. 'Hung herself? But you told us – everyone said that – that it was murder rigged to look like suicide?'

'Yes, it was very cleverly done. But the truth is just the opposite. Suicide rigged to look like murder. Even Bogan told the truth sometimes. You remember he informed us how Elizabeth had hinted at suicide to him – "I expect you'll be glad to have one hysterical woman off your hands"?'

'I am not to believe,' remarked Clarissa crisply, 'that Betty would take her own life. She was not a coward.'

'She wouldn't have done it for herself. I agree. But there was more at stake. The children. That's why she went in to say good-bye to them. That's why she seemed to the maid "excited". It was more than excitement. It was the exaltation of a person who is about to perform a purely altruistic act.'

'Eh? Altruistic? I don't follow,' said Hereward. 'You mean she sacrificed herself for the children?'

'Just that. Mind you, she was probably at the end of her

tether in other ways too. I doubt if we shall ever know for certain now, but the likelihood is that she believed Bogan had her in his power; partly through the hypnosis treatment, partly through his control of her drug addiction. What Bogan was after, we may never know either. Maybe he wanted her as his lover, maybe it was just his vicious lust for torturing people's souls. At any rate, I've no doubt in my own mind that the crucial moment for her came when he threatened to deprave John and Priscilla. The marijuana business makes it pretty clear what he was up to.'

'But I don't understand,' said Charlotte. 'Why couldn't she have broken off her association with him, told us what he'd threatened to do to the children?'

'First, because she may really have believed that the hypnosis treatment had put her in his power. Second, because no one but her own family – perhaps not even they – would have taken the word of a neurotic, unstable drug-addict against that of an eminent doctor. She had no *material* evidence against him, you see. He would have said it was a case of morbid delusions, if she had attempted to expose him. And, above all, she was deadly afraid of Bogan. She knew that, even if she managed to discredit him with her family, he would sooner or later get his own back.'

'I understand now,' said Dykes. 'She had to get rid of Bogan thoroughly, for good and all. So she killed herself in such a way as to throw the suspicion of murder on him.'

'Oh no. It wasn't that. You're leaving out too much of the material evidence. No, she hung herself and left a suicide note fastening the responsibility on Bogan. Bogan's reputation would have sustained any attacks a neurotic patient made upon it, but it would *not* sustain the police inquiry which would inevitably result from a patient's suicide.'

'Hold on,' said Hereward. 'That won't do, y'know. There wasn't a suicide note. We never found one.'

'No. Andrew destroyed it – or at any rate, removed it.'

Hereward goggled at him.

'Ah, now I understand what you meant about the sympathy between those two poor children,' said Clarissa.

'Yes. The physical agony, the extreme emotional disturbance which Betty experienced when she killed herself was communicated to Andrew, like her nightmares when they were children. He woke up, went to her room, found the door locked and no answer when he called to her. He picked the lock and went in. There was her body hanging, and the suicide note. Reading it, he knew that all his suspicions about Bogan had been justified. Now Miss Cavendish and I have had some long talks about Andrew's character. I won't go over them with you, except to say that her account of him confirmed my own belief that what happened to Betty in America maimed and permanently distorted his mind. My point is this: when he found his sister dead and read the suicide note, it merely set a keener edge on a deadly enmity against Bogan that had existed for years.'

'You mean, Bogan really was Engelman – the man who had ruined Betty?' asked Charlotte.

'*And* ruined Andrew's own life. Yes. He admitted to us that he thought he'd recognized Bogan as the marijuana-peddler. He was very adroit all the way along in not attempting to conceal his suspicion and dislike of Bogan. He emphasized this hatred, simply because he knew it would be impossible for him to conceal it. I'm convinced in my own mind that he recognized Bogan as soon as they met. You don't ever forget a man you've fought with, a man who has done you a mortal injury. Andrew's by-play with Scribbles, and during the Babes-in-the-Wood charade, was partly an attempt to find out what Bogan's game was with Betty, and partly just to unnerve Bogan. Then, when Betty died, it gave Andrew both an opportunity and a justification to be revenged on Bogan for the injuries he had done them both.'

'It was Andrew who made her death look like murder?' said Will Dykes.

'Yes. He arranged the set-up. He took down her body, and

then pulled it up by the rope so that, when we examined the rope, we should believe her murderer had hauled her up that way. He probably rearranged the room a little – remember, his aim was to make it look like a murder which the criminal had tried to fake as a suicide. The most brilliant and macabre touch he gave to this picture was done by making up her face.'

'Good God!' exclaimed Hereward.

'Yes. Pretty grim, that. I noticed that her mouth was not made up quite perfectly. Even Andrew's nerve failed a little there; but at the time this didn't mean anything to me. He locked the door from outside by the pencil-and-string method – another neat indication that it had been murder, and came away with the suicide note. After that, he remained quietly, but not altogether inactive, in the background. It was he who planted the burnt paper in Bogan's grate, of course. But the police still failed to arrest Bogan. And Bogan himself, who must have had a pretty shrewd idea of what was going on and who was behind it, decided to take a hand. He planted a cord of Dykes' dressing-gown tassel in the room. He had to deflect suspicion from himself, but he dared not hint to us that Andrew was trying to frame him, because that would have started letting all his own cats out of the bag. Andrew, in the meanwhile, came out with a theory of the relationship between Bogan and Elizabeth which was very near to the truth. Unobtrusively he handed us a motive for Bogan's having killed her. And *still* we didn't arrest Bogan. So Andrew arranged that rather clumsy business of the poisoned milk. He hoped we would interpret it as an attempt by Bogan to silence him too. But it didn't come off at all as he'd meant it. In fact, it turned the attention of the police towards Mr and Mrs Restorick.'

'Eh? You mean they actually –?' began Hereward, outraged.

'Of course they did, my dear,' said Charlotte. 'Go on, Nigel.'

'Bogan was on his guard against Andrew by now. So he answered this stroke by pouring some of the poisoned milk into the milk jug. It was a pretty intense duel that was going on behind the scenes, believe me – Bogan trying to anticipate what Andrew's next move would be, Andrew circling round Bogan looking for another weak spot, and both of them at the same time covering up from the police. Andrew enjoyed himself, I'm sure. But he'd made a mistake. He was far too clever to overdo the incrimination of Bogan: and, as a result, he underplayed it. After a bit, he began to realize that he'd not given us enough evidence against Bogan, and by that time it was too late to manufacture more. The trouble was, of course, that – if Bogan had intended to kill Betty – he'd have means to his hand, as a doctor, far safer than the one Andrew wished us to believe he'd adopted. It was this that stuck in our throats all along.'

'Just a minute,' said Will Dykes. 'You told Andrew and myself at your flat how the police were getting on to Bogan's illegal activities – the blackmail and drugs and so on. I wonder Andrew didn't let it go at that. Bogan was almost certain to get a long sentence and have his whole career ruined anyway, wasn't he?'

'Yes. But that wasn't enough for Andrew. He wanted the snake killed, not scotched. It was partly his personal hatred for the man, and partly a genuine and probably well-justified fear that, if Bogan was left alive, he'd take his revenge sooner or later – and take it on John and Priscilla, as well as on Andrew himself. So, when it became evident that Bogan was not going to be arrested for the murder, Andrew decided he'd take the law into his own hands. No doubt the pretended arrest of Dykes hurried on the process. But, since there was nothing about it in the papers, Andrew must have soon realized it was a fake. By now, however, he was too much in love with the thought of a personal revenge, of killing Bogan with his own hands, to retract. As Clarissa said to me, Andrew was a man driven by the Furies.'

There was a long silence, like the exhausted silence of convalescence. They would all recover, thought Nigel: even Will Dykes; perhaps Will Dykes most assuredly, for he had the creative principle strongest inside him. They could hear the snow slurring and pattering off the roof, melting away into musical rivulets. Gazing out of the french windows, Nigel looked over the terrace towards the low-lying countryside beyond, the woods and fields where two children had once roved, inseparable. The world had come between them, but in death they had returned to each other. He was humming to himself the air of 'The Enniskilling Dragoon':

> 'And light was her laugh like the sun on the sea
> Till the weight of the world came between her
>   and me.'

How did it go on? The second stanza?

> 'Oh what can man do when the world is his foe,
> And the looks of her people fall on him like
>   snow,
> But bend the brow boldly and fare away far
> To follow good fortune and get fame in the
>   war?'

As if continuing his thoughts, Will Dykes spoke in a whisper. 'I'm glad, somehow, that it wasn't murder. That Betty wasn't murdered. I don't know why. Yes, I do know. To kill herself – it was a voluntary act, even if the poor darling was half-crazed when she did it. But to be murdered, to be pushed out of life – no, it wouldn't have been a right end for her. She – it'd have been all wrong – like evicting a princess from her palace. Not that I take much stock in palaces. Oh well, it's over and done with.'

'Not for Andrew,' said Clarissa. 'What will happen to Andrew?'

'We shan't hear,' said Hereward, with unexpected warmth. 'He'll be too clever for them. Old Andrew always had the brains.'

'Yes, I dare say he's got away. He gave himself plenty of time, while the police were chasing after Bogan. And, the way he's knocked around the world, he'll have means of getting out of a country, even in wartime. But we shall hear from him. He's not the sort to let anyone else be put on trial for Bogan's murder.'

And so, indeed, it turned out. A few days later, Blount received a letter from Andrew with a Spanish postmark, containing a full account of Betty's suicide and the murder of Bogan. Nigel had reconstructed those events with extreme accuracy, as even the chief-inspector admitted.

'It was a bad blunder we both made at the start, though,' he said. 'After all, there *were* no marks of violence on the body, except for that rope-mark round the neck. We shouldn't have let him bounce us out of the suicide theory so easily.'

Nigel looked up from the last paragraph of Andrew's letter, nodding absently. Then he read it again.

'It's queer how revenge has an instinct for the melodramatic. I suppose it's rather cheap and obvious, but I can't help feeling a lively satisfaction that that devil, with his ice-cold heart and his "snow", should have ended up in a snowman, though I admit it was for expediency and not as an artistic gesture that I put him there ... Good-bye to everyone. I shall not "give myself up to justice", preferring a more productive end to a sadly unproductive life. By the time you get this, I shall be in Germany – I know quite a few ways of getting in. There, I shall do as much damage as I can before they find me out. I have friends who will be working with me. Salud.'

THE END

VINTAGE CLASSICS

Vintage Classics is home to some of the greatest writers and thinkers from around the world and across the ages. Bringing you not just the books you already know and love, but new additions to your library, these are works to capture imaginations, inspire new perspectives and excite curiosity.

Renowned for our iconic red spines and bold, collectable design, Vintage Classics is an adventurous, ever-evolving list. We breathe new life into classic books for modern readers, publishing to reflect the world today, because we believe that our times can best be understood in conversation with the past.

Editions from **VINTAGE COLLECTOR'S CLASSICS**

The Romantics

Pride and Prejudice	Jane Austen
Jane Eyre	Charlotte Brontë
Little Women	Louisa May Alcott
Wuthering Heights	Emily Brontë
Emma	Jane Austen

The Gothics

The Picture of Dorian Gray	Oscar Wilde
Frankenstein	Mary Shelley
Dracula	Bram Stoker
Dr Jekyll and Mr Hyde	Robert Louis Stevenson
The Fall of the House of Usher	Edgar Allan Poe